ANGEL HUNT

London in the late 1980s is an exciting but sometimes dangerous place to live for Fitzroy Maclean Angel, making a living partly through gigging as a jazz trumpet player, partly through taking illegal fares in his de-registered black taxi cab. When an old university friend plummets to his death through a skylight window it's just the start of Angel's troubles, as he gets his arm twisted by the police to help with their enquiries into a group of animal rights activists, who might just have something rather more deadly on their minds than a bit of foxhunt sabotage...

ROYAL BOROUGH OF GREENWICH

Follow us on twitter @greenwichlibs

Outreach Library Service
Tel: 020 8319 5875

New label May 2022

Please return by the last date shown

Blossom -- MAY 2022 Mummef -- NOV 2022 Pennyfield -- JAN 2023 Central -- MAR 2023 Tudor -- JUN 2023	G Akoel Time Cnt -- JUL 2023 SEP 2023	2ep WITHDRAWN

Thank you! To renew, please contact any
Royal Greenwich library or renew online or by phone
www.better.org.uk/greenwichlibraries
24hr renewal line 01527 852385

ANGEL HUNT

This one is for Charlie, Vonnie and Caro
and anyone from the old days who
still holds the negatives.

ANGEL HUNT

by

Mike Ripley

Magna Large Print Books
Long Preston, North Yorkshire,
BD23 4ND, England.

British Library Cataloguing in Publication Data.

Ripley, Mike
   Angel hunt.

A catalogue record of this book is
available from the British Library

ISBN   978-0-7505-2760-6

First published in Great Britain 1989 by Collins

Copyright © 1989, 2006 Mike Ripley

Cover illustration © Gwyn Jeffers by arrangement with
Telos Publishing Ltd.

The moral right of the author has been asserted

Published in Large Print 2007 by arrangement with
Telos Publishing Ltd.

Magna Large Print is an imprint of Library Magna Books Ltd.

Printed and bound in Great Britain by
T.J. (International) Ltd., Cornwall, PL28 8RW

CHAPTER ONE

It could have been the extra garlic I'd put in the Rogan Josh that woke me at 2.06 am, but it was probably the noise Billy Tuckett made falling through the bathroom skylight and killing himself.

I knew it was 2.06 am because the bedside clock told me so in orange digits big enough to divert aircraft if the curtains had been open. I knew I'd overdone the garlic in the Rogan Josh because I'd been trying to impress Zaria. I'd even gone to the trouble of finding a real piece of rattan jog – the dried bark that gives a deep red colour to the dish – in the fifth Punjabi deli I'd tried. (The first four had told me to cheat and use vegetable dye. I ask you!)

I'd been house-sitting for Nassim Nassim's cousin Sunil in Leytonstone for a week now, which meant that the five-day housewarming party where all my so-called friends drop in to see how I'm coping, how much booze I've laid on and what the music centre's like, had come to an end. Zaria, a relatively new old friend, had been persuaded to stay over that Sunday night as I had convinced her I was missing my faithful feline companion

7

Springsteen, who was back in Hackney guarding the flat we shared. Apart from her obvious advantages, Zaria also took up less space in bed. It could be a case of Back To The Futon for Springsteen at this rate.

Anyway, all that – and the Rogan Josh, which I'd taken real sweat over, right down to serving it with iced bottles of Kingfisher lager and quarters of lime and rice fried with egg, and to hell with the risk of salmonella – was before Billy Tuckett dropped in.

I mention the Rogan Josh because it must be the reddest red food going and, like all good things, it stains. I know this to my cost, as I spent the next few days discovering which Stain Devil cleaning stick was needed to remove most of my portion from Sunil's white bathroom carpet.

It turned out to be the one the manufacturers recommend for blood and milk stains. That had always seemed an odd combination to me. I mean, why should people feel so homicidal towards milkmen?

I needed it because, when I finally disentangled myself from Zaria's legs (another advantage noted: no claws), I padded over to see what the noise was. Big mistake.

At first I thought it had maybe been a cat on the roof, then possibly some inept burglar. There didn't seem to be any sound coming from the bathroom, so I opened the door and fumbled round the corner to find

8

the light cord. Second, really huge, mistake.

There was a Billy-Tuckett-shaped hole in the skylight, which was actually a big picture window rather than the old-fashioned single-pane type, and a Billy-Tuckett-shaped body lying in the bath, one arm and one leg over the side. I took a step forward so I could see over the edge. Third, really crucial, mistake.

If the fall hadn't killed him, the large diamond of glass he'd brought with him and impaled his neck on certainly had.

That's when I threw up on the carpet.

I have a Rule of Life (No 74, actually) that says that you can work your way out of most situations if you can give yourself enough thinking time.

With my head bent over the sink, I had plenty of time to work out my options. My problems were: I had a body in the bath right behind me, a girl I'd known for less than 24 hours in a bed in the next room; I was staying in the house of somebody I'd never met, who was currently at a family wedding somewhere north of Karachi; and somewhere down the yellow brick road, I had to call the cops.

I couldn't do anything about Nassim's cousin being in Pakistan, I reasoned as I rinsed my mouth for the hundredth time. And I couldn't do anything about the body, could I? (I did think about that one.) So that meant I had to call the police, always assuming that the local Neighbourhood Watch hadn't. But I could get Zaria out of there and home fairly quickly. Besides, I had something for her to do.

Good. Decision taken; something to do. I felt better already. I'd wake Zaria and get her out pronto, then bell the local Bill.

At the time, I honestly never gave a thought as to why Billy Tuckett had been poncing around on the roof in the wee small hours or why he'd chosen Sunil's bathroom to fall through. I only just remembered to put some clothes on.

Zaria snuffled and turned on her back as I put the bedside light on. The lamp had a 'gentle' yellow light bulb, which gave her skin an olive tinge. It was a pleasant sight, as all she was wearing was a gold throat chain that spelled out 'ZARIA' in half-inch letters. I don't know why she wore it; my memory wasn't that bad. Maybe hers was.

'Come on, shake a leg,' I said.

'That's not my leg,' she said, without opening her eyes.

'Really? Maybe that's where I've been going wrong all this time. Come on, get your ass in gear. And don't tell me, that's not...'

She flapped my hands away as she sat up.

'What's the problem?'

She stretched her arms out in front of her like a cat, proving that Springsteen was still behind on points.

'I think we've had a break-in,' I said, thinking it was the best story to push, and concentrating on pulling up my jeans.

'Burglars?'

'No, very persistent Jehovah's Witnesses. Now get dressed.'

I fumbled around on the floor and found her white boiler suit and one of her high-heeled shoes. From what I could remember, that was two-thirds of her clothing. I flung them on to the bed where she should have been, but wasn't.

'Where are you going?' I said in a loud whisper.

'I need to pee.' She rubbed her eyes with one hand and pointed in the vague direction of the bathroom with the other.

'Not in there you don't, believe me.'

It took a couple of seconds to sink in, then she was struggling into the boiler suit, using language, under her breath, that would have made treble word scores in Rude Scrabble.

While she was looking for her other shoe, I stuffed my feet into trainers – no socks – and pulled on my Steel Wheels Tour sweatshirt.

'There's something I want you to do, Zed,' I said to her perfectly-formed backside.

'What?' Her voice was muffled because her head was under the bed, still shoe-hunting.

'Post something for me.'

'It's the middle of the sodding night. Isn't

it?' She wiggled, and I almost lost my train of thought.

'In the morning. I'm going to be tied up with the cops, I expect.'

She froze.

'Is it anything shady?'

No, you silly cow, it's a book club return. 'Just something I was asked to look after, that's all.' Well, that was almost true.

'But it wouldn't look good if the police ... A-ha!' She started to snake out from under the bed, clutching the renegade shoe.

'Just do it, hey. Or do you want to wait until the Law turns up?'

'Shit, no. I'm outa here.'

She sat on the floor and fastened the ankle strap of the high-heel. I hadn't realised how small she was without them.

I held out my hand. 'Come on. Bag?'

'Charming. You've a really nice morning-after manner.'

'No, your handbag, you Doris.'

'Oh. Sorry. It's downstairs.'

We crept downstairs like naughty children, and Zaria collected a leather handbag no bigger than a small keg of beer from the hallway table.

'Wait here,' I told her. I hadn't put any lights on, so with a bit of luck she would stay there.

I fumbled my way into the living-room and closed the door behind me before hitting the light switch.

Whatever Nassim's cousin Sunil did for a living, he did it from an old-fashioned headmaster's desk and a small personal computer. Behind the desk was the room's single bookshelf containing one of the most boring selections of reading material I'd come across. There were about half a dozen tax manuals, some computer books, a large-scale London *A-Z* and a copy of Duke Ellington's book, *Music is my Mistress*.

Naturally, I'd found that soon after I'd arrived. In fact, five minutes after checking the record collection (nothing worth taping) and the obvious places where you'd lock the booze away from the hired help. With nothing else to read, it seemed to have the edge on the income tax manuals (though nonbelievers would say only just), so you can imagine how bad I felt when I opened it to find most of the pages had been razored to provide a nest for a small brown envelope.

The technique's not new. I have a bogus copy of Hugh Brogan's *History of the United States* that has been turned into a fireproof combination lock safe; but that was a professional job done by my mate Lenny the Lathe in return for a favour. This was decidedly amateur night, and if the book itself hadn't stuck out like a sore thumb among the reference works, then a quick look at the floppy spine would have given

13

the game away.

I removed the envelope and decided to dump the book, which, empty, was probably even more suspicious. The envelope was about six inches by four and almost an inch thick. It was sealed with Sellotape and staples, a real belt and braces job. I didn't know what was in it; I just had the feeling that Sunil wouldn't thank me if the boys in blue turned it over in their usual zeal to find something to donate to the Oxfam shop.

I found a felt-tip pen in the desk drawer and addressed the envelope to 'Mr F MacLean' care of a pub I knew in South-wark where they knew me by that name. And if there was any doubt, I always had a spare driving licence in that name anyway.

I grabbed my leather jacket from the chair where it seemed to crawl to no matter where I'd hung it earlier, and found the keys to Armstrong in one pocket and a screwed-up five-pound note in the other.

Zaria was hopping from one foot to the other.

'Do you think they're still here?' she whispered, reaching for the front-door lock.

'Who?'

'The burglars.'

'Oh yeah. Sure of it.'

Well, I was damn sure Billy Tuckett wasn't going anywhere.

Zaria lived just up Eastern Avenue – let's

14

face it, half the world lives up Eastern
Avenue – in Redbridge, in one of those huge
roadside vicarage-like houses that has had
to be turned into a rest home for the elderly
because no-one else could afford to pay the
rates. Well, if they could, they wouldn't live
on Eastern Avenue. Zaria was a day nurse,
not an inmate.

The journey there and back took no more
than ten minutes once I'd got Armstrong
fired up.

Armstrong is my wheels. He's a black
London cab, of the traditional FX4S design,
world famous on T-shirts, cheap souvenirs
and postcards. Even with a mileage clock
that stopped at about 190,000 miles, he still
runs to perfection, never gets clamped or a
parking ticket, and blends beautifully into
the city background. They're becoming even
easier to pick up once de-licensed nowadays,
thanks to the invasion of the upstart Metrocabs, which drive like a Panzer, look like an
undertaker's second-best hearse and give the
punters a ride that makes them think they're
in a telephone-box on castors. Not that I'm
biased, of course.

If Armstrong has a disadvantage, then it's
that he hasn't got a passenger seat. So Zaria
sat in the back, opened the glass screen and
whispered frantically in my right ear all the
way home.

Mostly she quizzed me about the burglars,

and I said they'd tried to get in through the bathroom window and one of them had put a foot through it, probably coming from the roof next door, and I generally made out that there was a whole gang of footpads up there lying in wait for Santa Claus. It wasn't until we got to Redbridge Station that she thought – and I could almost hear her thinking – about the envelope and the fiver I'd given her.

'It's not drugs, is it?' she said suddenly. 'I didn't think you did drugs, and I won't handle them.'

'It isn't, I don't and you're not,' I said, but I was only sure of one out of three. 'But it is valuable and it might just be what those guys on the roof were after.'

She swallowed this, or seemed to. Thankfully she was still half asleep.

'Well ... if you're sure ... I'll post it tomorrow in my lunch-hour.'

I pulled up outside the rest home she worked at and reached through the window to open the back door for her, the way real mushers do without getting out themselves. She leaned in and pecked me on the lips. 'You've got my number?'

I bit my tongue and simply said: 'Sure, I'll bell you tomorrow or Tuesday latest. Okay?'

'Not the mornings, remember. They tend to sleep in the afternoons.'

'Got it. See yer.'

I watched her until she'd unlocked the side door of the big house and turned on a light. You can never be too careful these days. The residents could have been waiting to mug her with a Zimmer frame.

She waved and I did a U-turn – taxis are ace at that – and headed back to the nightmare in the bathroom. Why me? Other people have spiders in their tubs.

En route, I spotted a litter-bin on a streetlamp and I screeched up to it, jumped out and deposited the hollow copy of the Great Duke's book.

If I'd known then what I knew later, the envelope would have gone in with it.

Hassle, hassle, hassle.

I suppose my call went through to Wanstead nick, but I didn't ask. The copper on the receiving end took the details twice, and I didn't blame him. You don't often get people ringing up in the middle of the night to say they've found a body in the bath. Well, not on Sundays anyway. I promised I wouldn't touch anything, having no intention whatsoever of going anywhere near the bathroom again. I hadn't anything left inside me to throw up.

The first two were traffic cops, and they were on the street cruising for the house number, no sirens out of deference to the ratepayers, within five minutes.

I made sure I looked as if I'd just got out of bed and dressed in a hurry – hence no socks and the sweatshirt – and went down to the front garden to wave them in.

The one who took the lead looked big enough and mean enough to relish a ruck if there was a chance of one. His colleague, smaller and older, made sure he was going to be second going into any dark places.

'A break-in, is it, sir?' asked the big one, tightening his black gloves like he'd seen on television.

I did a double-take before I realised he'd been talking to me. I wasn't used to uniforms calling me 'sir.' Come to think of it, even when the taxman wrote to me, he spelled it c-u-r; which is why I never wrote back.

'Er ... I'm not sure, officer. There was a guy on the roof and then suddenly he was in the bath.'

The big one looked down at me as if I'd just crawled out from under.

'The bath? Did you say bath? Or bath-room?'

'Both. He ended up in the bath which, in this house, is actually in the bathroom.'

Watch it, watch it. That lip of yours will get you into trouble one day.

'There's a window in the roof,' I said quickly. 'More a skylight, really. He fell through that. He actually landed in the bath itself.'

18

Quite convenient, really, thinking about the blood.

'I don't even know he was trying to break in,' I added lamely.

'Odd place to go for a midnight stroll, sir,' said the older one sarkily.

I didn't tell him I knew people who did much weirder things than that.

'And just how did he get up there?' The big one looked up at the night sky, seeking inspiration. Then, looking at me: 'Have you called an ambulance?'

'No. It didn't seem ... necessary. You see, he brought most of the glass with him and sort of ... slit his throat.'

'You haven't touched anything, have you, sir?' The older one moved forward to take command now that it was clear the Apaches weren't waiting in ambush.

'Not bloody likely,' I said, then wished I hadn't.

'Get the gloves, Dave.'

The big one looked slightly disappointed, then trotted back to their car and took a black shoulder-bag out of the boot. They came into the hallway before opening it and taking out rubber surgical gloves. Since the Aids scare, that was now standard operating procedure. It hadn't crossed my mind, but I was grateful now that I'd been too busy throwing up to examine the body too closely.

'Right, sir, lead on,' said the smaller one.

I turned on lights as we went upstairs.

'Lived here long, sir?' one of them asked as we got to the landing.

'I don't actually live here at all,' I answered honestly. (Rule of Life No 5: always tell the truth; not necessarily all of it and not all at once.) 'I'm house-sitting for a friend of a friend; well, a cousin of my landlord, actually. I've been here about five days.'

'And where are the owners?'

I noted that he'd forgotten to say 'sir.'

'Pakistan. Until after Christmas.'

'I see. And where exactly do you live?'

'Hackney.'

'Hah! Bandit country,' said the big one from behind us.

I let that one go as we'd got to the bathroom, and I opened the door and stood to one side to let them in. I could feel the cold draught from the hole in the roof, but I had no intention of getting any closer.

'Oh, sweet Jesus!' I heard one of them say, followed by a retching sound choked back in the throat.

'Fuck-ing Ada!' shouted the other.

Then the big one appeared in the doorway, ashen-faced and wide-eyed.

'Why didn't you tell us the floor's covered in puke?' he said angrily, hopping on one foot.

'Oh yes. Er ... sorry.'

By 4.00 am I had a houseful of them. A brace of ambulance men, assorted uniformed beat coppers, two plainclothes men and a white-haired, white-coated pathologist who chain-smoked Players Navy Cut. He looked pretty fit for 75, but for 51, which is what he probably was, decidedly rough.

I made a gallon or so of tea until I ran out of milk, then a pot of black coffee, and pressed every cup and mug in Sunil's fitted kitchen into service.

The extra vehicles in the street, with their flashing blue lights, had brought some of the neighbours to their doors or bedroom windows, and one of the uniforms was designated to go and ask them if they'd seen anything. From what I could see, peeping out from behind the lace curtains in the living-room, nobody was admitting to much.

The two plainclothesmen disappeared for about half an hour in their Ford Escort and returned from the other end of the street. Why walk round the block when you can drive?

They hadn't said much to me apart from announcing themselves as Detective-Sergeant Hatchard and Detective-Constable White, and even when they got back inside, Hatchard talked to the pathologist while White went off for a snoop around, as policemen do.

I took a mug of coffee up to the pathologist

so I could earwig what was going down. He nodded his thanks as he took it and flipped another cigarette butt into the toilet. Before it had hissed out, he was lighting another.

'Thanks,' he croaked. 'Four sugars?'

'Absolutely,' I said, with the conviction of knowing I was going to live longer than he was.

'Whatderwannaknow?' he asked Hatchard.

'Whatever you've got,' said the Sergeant, his hands deep inside his overcoat pockets.

They didn't seem to mind me hanging in there, but it was getting a bit like the ocean liner scene in the Marx brothers' *Night at the Opera*. Two uniforms were trying to put an extendable ladder up to the skylight – God knows where it had come from – over the bath without actually having to look at the body. Another civilian was trying to set up a camera and tripod to photograph the scene, and everybody was trying to sidestep the vomit on the carpet.

'If the fall didn't break his neck,' said the pathologist in a cloud of smoke, 'then the massive blood loss and shock did. There's a piece of glass the size of your fist in his neck. Damn near took his head clean off.'

I could have told him that, I thought, but kept quiet.

'Foul play?' asked Hatchard.

'*No Sex, Please, We're British!*' said the pathologist.

'What?'

'That's as foul a play as... Oh, never mind.'

The pathologist raised his eyes to the ceiling. I didn't think it was bad for off the cuff, but he'd probably used it a zillion times before.

'Unless someone dropped him from a helicopter,' he said patiently, 'then I think it fair to assume he was clambering across the tiles and slipped, though God knows what he was doing up there. If it was suicide, then it was a bleedin' elaborate way of doing it and he changed his mind halfway down.'

He looked at the puzzlement on my face and the blank unemotion of Hatchard.

'Does this house have red pantiles?' he asked me.

'I dunno,' I answered truthfully. Why the hell should I look at the roof except to see if there was a satellite TV dish? (Come to think of it, I had and there wasn't.)

'Bet it has,' he said, nodding to himself. 'Yer man here–' he jerked a thumb at the bath '–lost most of his fingernails trying to hang on. What he's got left have got red plaster and dust under them.'

'So he wasn't wearing gloves,' said Hatchard to himself.

'Pretty amateur burglar if that's what he was.' The pathologist looked at his own hands and stripped off his surgical gloves, dropping them into a plastic bag. 'I'll organise the meat wagon once David Bailey here's finished.' He nodded at the photographer and flipped another butt into the toilet, then pressed the flush. 'Another day, another half-dollar,' he said cheerfully. 'Nice to have a fresh one for a change.'

I suddenly realised why he smoked so much, and felt queasy all over again. I was afraid I was going to heave.

'Time for us to have a little chat, sir,' Hatchard said to me.

I was afraid of that too.

'Name, please sir?'

Here we go.

'Angel.'

'Pardon?'

'Angel – as in on top of your Christmas tree,' I said before anyone else could say it. Sometimes, I hate Christmas.

'First name?'

'Roy.'

'Is that your full name?'

'Won't it do?'

'Full names now save time later on.' I noticed he'd soon dropped the 'sir' as well.

'Fitzroy Maclean,' I admitted, not relishing the idea of 'later on' one bit.

'Fitzroy Maclean Angel ... bloody hell...' came a voice behind me. It was the other detective, White, who had come into the living-room far too quietly for my liking. I knew somebody else who could do that, but he had four feet.

'And you don't actually live here?'

'No, I'm house-sitting.'

'New one on me, guv,' said White, slumping in an armchair.

'It's like baby-sitting while the owner's away.'

'To keep the break-ins to a minimum, I suppose,' said Hatchard drily.

'I never said I was any good at it,' I offered.

'And just who is the lucky owner?'

'A man called Sunil.'

'First name or last?'

'Er ... I don't know.'

Hatchard put down his notebook and ball-point and reached for a cigarette. I'd given up about three weeks earlier, but I was ready to beg from him. Bodies in the bath I could stand. Answering questions like this was really stressful.

'He's a friend of my landlord – the land-lord of the place where I live. In Hackney.'

'Exactly where in Hackney?' Hatchard asked patiently.

'Nine Stuart Street. Flat Three.' My heart sank as he made a note of it.

'And your landlord's name?'

'Nassim.'

'Nassim what?'

Oh dear. He wasn't going to like this either.

'Nassim. No, really, Nassim Nassim. We

did ask his surname and he said it was too difficult, and we had to stick to Nassim. So...'

Hatchard shook his head slowly.

'His address?'

I said I wasn't sure, but I gave them a phone number that I knew to be Nassim's office above a leather warehouse in Brick Lane. I felt I ought to try and phone him at home to tip him off – if I got the chance.

'The uniformed officers said you told them you heard a noise, got out of bed, went to the bathroom and then dialled 999. That's it, is it?'

'Apart from throwing up, yeah.'

'You didn't touch anything?'

'No way.'

'And you were alone in the house?' This out of left field from Mr Nasty Policeman.

'Yes,' I said, looking at Hatchard, Mr Nice Policeman, instead.

'These your knickers, then?'

White flung the pair of lemon panties he'd had scrunched up in his coat pocket on to the arm of the chair I was sitting in.

'Not my shade.' I knew Zaria had forgotten something. 'OK – look, I had a young lady here earlier – last night, that is. I didn't think the owner would approve, so I said nothing, but she'd gone home by then. Went home in a taxi.'

Did I lie? But the last thing I wanted was

them chasing Zaria and her telling them about the package she was posting.

'Honest–' I floundered. 'She was gone. She never saw Billy. God knows, I wish I hadn't.'

'Billy?' they said together. Good, they'd already forgotten about Zaria.

'Yeah, the bloke in the bath. Billy Tuckett.'

They looked at each other. This wasn't in their script, actually having information volunteered.

'There was no identification on the body. Did you take it?' asked Hatchard, leaning forward.

'No, I told you, I didn't touch him. But I could see who it was.'

'And you knew him?' This from Mr Nasty.

'I used to. We were at university together, but I haven't seen him in – what – ten years? He hadn't changed much.'

Except for being much deader than I remembered.

'Why didn't you tell us who he was?' asked Hatchard. White just sat there looking flabbergasted.

'You never asked,' I said.

Well, had they?

CHAPTER TWO

Why did I tell them it was Billy Tuckett? I've wondered since myself. But they would have found out; slow they might be, stupid they ain't.

Putting me and Billy together ten years back would probably never have occurred to them. Why should it? But I knew that somewhere down the line there would be some formal identification or an inquest where, with my luck, I'd run across Billy's mum and the cat would be out of the bag, to coin a very sick phrase. That would look bad, and even Plod would put two and two together and make five. It's much better to give them two and one and let them make four. It's called damage limitation.

I'd met Mrs Tuckett only twice; once when she drove Billy down to university at the start of a term and once when she turned up to see him get his degree. (A lucky third if I remember, but I couldn't recall in what, just the class. My, but we're snobs at that age, aren't we?) I had a nasty feeling she'd remember me, because she was the sort of woman who would remember somebody offering to drink Newcastle Brown Ale out of her shoe on Degree Day. And when she'd driven Billy, a pimply second-year, up to my hall of residence at the start of his fourth or fifth term, I'd been on hand to help them unload her Mercedes estate car. Actually, I'd been waiting for somebody else, but I just happened to be on hand and I couldn't just stand there and watch her struggle with all those boxes, suitcases, typewriters, bicycles, stereo systems and so on. I remember I looked at the pile of Billy's goods and chattels, which were supposed to fit inside a 12-by-six-foot room, and saying: 'I came with a Sainsbury's carrier – and I had trouble filling that.' And Mrs Tuckett had shrieked with laughter, because she probably was the sort of woman who laughed loudly in pubs, but would never intentionally hurt anyone, and who would be cut to the marrow when she heard of her only son's death.

She could have changed, of course. Run off with the milkman, disowned Billy, got religion; but I didn't think so. 'You'll look after him for me, won't you?' she'd said to me after we'd got him unpacked and she couldn't think of anything else that might prevent her from leaving. Billy had just shuffled from one foot to the other and blushed as all dutiful sons should do. I'd told her not to worry and that he was one of the lads, although I'd never seen him before, and we were just waiting for her to go before we started the party.

She'd laughed at that and resisted the urge to cuddle him in front of one of 'the lads' and had gone. I remember I said to Billy something like, 'I thought she'd never go. Where's the corkscrew?' and he'd answered – dead straight– 'What do you want a corkscrew for?' and so I'd made an excuse and left quickly.

I tried to think of when I'd seen him after that, apart from when we got our degrees – him proud and posing for the family album, me drunk and disorderly. I knew I had, on a couple of occasions, at student union meetings, but I couldn't think why, as he certainly wasn't a political animal. It would come to me eventually. I have that sort of brain. I can remember stuff they thought too petty for Trivial Pursuit and then some days I have to look up the instructions on my bootlaces.

But when I finally got to bed again it was well into Monday morning, and it was Monday afternoon when I surfaced and there was a policeman on the door and it hadn't been a nightmare after all.

The uniformed copper on the door told me he was only hanging about until he got the word on his 'talking brooch' radio that the forensic boys hadn't forgotten anything and wouldn't need to come back. He personally couldn't give a monkey's whether I went out or not as long as the CID boys knew where they could get me. I said they did and offered to leave the door on the latch so he could sneak in for a bit of a warm.

Before I left, I tried to ring Nassim Nassim, my erstwhile landlord and Sunil's cousin and, I'd decided by now, the man who had got me into this mess. It was odds on that the cops had got to him by now, but in case they hadn't, it might pay me to square things with him.

Nassim was not available, a female voice told me. I knew it was unlikely to be Mrs Nassim as she refused to get involved in his business activities even to the point of answering the phone. Well, that's what Nassim had once told us. I think it was his flimsy excuse for employing a procession of nubile young secretaries. Just in case this was one of them, I left my name and number, pointing out that it was the Stuart Street property and part of Nassim's empire, which made us almost family, didn't it?

I just managed to get in the fact that it really was quite important before she hung up. You can't win 'em all. One or two now and then would be nice, though.

I got Armstrong fired up and headed towards Hackney, using the back streets to avoid the worst of the rush hour. In effect, I'd lost a day, and I wondered if there had been something I'd planned to do that

Monday, like work, for instance. I couldn't think of anything I'd promised anybody and I hadn't anything musical on for a few days, so that was all right. Being self-unemployed has its upside.

In Stuart Street I had a choice of parking spaces outside No 9. It wasn't so much fun nowadays, not since Frank and Salome Asmoyah, the black Yuppie couple who used to have the flat above me, moved to their much plusher Limehouse pad complete with mortgage repayments delivered in envelopes with black edges. My going-away present to them had been a pair of inflatable yellow wheel-clamps, which I'd attached front and aft to their VW Golf. Nothing could be more guaranteed to induce apoplexy in a London driver, though I never could get onside with that sort of paranoia. Have you ever seen a taxi wearing a Denver boot?

As I got out, I caught the enigmatic Mr Goodson sneaking in through the front door, but if he'd seen me pull up, he didn't wait to say hello. That wasn't unusual, though. I knew he'd be inside his ground-floor flat with the door locked before I could get into the hall, no matter how fast I was. He rarely spoke to the rest of us peasants in the house, though when he did, he was nothing but polite. He didn't play music loud, drink to excess, have phone calls, watch television or go out at all at weekends. I tell people he's an alien. If I told them he was a quiet, shy, unassuming minor civil servant who read a lot of books, they'd have the weirdo squad from Social Services round straight away. After all, this was Hackney, and there were probably by-laws about such things.

I sneaked up the stairs to Flat 3, tiptoeing by the door of No 2 so as not to disturb Lisabeth and Fenella, the two dragons who inhabited that particular dungeon. It wasn't that we didn't get on; we did – surprisingly well, in fact. But while I'd been house-sitting for Nassim, Fenella had been cat-sitting for me. Not that that required much; it's just that not even Springsteen has mastered the tin-opener yet, though he's working on it. Unfortunately, Fenella takes her duties terribly seriously, and would have a minute by minute report of what Springsteen had been up to while I'd been away. Lisabeth, on the other hand, regards anything male (about 48% of the population) and anything that moves faster than she does (the rest of the animal kingdom) with deep suspicion, and the combination of her moaning and Fenella enthusing was too much for me.

Springsteen was out, but there were tell-tale signs that he'd been ruling the roost and no evidence that he was pining for my return. There was a dish of cat food down for him, plus a dish of tuna fish chunks (in soya oil as he likes to preserve his kittenish figure) and a saucer of rapidly separating cream. He had a cat flap in the flat door if he wanted to get into the rest of the house, and Fenella had thoughtfully left my kitchen window wide open so he could come and go that way via the flat roof of the kitchen extension next door. She'd also left the heating on for him, which was doing nothing except heating the window-sill for the pigeons and running up my bills. It looked as if I would have to have a go at the electricity meter with an electromagnet again. It also seemed, from the feathers on the kitchen floor, that one of the pigeons had come down for a warm and had got too close. Ah well, one less tourist attraction.

I peeled off my clothes and took a long shower – it would be a long time before I took a bath again, and certainly not round at Sunil's – and treated myself to a proper shave with hot water and a razor. I had been using my travelling battery shaver while house-sitting and, despite what Victor Kiam says, nothing beats hot water and cold steel.

I had just time to pull on a clean shirt and a pair of chinos – Springsteen's favourites as they show up his black hairs to best effect – before the local news came on the TV. I flicked on the box and took a can of lager from the fridge. The news finished at the same time as the lager. It hadn't been a busy day in London town, but there was no mention of anybody falling through windows in Leytonstone.

I opened another can and wondered what to do next. About the only practical thing I came up with was that I probably ought to start smoking again. That was more than a tad retro, so I distracted myself and put some music on.

I fed a CD of Hugh Masekela into the machine and fought back the urge to get my trumpet out and play along, ruminating on the injustice of a world that had taken so long to discover him. No doubt somebody had held a torch for him. As a student, with everybody into punk in a big way, I'd regularly paid over the odds for Chuck Mangione imports. So much music; so little time. And always the social pressure to keep up to date and with the scene.

I remembered the larder was bare and took a snap decision (actually, 'going snap' on a decision was the latest buzzword) to hit the local late-night deli. I picked up my wallet and a bright blue blouson with 'Status Quo – 19th Farewell Concert' on the back in day-glo gold. You see what I mean about having to keep up with things.

I was almost at the corner of Stuart Street when a car slowed up into the corner of my eye. I was either being kerb-crawled or a bunch of Quo fans were after the jacket.

It was Nassim in a battered red Nissan,

and if he was a Quo fan, he'd never admitted it. I had never had him down as a kerb-crawler either, but from the state of the car, it looked as if it had had a good kicking. He leaned over and opened the passenger door so he could yell at me.

'Hey you, Angel. I'm coming to see and you are leaving. You said urgent so I am come straight away.' He narrowed his eyes. 'The house is okay, isn't it? You haven't set fire to nothing, have you?'

I put on my best butter-wouldn't-melt expression and stuck my head inside the car.

'Sometimes, Mr Nassim,' I said politely, 'I think you have a very low opinion of me.'

He shuffled a bit at that, shrinking into his green trench-coat, which someone had told him was Yuppily fashionable.

'And anyway,' I went on, 'the insurance will cover it.'

'Well, that at least is something,' he said. Then: 'Cover what? Hey, Angel, wait...'

But I'd closed the car door by then and was heading for the deli.

I waved to him to follow me in, and he snuffed the Nissan's engine and climbed out. Then he got back in and came out holding a mobile phone, which he crammed into a coat pocket.

'Is that a mobile phone or are you just pleased to see me?' I asked as I held the deli door open for him.

36

'Eh?'

'Skip it. How long have you been driving that piece of rust?' I nodded to his car.

'You think I'm going to park the BMW in Brick Lane?' He had a point.

'Now what's this about insurance? Why do I need insurance?'

I handed him a wire basket and put a box of eggs in it. 'Not you, your cousin Sunil in Leytonstone.'

'What have you done? You said you would look after things. That's why I give you three weeks' rent amnesty.'

You noted that. Other landlords would have said three weeks 'rent free' or 'credit' or something. Nassim called it amnesty. I added some goat's cheese to the basket.

'I haven't done anything, except spend most of last night and all of this morning keeping the police off your back. Can you reach the milk?'

Without thinking, he added a carton of milk to his basket. From behind her checkout till, Mrs Patel looked at us curiously over the top of her blue-framed spectacles. 'Police? What police?'

'Tall guys in blue uniforms and cars with flashing lights on top. You must have seen 'em. Butter, please.'

'Why police? Were they looking for Sunil? I've never trusted that damned boy.'

'No, it's nothing to do with him. Put that

back, will you, and get the slightly salted type. I know it's bad for you, but what isn't these days?'

I winked at Mrs Patel and to my surprise she winked back.

At the meat fridge, I picked up a pack of ground beef. 'They used to call this mince until people started making their own hamburgers, you know. I always use garlic and a smear of tomato puree in mine.'

By now he was totally bemused.

'Look,' I said, to put him out of his misery, 'you know that big skylight Sunil had put in the bathroom when the house was done up?'

'Of course I do. I paid for it. His damn wife said it was not natural to have a room without a window. Sunil would not buy the place until it had been done. Why? Why are you asking?'

'Because you're going to need another.' I snapped my fingers as if I'd forgotten something. 'Yoghurt. Plain sheep's, please. It's back there with the milk.'

It was only after he had reached for it that he realised he was carrying my groceries around. Huffily he pushed the basket at me.

'So what happened? Drunken party, I expect. Throwing beer bottles through the window. That it?'

'Not quite. Someone sort of ... dropped in.' I couldn't think of any other way of saying it. 'A guy had been on the roof. Maybe he was doing a bit of breaking and entering.' Well, he certainly did that. 'And he sort of came through and landed in the bath.'

'In the bath?' Nassim's eyes were out like organ stops by this time. So were Mrs Patel's, who had cocked her head on one side to listen better.

'I can see nobody is going to believe this story first time, are they?' I said resignedly. 'Yes, he landed in the bath and the fall killed him.'

'He's dead?'

'Mostly.'

'But it is nothing to do with me,' he squealed, turning to Mrs Patel for sympathy. She shook her head slowly and tut-tutted to herself. I hoped I never got her if she did jury duty.

'No-one's saying it is, but I'm in the house because I'm doing you a favour. I don't know Sunil from Adam–' and I went on before he could ask 'Adam who?' '–and naturally, the cops will want to check that out. They might ask if you know if Sunil had any dealings with Billy Tuckett...'

'Who is this Billy person?' Nassim's arms started whirling. Not a good sign.

'The man who fell through your window.'

'It is not my window, it is that good-for-nothing Sunil's window.'

'And what does good-for-nothing Sunil do for a living?'

'Nothing. He works for me.'

Fair enough.

'So that's all you have to tell the police.' I put a hand on his shoulder. He looked at it suspiciously. 'In fact, all they'll probably do is ask if you can get in touch with Sunil for them. They don't know that Billy Tuckett was actually making for Sunil's house. It could just have been bad luck.'

'Who is this Billy Tuckett person?' He was getting close to foot-stamping time.

'The man on the roof.'

'What are these men doing on my cousin's roof? Just how many people are going on roofs? I don't have anybody on my roof.'

I nodded to where Mrs Patel had strung 'MERRY CHRISTMAS' in large red letters across the drinks shelf, anchored by a bottle of Bailey's Cream at one end and a six-pack of headbanging lager at the other.

'Well, if *you* don't have a visitor on your roof at this time of year, it probably means you've been naughty, not nice.' I handed my basket to Mrs Patel. Next to the till was a box of chocolate Christmas tree decorations. I picked out a chocolate Santa Claus and showed it to Nassim.

'He checks twice, you know.'

I cooked and ate and even washed up; tried to get into some music; and resisted the temptation to open a bottle of wine.

Nothing worked. My sleep/wake clock had bust a spring, and I was worried about the fact that it had been Billy Tuckett who had dropped through the skylight. Why couldn't it have been a total stranger? Then I could have left it alone.

Instead I rang Bunny, which nine times out of eight is a dangerous thing to do. I didn't ring him to borrow money, because he never has any to lend. I didn't ring him because he plays a mean alto-sax, though he is one of the best reed men currently not working out of a studio in the Windward Isles (wherever). I didn't ring him to ask his advice on how to pick up women – and if I did, it would only be to find out where he buys his chloroform.

I rang Bunny because he too had been at university with me, though, funnily enough, I didn't really know him until later. As a student, he had very quickly shacked up with a second-year chemistry undergraduate who had very definite ideas that Degree Day was rapidly followed by Wedding Day. And once Bunny graduated, so it did. He got a job in insurance, and the marriage lasted about three years and three months, then Bunny found out that his quiet, dutiful wife had been having an affair with her boss at the food research place where she worked for roughly three years and two months. Bunny threatened to chainsaw the flat in Muswell

Hill and torch the goldfish, although maybe it was the other way round. What in fact he did was give up his regular job, take his half of the Muswell Hill flat in cash and go out and buy an alto, followed by tenor and then soprano saxes. Then he dedicated his life to music and the pursuit of women, and we found we had something in common.

Music, that is.

A female voice answered Bunny's phone and told me he was out seeing a man about a second-hand tenor sax but I could leave a message after the beep. Then she yelled 'Beep' so loudly I ended up a yard away from our communal house phone, which is nailed to the wall just inside the front door. I wondered where Bunny had found her.

I played along, saying I was acting on behalf of Boot-in Inc Recording Studios – an outfit Bunny and I had actually done some backtrack recording for when they wanted a sound they couldn't synthesise – and that it was vital that I contact Mr Warren immediately to consult on his availability for a major recording contract, and which pub was he in anyway?

'Calthorpe Arms, Grays Inn Road,' she said, and I said thanks and hung up.

As I turned from the phone, I realised the stairs were blocked by Lisabeth, hands on hips, outside her flat door.

'What are you doing here?' she said, as if

reading from a Gestapo training manual.

'I live here,' I said innocently.

'You're supposed to be away for the week.'

The prosecution rests, m'lud. Case closed. Pass the black cap.

'I'm back for a couple of nights,' I said weakly. Why did I feel intimidated? Maybe it was because she had the advantage of the high ground and was looking down on me.

No. It was because she was Lisabeth.

'Fenella's out at her French lessons,' she said, dead straight.

I bit my tongue and simply said: 'So?'

She brought her hands away from her hips, which had hidden them quite well, and let a tin-opener and a tin of Whiskas drop onto the stairs.

'So feed your own damned livestock.'

And off she flounced.

I trudged upstairs and picked up the tin and the opener. Outside Lisabeth's door, I said in a loud voice, as if talking to someone: 'That's the trouble, you just can't get the staff these days...'

Then I ran the rest of the way just in case she'd heard.

The Calthorpe Arms at that time on a Monday evening was so busy that you could hear a beermat drop. There were about a dozen customers, mostly middle-aged men sitting alone reading *Evening Standards,* who troubled the barman only to the extent that occasionally he had to turn down the corner of a page of his Stephen King paperback. It must really be business that had brought Bunny here, as it wasn't his sort of pub. There were no women. Come to think of it, I wasn't that keen on it either, though it did serve a cracking pint of Young's bitter.

So good, I ordered a low-al lager so as not to get locked into a session.

Bunny saw me and gave me a brief nod, then went back to talking to a young black dude wearing a blue trenchcoat and nursing a colour-coordinated Filofax. Only the die-hards used them now; that was the first one I'd seen in captivity for some months. Maybe only the really bad cases, those who were hooked, had to keep their habit going.

After five minutes or so, they did their deal and the black guy left in a jangle of car keys, a big bunch on an ostentatious metal Mercedes key-ring. I bet myself he had a Skoda parked round the corner.

Bunny joined me at the bar and bought us both another drink. 'This isn't your turf, is it?' he asked, checking his change carefully and obviously in front of the barman. Bunny knows lots of little irritating bits of behaviour.

'No, I was looking for you, and I wouldn't have figured you for this particular humming and vibrant example of the capital's nightscene.'

'Business.' He shrugged. 'Had to see Elmore there about some instruments. Also got a job if you're interested, on Wednesday.'

I hesitated just that millisecond too long. Bunny works on the principle that if he asks every woman he meets to sleep with him, a certain percentage are going to say yes. If they say no straight away, he moves on. If they hesitate, he reckons he's in with a chance. He gets a lot of noes that way, but a remarkable number of yesses, and when he didn't register an instant negative from me, I was as good as signed up.

'It's a peach of an earner,' he went on quickly. 'And it'll be a giggle, guaranteed.'

'All that means is it's cash-in-hand and there are women involved somewhere. Where, when and, lest we forget, how much?'

He looked at me disapprovingly. Well, he tried to.

'You can be really mercenary at times, Mr Angel. Don't you ever think of anything but dosh?'

'Of course. I've got a lot on my mind: the state of the economy, interest rates, disarmament in the Warsaw Pact, lead in petrol, why nobody lets England win at cricket any more, does the Aids scare mean we'll never have another vampire movie, are 48 satellite TV channels enough...'

'Okay, okay, lay off the ear-bashing. Do you know St Christopher's Place up West?'

'The precinct, off Oxford Street?'

'That's it. All the shopkeepers there have chipped in and hired a promo agency to drum up Christmas trade. One of their ideas is to put a band on a lorry and drive round the block at lunchtime belting out the old traddies – the stuff you play. If nothing else, it'll annoy the hell out of Selfridges.'

'And on the lorry will be a clutch of nubile young ladies in red Santa Claus miniskirts and fishnet tights handing out leaflets saying "Come and shop in St Christopher's Place."'

He looked staggered.

'Somebody's asked you already?'

'No, Bunny, I just know the way your mind works.'

'There's 50 in it for you. An hour's work. Two, tops.'

'Who else is playing?'

'I've got Trippy on piano...'

'Does it have a full set of keys?'

'The piano does. I don't know about Trippy.' I nodded in agreement. 'He's got his mate Dod bringing a snare drum and high hat – I didn't think there was much point in a full drum kit.'

Again I agreed. I didn't personally think having a piano on the back of a truck was much use either, but it looked good and gave the band somewhere to balance their beer cans.

'There's me on clarinet, you on horn, and

I've a tuba player called Chase. Know him?'

'He's a miserable git, isn't he?'

'That's him. I'm still short of a trombone, though.'

I took a felt-tipped pen out of his jacket pocket and wrote a number on a beer mat.

'Ring this first thing in the morning. It's a direct line into the BBC. Ask for Martin. He's very good and he'll probably do it for nothing if he can get a couple of hours off.'

'Cheers,' said Bunny, pocketing the mat as he'd done a million others, though the phone numbers on them weren't usually trombonists'. 'What *are* you doing here, anyway?'

'Came to see you. Your answering service said you'd be here.'

He looked down into his glass.

'Ah yes ... Edwina.'

'Edwina? Where did you find her?'

'She found me, and I'm having trouble getting rid of her.'

'I never thought that was your problem.'

Bunny pursed his lips and whispered: 'Bitch.'

'I wanted to pick your brains,' I said.

'Find 'em first.'

'Think back to your carefree youth before the cares of the world descended on your manly shoulders.'

'Last week, you mean?'

'Ha-chortle-ha. A bit further back, to uni days. Remember a kid called Billy Tuckett?'

He thought for a minute.

'Yeah – vaguely. What's he to anybody?'

'I ... er ... came across him the other day, that's all.'

I indicated that Bunny's glass was empty, but he shook his head. 'I've been trying to recall what Billy did at uni, or afterwards,' I went on. 'Did you ever come across him?'

Bunny looked at the ceiling.

'Didn't we used to call him...'

'Yes, of course we did, but we were young and unsophisticated then.'

He nodded agreement.

'Yeah, I've caught him a coupla times. I think he lived out Romford way, but I never had much to do with him. I saw him at the odd university reunion. You know, when I was married to that ball-crushing, vicious old cow Sandra.'

'I'm glad to see you've got over your matrimonial difficulties without rancour,' I said, draining my glass, knowing he wasn't listening.

'We used to have to go to them all and raise funds for the old *alma mater*. Actually, that sow Sandra only went to see how we were doing in the rat-race compared with her contemporaries. Obviously we weren't keeping up with the Joneses, so she started screwing the boss.'

'And Billy used to go?' I tried to get him back on to the subject.

'Oh yeah, hanging around moonfaced like he did ten years ago, all ill-fitting clothes and two halves of shandy because he had his pushbike with him.'

He saw my expression.

'No, straight up, he always rode a push-bike. Never learned to drive. It was against his principles. Cars pollute the atmosphere, all that shit.'

'Is that why I remember him? He was into the environment? A Green?'

'Sure, anything like that. He was in all the conservation groups when he was a student, but his big thing was animals.'

'Animals. You mean like "Save the Whale"?'

'And the rest.' Bunny zipped up his jacket and made to go. 'Save the Whale, rescue the rabbit, free the anaconda. Stop animal experiments, stop fox-hunting, abolish police horses, vote your gerbil into Parliament.'

'That's been done. Many times.'

'Too bloody right,' he grinned. 'He couldn't hold a conversation about anything else. That was Billy. Any chance of a lift?'

I said okay and we wandered out. The barman didn't say goodbye.

On the street, as I unlocked Armstrong, Bunny said: 'You never got conned into any of that, did you?'

'What, the rat-race or going to uni reunions?'

'Both.'

'No, that's right,' I agreed. 'I never got into the rat-race – or the brat-race as it is now – because I never wanted to. And I only ever went to the first reunion after graduation.'

'Couldn't hack it, eh?' he asked, climbing in the back.

'No, I was barred after the first one.'

CHAPTER THREE

The heavy mob came round the next morning; all one of him.

He said he was called Prentice and he was a detective-sergeant and he'd been well trained in the most vicious of police techniques: politeness and reasonableness. From the off, he had me convinced that by helping him I was doing no more than carving out a new life for myself as a better citizen, a better human being. Maybe this was my chance to make up for all those little oversights and lapses in the past, which we all have no matter how hard we try to forget or overlook them. If I could help him – and, after all, he was only doing the job we paid him to do, wasn't he? – then it would be a personal shot at redemption on my part.

He almost had me going, but my Rule of Life No 14 is that when somebody offers you the chance of a lifetime, they usually mean theirs, not yours.

I was on the communal house phone, which is chained to the wall tighter than a medieval Bible, when the doorbell rang. Most everybody in the house had gone to work, or whatever it was they did during daylight, and as I was only two feet away, I reached over and slipped the lock, taking the phone receiver with me.

'With you in a tick,' I said, signalling at the phone.

He nodded politely and showed me the palm of a gloved hand. I went back to sorting out a schedule for the day with Simon, the proprietor of Snogogram International. But I felt the hairs on the back of my neck stand up and decided that maybe I'd better not say too much in front of the stranger.

'Okay, Simon, 12 sharp down in Southwark. You can fill me in then,' I said, and hung up.

I took a closer look at our visitor. The soft, black leather bomber jacket, the steel-rimmed glasses, the light blue Ford Escort parked out in the street behind him. I should have known immediately. If he'd actually had a flashing blue light on top of his head, I might have rumbled him sooner.

'Mr Angel? Glad I caught you in. My name is Prentice. Detective-Sergeant.'

'I suppose it's about...'

'Yes. Mind if I come in?'

I couldn't think of a good reason why not, so I ushered him towards the stairs and told him I lived in Flat 3. Half way up, Springsteen shot through his legs and passed me at about Mach 5, doing a handbrake turn at the bottom of the stairs and heading for the back door. With his eyes flashing, he looked like a black, furry guided missile.

Prentice turned his head to see what had just missed him, making the finger-rubbing gesture and whispering 'Puss ... puss...' which is something I've noticed a lot of people who haven't met Springsteen do. Maybe it works on other cats, but I wouldn't attempt it without asbestos gloves.

'Yours?' he asked.

'I pay the rent and he lets me sleep here.' I shrugged as I opened the flat door. He waved me in first.

'I'm a dog man myself,' he said conversationally.

'Well, naturally. Dobermans, Rottweilers, attack Alsatians...'

He pushed his spectacles back into his face with the middle finger of his right hand. I was to learn that it was his way of controlling his temper.

'Jack Russells, actually. My father bred them. Of course, it's not fair to keep dogs like that in London, not natural hunters like them.'

So that's where I was going wrong with Springsteen. Maybe I should buy him a place in the country. Maybe a foreign country.

'Is this going to take long, Sergeant? I have to go to work, you see.'

'I shouldn't think so. Just what exactly do you do, Mr Angel?'

Now I had a number of answers to this. Self-unemployed was the usual one, though I didn't think that would wash with Prentice. And I would never say that to anyone who was unemployed but didn't want to be. To anyone who was claiming unemployment benefit or social security, which I don't, I would imply that I'd registered as 'outdoor clerical' or similar, and wasn't it a disgrace they couldn't find me a job? Sometimes I stick to 'driver' – well, I have a cab (though you'd better not be talking to a real musher), and a Heavy Goods Vehicle licence. But 'driver' has dodgy implications if you're a copper. So I compromised.

'I'm a musician.'

'Oh, so you have a degree in electronics?'

He said it with a faint smile. I knew what he meant. Possibly he was human after all.

'Not me. Strictly crash-bash saloon bar trad jazz.' I pointed to where my trumpet was balanced on top of one of the stereo speakers. People think I put it there as a piece of pop art to decorate the room. Only I know I forgot to pack it away.

'Have you done the "in" clubs? You know, Jazz Cafe, the Wag Club, places like that?'

He was well informed, probably more up to speed than I was.

'I'm not into Yuppie-jazz, so I'd never get asked to the Jazz Cafe, though they get some good people there.' That was true; in fact, Stoke Newington was turning into the Storyville of British jazz. 'But I never get past the bouncers at the Wag.'

'Me neither,' he grinned.

Maybe I could do business with this guy, I thought. Sometimes I have the weirdest thoughts, and I always promise to give up eating cheese late at night but never do.

'Time for a cup of coffee?' I asked, not keenly.

'Sure,' he said, moving a pile of paperbacks and sitting down in my fake Bauhaus leather and steel chair (one of a set, of one).

I went into my kitchenette and flicked the kettle on. His voice carried after me.

'Interesting mixture of reading material,' he yelled.

'I try to keep the grey cells working,' I shouted back, more to reassure him that I hadn't done a runner out of the kitchen window.

'Bit of military history, detective stories – is there any money in these old Penguins?– PJ O'Rourke, essays by Gore Vidal, the new Jeffrey Archer–'

'Sorry, somebody must have left that here,' I yelled.

'What did you read at university?'

'History,' I shouted, pouring water.

'Billy Tuckett did Chemistry, didn't he?'

End of polite chit-chat. Rule of Life No 61: there's no such thing as off-duty.

I carried the coffee jug and filter and two cups back into the living-room and put them down on my coffee table, which sounds posh but in fact it doubles as a dining table, poker table and ironing-board.

'Real coffee,' said Prentice. 'That's a treat.'

'Never been able to drink instant since I went to America the first time. I've no milk, but there's sugar somewhere.'

'That's okay; as it comes.'

I moved a pile of CDs off the sofa-bed and sat down, balancing my 'I LOVE HACK-NEY' mug on one knee.

'I didn't know Billy that well, in fact hardly at all. But yes, I think it was Chemistry. Is that relevant to anything?'

'No.' He buried his face in his mug, which didn't say anything but had a picture of a cat rolling a joint. 'But it was a hell of a coincidence, wasn't it?'

'What was?' I asked, playing dumb.

'Billy Tuckett being the person to drop in on you like that.'

'He couldn't have known I'd be there. I didn't know myself where the house was until the week before last. And anyway, I haven't seen Billy for Christ knows how long, and I never knew him well. And–'

'Okay, okay.'

'–another thing: what the fuck was he doing on the roof in the first place?'

'Ah, now I think I have a theory about that.' Prentice leaned forward and put his mug on the table. 'Can you spare me an hour or so?'

'What for?' I asked suspiciously.

'I want you to come out to Leytonstone with me and let me show you something.'

'Well, I... Look, Sergeant, just what have you got on me? There is no way I had anything going with poor Billy, and no way he knew I'd be in that house.'

'Of course not, Mr Angel.' Prentice smiled, and that made me more nervous than anything. 'It's such a bleedin' long-shot set of coincidences, it has to be true. Nobody, but nobody, would be daft enough to stick to a story like that if it wasn't.'

I was glad somebody else saw it my way.

'I think I know why Billy was heading for that house,' Prentice went on. 'He knew someone who used to live there before it was owned by a Mr...'

He reached inside his jacket for his notebook but I said 'Sunil' before he could clear his shoulder-holster, or wherever it was he kept it.

'Yes, er ... Sunil. Now he's–'

'In Pakistan, I believe.'

'Been living there about a year, is what I was going to say.'

'Oh, sorry.'

Rule of Life No 37: when a policeman's talking, shut up.

'Before that, the house was occupied by a Miss Lucy Scarrott. Does that ring any bells?'

'Should it?'

'I happen to know that the late Mr Tuckett was very close to Ms Scarrott.'

'But not close enough to know she'd moved out?'

'Possibly,' he said slowly.

'Or maybe she sent Billy back to turn the house over; is that what you're thinking?'

He smiled, and I felt the hairs on the back of my neck go rigid. 'You've got a devious mind, Mr Angel. Ever thought of a career in the police?'

'Blue's not my colour.'

'I've heard worse reasons.'

'I can't possibly be tall enough.'

'They're very flexible about that nowadays.'

'I've got a degree,' I said, getting desperate.

'So have I,' Prentice checked me.

'I couldn't stand the short working week, and I really wouldn't know what to do with all that bribe money.'

'Ah, there is that,' he said, as if thinking it

over. 'But then, you don't go into the CID straight off...'

I licked a forefinger and made a 'nice one' stroke in the air. He was okay, but (Rule of Life No 38) the time to start worrying was when the policemen got nicer.

It's not that I have anything against them *per se,* of course. It's just I like to know where I stand and which bit of me to tense up before the rubber truncheon lands. It's the same in power politics. The Russians would much rather deal with a right-wing conservative any day, because they know where they stand, rather than a left-wing liberal who might do something off-the-wall, like act on principle, for heaven's sake. I had the feeling that Prentice was out to kill me with kindness, or at least make me put my hands up to something I hadn't done. But what?

'Look, Sergeant, what's the deal? I recognised Billy Tuckett from way back and thought I'd save you guys some time by giving you his name. I could have kept the lip zippered. I don't know this Lucy Scarrott female and I don't know what Billy was doing on the roof. What can I tell you?'

'Maybe nothing,' he shrugged. 'But I'd value your input.'

'You're not thinking of opening a sperm bank, are you?'

'Sorry,' he laughed. 'Got to watch the jargon.'

'You probably use a lot down Wanstead nick.'

'I don't work out of Wanstead,' he said carefully, but went no further.

'So what exactly do you want from me?'

'I want you to come with me to Mr Sunil's house and let me show you what I think happened to Billy Tuckett.'

'What good would that do?'

'I'm not sure, but you might be able to fill in the odd gap.'

I shook my head in despair.

'How many times? I haven't seen Billy in years and I don't know why he decided to have a night on the tiles on Sunday. Why don't you try this Lucy Scarrott bird?'

'We can't find her. Bit embarrassing, really; she's supposed to be on probation, but her probation officer sort of lost her about a year ago.'

'And I'm the next best thing?'

'The only lead to Billy we have, and, I admit, a pretty slim one.'

'As long as we understand each other on that score, fair enough.' Going along with him seemed to be the best way of getting rid of him. 'But I have to ask, though I think I might regret it, what is Lucy Scarrott on probation for?'

'Breaking into an animal research centre.'

Oh-oh. Animals again.

I followed Prentice's Escort over to Leytonstone in Armstrong. I told him I wanted to go on to work afterwards, but really I needed thinking time to try and figure him out.

We turned into Dwyer Street and I still hadn't made any headway. Then I realised he wasn't stopping outside Sunil's house, but carrying on to the other end of the road. He parked ten yards or so after the last house, outside a wire-mesh fence in front of a late 1950s prefabricated school. There was a handkerchief-size tarmac playground in front and a wooden sign, which somebody had tried to set fire to, saying Dwyer Street Infants' School.

Prentice got out of his Escort and locked it, then pointed to the gate of the school yard. I pulled Armstrong in behind his car, got out and joined him by the gate. There was no padlock on it, and it squealed as Prentice pushed it open.

'Your motor?' he nodded towards Armstrong.

'Yeah, and it's taxed.'

'You can pick up second-hand Metrocabs now, you know.'

'Wouldn't have one given,' I said firmly.

'Why? Not as economical on the fuel?'

'No, just no character.'

He gave me a quizzical look, then indicated to the left side of the school.

'Come round the side,' he said, and I

followed him down the tarmac path, which was about a yard wide, between the school building and a six-foot wooden fence that isolated the first house in the terrace.

'It's not a school any more,' he said over his shoulder.

'Well, they have to hide the Cruise missiles somewhere,' I said, zipping up my fleece-lined leather jacket against the rain, which had started coming down in ominous big spits.

I had a sudden pang of conscience about the hole in Sunil's roof where the skylight had been. But it was only a brief pang.

Prentice was ignoring my backchat.

'It's a local community centre, Scout hut, adult education centre and creche. In fact, it's probably used more now than it was when it was a school.'

He'd stopped in front of the side door, a flimsy hardboard affair with a Yale lock, distinguished by a fist-sized hole to the side of the metal keyhole.

'Now who do you think would want to do that?'

Prentice put his left hand through the hole and flicked the lock from the inside.

'Someone who wanted to do what you've just done,' I said as I followed him inside. 'But they had a sledgehammer, not a key.'

We were in a kitchen of sorts. I presumed it had once been the school's dinner ladies' empire, and there was still a stove and tea-making gear but not much else except a funny smell. It was musty and earthy and oaty all at once.

Prentice was watching me. He didn't say anything, just nodded towards the big enamel sink, which had a single cold water tap and a rickety hot water geyser above it. (These 'butler's pantry' sinks are worth a few bob these days, either to the dockland Yuppies doing up houses Jack the Ripper wouldn't have been seen dead in, or to amateur photographers who use them in their darkrooms. I'm not sure what for.)

To the side of the sink, under the draining-board, were half-empty sacks and bags that contained cereals, wood shavings and what looked like the sort of seeds you feed to birds rather than the ones you roll with tobacco.

'Either school dinners have really gone downhill, or there's one hell of a big parrot on the loose round here.'

'You're getting warm,' Prentice said. 'Come here.'

He opened a door into a corridor, and I followed him down it. The doors of the class-rooms along it had handwritten cards draw-ing-pinned to them saying things like 'Course 21B: Italian' or 'Over 60s Metalworking,' and one that said 'Blue Tit Patrol' pinned high enough up to avoid any graffiti. At the end was a fire door with a push bar. Prentice opened it and wedged it open with a rusted chunk of iron left there for that purpose.

We were in a small courtyard into which had been crammed half a dozen hutches and garden-shed-type constructions. There was also a ten-foot square pen of some sort like a small corral, made out of odd bits of timber, and in one corner, a pile of what was unmistakably manure.

'It's a frigging zoo,' I said.

'Got it in one,' said Prentice smugly.

'Now hold it a minute,' I said, holding my hands up. 'Are you telling me Billy was here Sunday night, and it had something to do with animals. These–? There aren't any fucking animals here!'

'The place is closed for the Christmas holidays, and the RSPCA takes care of the livestock until January. It started when it was a school. You know the score; give the urban kids a slice of country life. Some teacher must have found out that most of his class had never seen a duck before, so they started an urban zoo. There were quite a few of them back in the '70s. When the school closed, they kept the animals on for the toddlers in the local playgroups. They use the place most mornings. And the old caretaker lives next door, so he feeds them and mucks out. It was no big deal; just a few chickens, a couple of rabbits, hamsters, gerbils and a donkey.'

'A donkey?'

'Yes. Early retirement from Southend beach, I understand.'

'Strewth, they're even laying the donkeys off now. Times must be hard.'

'It's the cuts,' he said, playing along.

'And you're fingering Billy to have been here on Sunday on some sort of animal liberation commando raid?'

'If that's what it was, they were too late. The animals were shipped out on Friday, but maybe they didn't know that. And yes, I think your mate Billy was here ... broke in here ... on Sunday. Didn't you say he was keen on animal rights when he was a student with you?'

'No, I don't think I did,' I said, looking him in the eye. 'And anyway, how did he get up on the roof?'

'I'll show you; but first, look inside the huts.'

'Which one?'

'Any of them.'

I opened the door of the nearest one, but gingerly in case there was a puma or something the RSPCA had forgotten. The interior stank of wet fur, and there was dirty, dried straw on the floor. It was ten seconds or so before I realised I was supposed to be looking at the inside of the wooden door. Someone had spray-painted, about a foot high, in bright red, 'AAAA,' so the letters overlapped.

'Aaaarg?' I asked Prentice, but this time he

didn't smile.

'The four As. Sometimes they just put figure 4 and capital A. It stands for Action Against Animal Abuse.'

'So we are talking animal libbers.'

'Not your average flag-day collectors or the sort who give out leaflets on market day. These are the animal fundamentalists organised into hit squads. The SAS of the animal rights movement. Let's get inside, the rain's set in for the day.'

Prentice kicked the iron block away so the fire door slammed behind us. He motioned towards the classroom door with the 'Blue Tit Patrol' sign.

'Look in here.'

I went in first, and all I saw was a standard classroom with a blackboard down one wall, two lines of plain tables and some wooden chairs. A broken chair lay on its side in the far corner, its two front legs about a yard away.

'So?' I shrugged.

'The caretaker swears blind that there were no broken chairs in here on Friday.'

'You've lost me,' I said truthfully, parking my bum on the edge of a table.

Prentice pulled out a chair and sat down.

'I think your friend Billy and his fellow commandos were a bit peeved to find themselves here after the horse had bolted, so to speak.'

'Or the donkey,' I added helpfully. He

ignored me.

'I think there's a good chance that Billy was brought in here and asked a few nasty questions by his fellow liberationists, and maybe there was a fight.' He stood up and picked up his chair in a sweeping movement.

'I think Billy might just have been desperate enough to smash that chair over somebody's head so he could make a run for it.'

'Hang on a minute. Just rewind that, would you. Why should Billy's Action Man friends take it out on him – unless they thought he'd set them up?' I was getting a bad feeling deep down about what I was saying. 'Unless they thought he was a plant or a snitch?'

'You've been watching too much *Hill Street Blues,*'he said. 'We still call them grasses over here. And yes, Billy was contemplating becoming my grass.'

'You make it sound like a mid-life career move. Does it come with a personal pension plan?'

'Billy was into some serious shit with these loonies. It sounds trivial – what's a bit of spray-painting? Who would notice? But believe me, whatever they had really intended to do here was just the opening shot in their Christmas campaign nationally.'

'And they aim to be in Paris by spring?' I did my 'Let's invade Poland' impersonation, which isn't very funny at the best of times. It didn't impress Prentice one bit.

'Don't underestimate these people,' he said seriously.

'Why should I?' I asked, meaning: what business is it of mine?

He didn't answer, and I should have walked away then and there. If I'm not more careful, I won't live to see 30.

Again.

'I figure he went over the fence here,' said Prentice when we were outside in the rain once more.

'Why not go out the front gate, the way they came in?'

'Perhaps there was somebody on lookout in a car or something. They must have had transport. I found some fibres here.' Prentice pointed to the top of the fence. 'Almost certainly from Billy's jeans. And there was a rubber skid mark from his shoes.'

'And then where?' I asked, adding: 'Not that I'm interested, but you're going to tell me.'

'Take a look.'

I grabbed the top of the fence and pulled myself up until I could rest my forearms there, keeping myself about a foot off the ground by skidding the toes of my trainers – only cleaned the previous week as well – into the wet wood.

On the other side was the back door of the first house in the Dwyer Street terrace, which ended down the road with Sunil's at No 16. Although probably built as a row by some Victorian property magnate, all the houses were slightly different from the front and all had been built on to or extended differently at the back. This first one would be No 2, with odd-numbered houses on the other side of the road. Somebody at some time had converted the scullery and outside privy into a modern, one-storey kitchen. I leaned further over until I could see down the line of houses. Most of them had similar extensions.

No 2's fitted on to half the back of the house, leaving a downstairs and an upstairs window free. The extension's roof sloped up at 45 degrees to within about four feet of the roof proper. The owner, wisely not trusting London tap water for his greenhouse, had installed a network of guttering to catch rainwater in a pair of large, aluminium beer barrels (worth over a hundred quid to the brewery and a thousand a ton to the illegal smelting operations over in Barking). The barrels had holes cut in the top to funnel the rainwater in, and plastic taps knocked into the side to let it out.

It was perfectly possible to see how Billy could have vaulted the fence, got onto the kitchen roof via one of the barrels and from there onto the main roof and all the connecting ones down to Sunil's house. If you were desperate enough, it was the only way to travel, but on a frosty night in the middle of December, you had to be desperate.

'The caretaker's house?' I asked.

'He didn't hear a thing,' Prentice said, nodding.

Well, neither had I until Billy had either slipped or tried to open that skylight window. I lowered myself down off the fence.

'So?'

'So Billy Tuckett gets badly scared and starts running for where he thinks his old friend Lucy Scarrott lives.'

'I'd got that far. I meant, so what's it got to do with me?'

'You knew Billy...'

'Like hell. Briefly and very much in the past tense, and I don't mean 'cos he's dead. I knew him once, a long time go. I don't see where I come into this at all.'

'What if Billy knew Lucy wasn't there and it was you he was running to?'

'Impossible.'

'Sure?'

'He hasn't seen me or thought about me for ten years, as far as I'm aware, and he couldn't have known I'd be in that house. How many more times?'

'Okay.' He put his hands in his pockets and walked off. I caught up with him halfway to the gates.

'You said Billy was your grass. Who was he grassing on?'

'I don't know.' Prentice didn't stop walking, but he slowed. 'We never got that far. He was worried about what the cell was planning, thought they were going too far, and he was almost ready to come over.'

'Cell? What are you talking about?'

Prentice began to swing the schoolyard gate shut.

'The 4As are organised on a cell basis, with four or five members per group. Each acts independently but to a central timetable. This – whatever it was they planned – was just one of eight incidents across the country on Sunday night. This one came to nothing, but you must have read about the others.'

'No, I don't take much notice of newspapers.'

His look made me feel guilty, though I couldn't think why it should.

'We found incendiary bombs in department stores in Leicester and Huddersfield – fortunately before they'd gone off. A chicken farmer in Norfolk had the front of his house sprayed with liquid manure, and a pharmaceutical laboratory was broken into in South Wales and about 50 white mice released.'

'That means there'll be a hundred on the run by now.'

He squared up to me.

'These people are not funny. 4A is out on a limb compared with any of the animal rights organisations that have gone before.

70

Pretty soon they're going to kill somebody.'

'Aw, get out of town. You're winding me up.'

He began to unlock his car door.

'If you won't help, fair enough. I'll see you at the inquest.'

'Help? How the hell can I help? And why should I?'

He held the Escort door open.

'Billy came to me because he was in with a bunch of fanatics. That's what he called them, and he was worried because something big was coming up and it would get out of control. He wouldn't say any more until he'd had a chance to talk it over with a friend, he said.'

'And you think that was me?' I snapped. I was getting ratty, and the rain was going down the back of my neck.

'Or Lucy Scarrott, or maybe somebody else. You knew Billy, You could find his friends, find out what he was into.'

'A bit thin, isn't it?'

'You're all I've got.'

'And why should I?'

He exhaled slowly and rested a forearm on the top of the car door.

'Billy dropping in on you was a big coincidence, and we don't like coincidences, so further investigation may be necessary.' He put his head on one side, but kept a straight face. 'If I read you right, you're not the kind who would welcome further investigation much.'

'You mean really deep, persistent scrutiny and monitoring of my day to day existence? What a less law-abiding, trusting soul might well call harassment, if they were feeling uncharitable?'

He smiled and climbed into his car.

'Remember, the Force is with you.'

I let him get clear before I turned Armstrong around and cruised down Dwyer Street.

Nassim's battered Nissan (Nassim Nassim's Nissan? Why couldn't he have a Ford?) was outside No 16 and there was a builder's flat-backed truck parked in front of it. They would be repairing the skylight, I guessed correctly, and were probably a firm Nassim had shares in, so he could fiddle the invoices for the insurance company.

I popped in to see what the form was, and to find out if I'd been fired as a house-sitter. That was all I had in mind, but I ended up, five minutes later, knowing something the police and the probation service didn't know.

I found out where Lucy Scarrott was living.

And I should have kept it to myself.

CHAPTER FOUR

Of course, I didn't realise at the time just how deep I'd get in, and I can't be blamed for not seeing what would happen in the end. As far as I'm concerned, a Tarot card is of no use unless it fits one of those hole-in-the-wall banks, preferably on somebody else's account. (The bank card I want to get hold of is the one issued by an Arab bank called Watani Express. No kidding, a credit card with a camel instead of a hologram!)

To be honest, I didn't give it much thought. The morning was wasting away and I was on a promise to deliver women for Simon down in Southwark.

Simon the Stripping Vicar had also in his time been Simon the Sex Ton, the Curvy Curate and even the Randy Rabbi. You name it, he's taken off the clothes for it. He used to work for an outfit in the City called Even Rudergrams, but about a year ago the market fell right out of the bottom of the stripping kissogram girl (or boy) business, and the company packed up and moved into something else. Probably private health insurance or personal pensions. Ever wondered where the old door-to-door encyclopaedia salesmen went?

Simon bought up the costume store and set himself up in premises in Southwark, under the name Snogogram International. It was basically the same old idea of stripping kissograms, but he had one or two speciality lines. The most popular was undoubtedly the stripping policewoman or traffic warden – always good for a laugh among London's paranoia-ravaged motorists. Once, when very drunk, Simon had phoned me late one night to try out a new concept, the 'Uzi-O-Gram,' which had the catchline 'Shoot up your girlfriend's wedding, just for fun!' I had explained that while this was probably in the best of taste and unlikely to be very illegal, it was already being done in California and he'd be pushed to get third party insurance cover. This latter piece of logic had been the clincher, and he'd dropped the idea as soon as he'd sobered up, the following week.

He had come up with one idea, though, that had turned out to be a blinder at Christmastime. He called it Boozebusters, and the idea was that wives (and, more rarely, husbands) who were fed up with their partner's non-stop round of office parties would hire a Boozebuster squad to snatch the miscreant from the pub or wine-bar or restaurant, or even the office itself at a pre-arranged time. Needless to say, the 'snatch squad' (yes, I know, but that's what they called them-

74

selves) were usually scantily-clad kissogram girls armed with water-pistols and cans of projectile shaving foam. The girls all had wodges of visiting cards in their stocking tops, which they threw as they grabbed their victim, and these had the Boozebusters logo – a picture of a drunk in a red circle, with a red slash – and Simon's phone number on them. That Christmas, the Boozebuster girls were the sharpest thing in town.

Naturally, Armstrong was the perfect vehicle for transporting a hit team, especially if they were dressed as policewomen. At Christmastime in the City these days, there were more fancy dress police than real ones.

I checked in with Simon just after 12.00.

'Got a good one for you, Roy,' he said. 'A four-hander at the Princess Louise in Holborn. Know it?'

'Do fish swim? There's no parking around there.' I like to think Simon paid me for my expertise.

'That's why I wanted Armstrong,' he said.

Okay, so he paid me for my taxi. I didn't mind; I was happy that he still talked to me at all. I'd once had to miss a rendezvous with him after he'd done his own stripping vicar act for some giggling secretary's twenty-first birthday, and he'd shot out of the pub stark bollock naked to find me somewhere else. Ever-resourceful, he'd stolen a copy of the *Evening Standard* to hide his blushes and gone home by Underground.

The Snogogram building wasn't really a building, it was a converted railway arch. There was just one room, rather like a small warehouse. Simon had a desk and three telephones near the door, and the rest of the place was taken up with racks of costumes and boxes of party stuff such as balloons and streamers. There was even a cardboard birthday cake about ten feet across, which a couple of girls could leap out of if somebody paid for their time and the hire of a van.

I sat on the edge of Simon's desk, as there were no chairs. Behind it were several sets of screens at different angles, behind which the stripogrammers or Boozebusters got changed.

'What time?' I asked him.

'About two-ish. It's some guy called Harding, and its his last work day before he goes on holiday. His secretary–'

He broke off as a natural brunette called Kim came from behind one of the screens. She was wearing a red basque and matching knickers, with four suspender straps hanging loose around her white thighs. It was a nice piece of lingerie, but I'd never worked out why they named it after Spanish terrorists.

'Will you do this bleedin' thing up for me?' She offered Simon the drawstrings round the top of the basque. 'Oh, hi, Angel. Christ, but it's as cold as a witch's tit back there. Ever thought of investing in any heating, Simon?'

Simon didn't answer, just turned in his swivel chair and began lacing up the front of Kim's basque while still giving me my instructions.

'–his secretary has ordered a full four-hander policewomen buster to make sure he's back in the office by two-thirty so he can sign all the staff's petty cash vouchers. He is a bit of a late lunch merchant, by all accounts.'

He finished tying a big bow dead on Kim's cleavage and, as she turned to go, she winked at me.

'Here's his office address.' Simon had swivelled back to me and handed me a piece of paper with an address in Theobalds Road.

I was watching Kim walk back to the screens. She was holding a suspender in each hand like she had a skipping rope. I had a bizarre thought. Maybe they named the Spanish terrorists after…

'No problem,' I drawled, checking the address. 'Who else is coming?'

A full four-hander meant that two girls dressed as policewomen would go into the pub, locate the victim and intimidate him in front of his office cronies, then start taking their clothes off. Two others, wearing raincoats over their underwear, would be waiting at the bar or similar, ready to join the fray shouting 'Boozebusters' and things like 'Your wife/secretary/boss is taking you out of here now!' And then they would spray foam, throw cards, pop party-poppers and so on and drag the victim out to a waiting fast car. Or in this case, Armstrong. Suitable scenes of red-faced hilarity would occur back at the office, as someone always tipped off the entire staff to be ready at the front door. It was not unusual for the orderer of the Boozebuster to specify a long route back to the office, to give the victim's fellow revellers time to get back ahead of him.

'Kim and Jacqui will be the cops, Frances and Eddie will shadow them with the shaving foam and stuff,' said Simon, like it was Normandy beach 1944.

'And my mission, should I decide to accept it?'

He looked at me blankly. Surely he wasn't too young to remember *Mission Impossible?* Oh God, he couldn't be, could he?

'Make sure they don't leave their coats – or their underwear – hanging over the beer pumps.' He looked up at me sharply. 'This time.'

I looked suitably abashed. I honestly thought he would have forgotten the Marquis of Granby incident.

I looked at my watch.

'Have I got time to do a quick errand? Just round the corner.'

He looked at his watch; a liquid crystal

Roger Rabbit affair. Trendier than my Tissot Seastar, but not as expensive. It's the little things that count, I always say.

'I was hoping you could pick up Eddie from the Blackfriars at one sharp. She's doing a birthday kissogram before she shadows the Holborn job.'

'Can do. I only want to pick something up from Union Street, so it's on the way.'

'Don't be late,' Simon said seriously.

'I won't be,' I answered, equally straight.

I'd worked with Eddie on a Boozebuster before. She was a large lady, happily married with three kids, without a chemical trace of inhibition in her body. If any Boozebuster victim decided he didn't actually want to go back to the office or home to his wife, Eddie would gently, but very publicly, take hold of him by what she called his 'wedding tackle' and lead him out of the pub. I wouldn't have believed it if I hadn't seen it with my own, slightly watering eyes. No way would I keep Eddie waiting.

I yelled a 'See yer' to Kim, along with some friendly advice about not letting her thighs get too cold. Simon muttered something under his breath about 'That would show up the teeth marks,' which both of us hoped she didn't hear.

I knew the Blackfriars well enough. It was a smartly restored pub that lovingly recreated the interior design of its psychopathic creator a hundred years ago. The main bar had an alcove with more marble than Lord Elgin could have handled, and, at the northern end of Blackfriars Bridge, it was over-popular with the lunch-time City crowd who thought it daring to venture across the river.

This close to Christmas, it would be packed solid, and I doubted if Eddie would be out on time, but I wasn't going to risk it.

I stopped at the Duke of Wellington – a scruffy corner boozer off Union Street – just long enough to buy two cheese rolls and a can of low-al lager to go. There were few customers, and the landlady had been leaning over the bar reading the *Daily Mirror.*

'Haven't seen you for a while, Mac,' she said, tight-lipped as she dropped the cheese rolls into a brown paper bag.

I suddenly realised she was talking to me. She thought my surname was Maclean.

'I've been working up north,' I smiled, convinced that for her the North began at Cannon Street.

'That's rare.'

I wasn't sure whether she was referring to regional unemployment figures or the fact that I claimed to have actually worked for once.

'Sound system okay?' I nodded to the twin tape-deck behind the bar as she counted out my change. I'd rigged it for her a while back in part payment for temporary accommo-

dation after the house I'd lived in in Southwark had accidentally been sort of totally
damaged. I'd recorded some background
music for her too, and it didn't sound as if
she'd added to her collection.

'Not much call for it these days,' she said
sullenly.

I gave up trying to remember her hus-
band's name so I could ask after him. From
the look of things, it was odds on he'd done
a runner with either the till, a barmaid or
the Christmas Club fund. Maybe all three.

'There hasn't been any post for me by any
chance, has there, Iris?'

She shook her head. 'Phone bill, electricity
bill and a notice saying the rates are going
up. And that was just the second post.'

'I'm expecting something from an old
friend, and I just remembered he only has
this address for me.'

'Nothing's come here, luv. I'll keep it for
you if it does. It'd be quite exciting to get
somebody else's mail for once.'

She went back to her *Daily Mirror.*

'Well ... er...' I couldn't think of much else
to say. 'I'll call in tomorrow, just in case.'

'You do that, Mac,' she said, without looking up. 'Maybe we'll be less busy. Maybe
you'll have a drink next time.'

No wonder the customers were staying
away in droves.

I picked up Eddie just as it started to rain again, and we chatted all the way back to Simon's office while she dressed herself in street clothes from a Sainsbury's shopping-bag. (That's how you know when you're going to be kissogrammed. Watch for the woman with her hair up, dressed in a rain-coat, who leaves a shopping-bag near the bar after a quick word with the barman. Of course, if you get it wrong, she's a terrorist and you've got about ten seconds to finish your drink.)

After she got out, more or less decent now, I readjusted the rear-view mirror back to its driving position and followed her in.

Simon was on one phone at his desk, grunting a lot but not saying much. I motioned to the other phone, and he waved me go ahead, so I parked a buttock on the edge of the desk and fished out a scrap of paper – a cigarette paper – from my wallet. The number pencilled on it was Zaria's workplace. Or so Zaria had assured me.

'Aurora Corona,' said a fruity voice.

'What?'

'Aurora Corona Rest Home. Who is this?'

Where did they get a name like that? I thought that was a Mexican beer.

'Er ... I'd like to speak to...'

'No telephone calls accepted for residents–' I wondered how long it had taken him to break the habit of saying 'inmates' –

'during luncheon.'

'Actually, it was one of your staff I was–'

'I'm sorry–' Oh no you weren't – 'but we do not accept personal calls until after four pm.'

'But it's important.'

'Who did you wish to speak to?' he mellowed.

'Zaria.'

'Hmmm. Is it an emergency?'

'Yes.'

'Are you a relative?'

'Yes. It's family business.'

'Zaria who?'

Oh shit.

'Pardon?'

'Which Zaria? We may have several on the staff.'

You bastard.

I hung up. That would teach me to pay more attention, to put names to phone numbers. Now they were unfashionable, maybe it would be okay to get a Filofax. No. Things weren't that bad.

The Boozebuster went off without a hitch. The unsuspecting and very sloshed Mr Harding was bundled out of the pub and into the back of Armstrong with the four girls in various stages of undress. It was a bit of a squash, but he didn't seem to mind, and I'd put on a tape of golden oldies (stuff from around 1985) for them to sing along to.

Before we got to his office, he'd persuaded Kim and Eddie (with a fistful of notes) to come with him and start another party at his local wine-bar after he'd 'cleared his desk.' I took Jacqui and Frances back to Southwark and collected my wages from Simon.

Then I headed north in the general direction of Redbridge to the Aurora Borealis Bide-A-Wee rest home, or whatever they called it, determined to get Zaria well sorted.

The clever devil who'd answered the phone had said private calls after 4.00 pm, which I guessed would be a shift change for the staff. I remembered something Zaria had said about clocking on at 8.00 in the morning, and 8.00-to-4.00 seemed a reasonable working day. Well, to some people. To me, it sounded depressing.

With the traffic thickening and the street lights coming on, it would be after 4.00 when I got there. London traffic now moves at an average speed of 11 miles per hour. Cabs carrying Sherlock Holmes did better than that, and you couldn't grow roses using Armstrong's exhaust.

I was thinking about life, the universe and how much I liked Kim Carnes's voice (a voice that makes you regret moving to filter cigarettes) on the tape-deck when I began to conjure up a mental picture of Billy Tuckett. At first it was back in university days again, and then, suddenly, him lying all bloody in

Sunil's bathtub, and it wasn't even funny bizarre any more.

It wasn't a vision or a psychic experience or a message from above. (Falling over is God's way of telling you the bar's about to shut, in my book.) Maybe it was delayed shock. Maybe it was drugs. I made a note to get some.

I don't know what it was. I just found Armstrong heading towards Lucy Scarrott.

On the speakers, Kim Carnes was feeling it in the air and praising the Universal Song. I just love the old romantic ones. So I'll blame her.

When I'd called in at Sunil's place after Prentice had driven off, Nassim was on the landing yelling orders to the builders, who were crashing around in the bathroom. It was as if he didn't actually want to go near the scene of the crime, and I couldn't blame him. The police had done a reasonable job of cleaning up and had put a plastic sheet over the hole in the window to keep the rain out. A couple of lads, who looked as if they were moonlighting from a Youth Training Scheme, were trying to re-glaze the window from the inside, underneath the plastic so their haircuts didn't get damp.

I hoped Nassim was making enough on the insurance claim to have the job done properly in the not-too-distant future.

'Everything okay?' I asked cheerily.

'No more dead men, if that's what you mean,' snarled Nassim. 'You be careful of those tiles!' he yelled towards the boys in the bathroom, who were setting up a step-ladder in the bath. 'You'll make good any damages.'

'He wasn't a burglar,' I said, joining Nassim at the top of the stairs.

'Who is a burglar?'

'Nobody is. The man who fell through the roof wasn't after any of the family jewels. He didn't have a striped jersey or a bag marked "Swag," as far as the Old Bill are concerned.'

Nassim winced at the sound of breaking glass from the bathroom, but it was only the remaining splinters of the old stuff coming down. I got interested as well. I love to watch people work when they obviously have no idea what they're doing.

'What are you talking about? Can't you see I'm busy?'

'The dead man wasn't a burglar is what I'm saying. You can relax on that score.'

'Not my house,' he said, not looking at me but straining to see round the bathroom door. 'Just my bloody money!'

At last, emotion. I was getting to him.

'Okay then, Sunil can relax.'

'He's coming home. Mind that paintwork, you!'

'What?'

'I rang him last night, and he's flying back

86

today or tomorrow. I think it a good excuse to get away from his family. I don't blame him. I don't like them either.'

'I thought you were related.'

He looked at me as if I'd crawled out from under the Axminster. 'We are. Hey! That toilet seat just will not take your weight!'

I shook my head and wondered if there was any room spare on the next space shuttle.

'Well, you won't be needing me here then, will you?'

'Correct.'

'I'll get my gear together, then.' That wouldn't take long. I was wearing most of it. 'I suppose the rent amnesty's off as well?'

'Double correct.'

Merry Christmas.

'Anyway, tell Sunil it wasn't my fault.' He looked daggers at me, so I pressed on before they drew blood. 'The guy wasn't a burglar, he was coming here because he used to know someone who lived here before.'

'Oh, the Cat Woman,' Nassim said casually, then yelled: 'Careful!' as part of the window-frame dropped onto the bathroom carpet.

'I know I'm going to regret this,' I said, but still said it. 'This ... er ... Cat Woman, she wouldn't be called Scarrott, would she?'

Nassim still kept his eyes on the lads in the bathroom, one of whom had produced a seven-pound hammer from his tool-bag, but reached for his wallet pocket and produced a broken-spined red leather diary. He wet a finger and flicked through some of the loose pages at the back.

'Here we are. Lucy Scarrott, 28 Geneva Street, Highbury.' That was up near the Arsenal football ground. I knew that from when I'd gone to watch them play in the past; but I'd been cured of insomnia for some time now.

'How do you know that?'

'Know what?'

'Where she lives?'

He looked at me pityingly.

'When we bought this place from her, she had nowhere to go. She did not tell Sunil this until the exchange of contracts. She was one totally disorganised lady. So I – I–' he jabbed himself in the chest with a finger '–had to find her alternative accommodations.'

'One of your bedsits?'

'For a couple of months, yes. Her and her smelly cats. I do not approve of animal pets in my properties.'

'And why should you?' I asked, looking down at my feet.

'And I also had to take her furniture into store until she found this house in Highbury. Then she telephones one day and says she wants her stuff delivered bloody quick. Not one word of thanks do I get from her or from Sunil or his wife... Hey!'

One of the apprentice glaziers had lit up a

wide-mouth blowtorch.

'When was this?' I asked quickly.

'Six, seven months ago.'

'And she bought this place in Highbury?'

'Bought? Rent? How should I know? Said she wanted somewhere better to bring up her baby.'

'She had a baby?'

'One baby and maybe 27 cats. The place smelled awful as soon as she moved in. What is he doing?' He pointed to the lad with the blowtorch.

'I think he's going to weld the new window into place. Have a nice day.'

I jogged down the stairs while he began to argue with the builders. I didn't fancy being around when Sunil got back to check his library.

So that's how I was heading north-west towards Highbury and Lucy instead of north and east to Zaria. I'd get to her later; hopefully before Sunil got to me. But I still wasn't sure why.

Perhaps it was Nassim's mention of the baby that sparked me off, however subconsciously. Perhaps I thought that if it was Billy's kid, then somebody had to tell Lucy the bad news, and if she was skipping probation, it had better not be the cops. But then, if it was Billy's kid, why didn't he know she didn't live on Dwyer Street any more?

One fact I did recognise and hang on to was that late afternoon was the best time to find a young mother at home. Even if you didn't know anything about baby-feeding times, a quick look at the TV schedules would tell you that. The programme planners assumed that most women's brains came out with the baby. If I was a young mother, I'd write in and demand re-runs of Joseph Losey movies or continuous showings of *Jewel in the Crown,* but then I'd never get to learn about biological cleaners working at low temperatures.

Geneva Street was a row of identical terraced houses without even different front-door paint-jobs to distinguish them. No 28 was noticeable only because it did not have net curtains, just long, dark purple ones that were almost drawn across the front room window. I could see the flicker of a television set reflected in the glass, though. I'd been right about the biological cleaners.

I parked Armstrong round the corner and walked back to press the doorbell of 28.

Before the two note ding-dong had faded, a baby had started to howl inside. And howl, and howl.

Eventually, the door opened an inch on a chain thick enough to restrain a Rottweiler. A lock of blonde hair and the edge of some round, gold-rimmed glasses appeared at my chest height, and I'm not that tall.

I almost asked if her sister was in; then the

tone of voice that said, 'Yes, what is it?' told me that wouldn't be too clever.

'Er ... Lucy Scarrott?'

'Who wants to know?'

I couldn't blame her. I do the same if someone I've never seen comes up and uses one of my names. Sometimes I do it if I know them quite well.

'My name's Roy,' I said round the corner of the door. 'I wanted a word about Billy Tuckett.'

'Billy's not here. I haven't seen him in over a year.'

From behind her, the baby's howl turned to a high-pitched whine, like Concorde warming up.

'I've got to go. Tell him he'll have to stand on his own two feet.'

The door began to close and I put out a hand to stop it.

'I can't. There's been an accident.'

The door eased back against the chain.

'How bad an accident?'

'The worst kind,' I said, hoping it didn't sound flip.

'He's dead?' said the blonde voice, after ten seconds silence.

'I'm afraid so.'

More silence, then she said: 'I'm sorry. Thank you for letting me know.' And then she closed the door, leaving me on the step in the rain.

For a minute or so, I just stood there. I hadn't really known what to expect, but it wasn't this.

To my left, I saw the long purple curtains twitch in the window, and for a moment I thought it was her just making sure I'd gone. But then they twitched again, and I looked down to see, just above the sill, the curls and bright blue eyes of a snub-nosed child.

I crouched down so that we were eyeballing each other and began to pull funny faces; the sort of expressions you do in traffic jams when you don't think anyone's watching. The kid began to laugh and steam up the window-pane, then started slapping the glass with a tiny hand, leaving greasy fingerprints.

After about two minutes of this, I heard the door open.

'Was there anything else you wanted?' she said.

I had to take my thumbs out of my nostrils and uncross my eyes before I answered.

'I wouldn't mind a chat about Billy, if that's all right.'

I drew a pattern in the raindrops on the window for the kid while she thought about it. The kid laughed loud enough for me to hear, and then the chain snicked off.

'You'd better come in,' she said. 'Before the Neighbourhood Watch get you.'

It wouldn't be the first time, but I didn't say it.

She led me into the front room where, defensively, she picked up the baby. She was only about five feet tall, if that, and the kid, a big, healthy specimen, seemed to be only a few inches off the floor. Lucy and the kid were wearing matching outfits: jeans and blue sweatshirts with World Wildlife Fund patches. The kid had bright yellow socks on; Lucy was barefoot and her hair was longer and she wore glasses. Otherwise, there wasn't that much difference.

The baby pointed at me and said: 'Der ... da-dat...'

'You have a lovely daughter,' I said, shaking my head slightly to stop raindrops running into my eyes.

She looked impressed.

'Most men think Cleo is a boy, just because I don't dress her in pink frocks.'

It had been a 50-50 chance, but it's better to be lucky than good. (Rule of Life No 1.)

'The pink for a girl, blue for a boy thing was probably thought up by men just to help them identify their kids without having to resort to close inspection. How old is she?'

'Sixteen months.'

'So she was born when you lived in Leytonstone?'

'What is this? What the hell has that got to do with anything?'

'I'm sorry.' I must have moved towards her, as she took half a step back. I indicated a chair, and she nodded that it was okay for me to sit down.

She relaxed visibly as soon as I did so. Now she was looking down at me.

'I'd better come clean,' I said. 'I was in the house you used to own in Dwyer Street on Sunday. Billy Tuckett fell off the roof and killed himself.'

'What?'

She let Cleo slide over her thigh and down onto the floor. The kid toddled off like a drunk trying to balance two pints of beer.

'I don't know any other way of saying it.' I did, but not so she wouldn't scream. 'He fell off the roof and killed himself.'

'Suicide?' She sat down herself, but her face remained blank. In a good light she could pass for 16.

'No, no way. It was an accident. We think he might have been trying to find you.'

'We?' Suddenly suspicious. 'Just who is we?'

'Look, lady–' Little Cleo staggered back into the room clutching a bright red balloon '–I just happened to be there, looking after the place while the owner was away. That was my first bit of bad luck. The second bit was that I had to identify Billy. I knew him, back in student days, but I hadn't seen him for ten years.'

Cleo ran to Lucy and hit her around the knees with the balloon, shouting 'Doon ... doon.'

Lucy reached out and ruffled Cleo's curls. 'I haven't seen him myself for about a year,' she said quietly. 'He called round one day and saw Cleo there and after that... I think Cleo was a shock to him.'

'Is ... was...?'

'Don't be embarrassed; I'm not. No, Billy wasn't the father. That's why it was a shock to him.'

Cleo tore off towards a fold-up dining-room table on which a hairy brown cat I hadn't noticed until now had begun to stir and stretch.

'Dat ... dat ... dat...' yelled Cleo, pointing at the animal, which wisely stayed just out of her reach.

'Cleo's a constant source of worry,' said Lucy vaguely.

'Seems fighting fit to me,' I said.

'It's her words,' Lucy went on, almost as if I wasn't there. 'Everything she says starts with a "D." She can't seem to get her mouth round anything else.'

'Don't worry, it'll come,' I said paternally, but not too much. 'Was ... er ... Billy...?'

'Expecting to be the father? No. I think even Billy knew you had to sleep with some-body before that happened. Billy and I were just good friends, really good mates. That's all. Can you believe that?'

'Sure. Why shouldn't I?'

'Most men can't, or won't.'

Cleo did another circuit of the room and emerged from behind a chair with a well-sucked teddy bear. 'Ded ... Ded...' she cooed as she hugged it.

'Billy moved away to work–' she hesitated for a fraction of a second '–out of London about three years ago, and I started seeing someone and Cleo was the result. Billy came back just before I sold the house in Dwyer Street and saw her when she was a baby. Yes, I can see what you're thinking. He was disappointed in me, I think. I didn't see him again. And now I don't suppose I ever will.'

She leaned over and hugged Cleo, who put a delicate finger on her mother's nose as she whispered: 'Dose...'

'Did you tell Billy you were moving out?'

'I didn't tell *anybody* I was...' She looked at me accusingly. 'How the hell did you find me?'

'Mr Nassim,' I said quickly. 'The guy who looked after your furniture. The guy who helped buy your house. He's my landlord. I was doing him a favour looking after the house over Christmas.'

'Have you told anyone else?'

'No. Any reason why I shouldn't?'

'I don't want Cleo's father to find us.' She stood up. 'I'm sorry about Billy, but I don't see what it has to do with me or how I can help you. Just what are you trying to do anyway?'

'I'm not sure,' I said, more or less honestly. 'Maybe just laying a ghost. There'll have to be a funeral.'

'There usually is. Thanks, but no thanks. I have my own problems.'

Just for a moment, I thought I saw a flicker of emotion in her eyes, but it was probably a trick of the light.

'You and Billy were into animal rights campaigning, weren't you?'

That stumped her for a few seconds, then she opened the door to the hallway for me.

'That was a long time ago. You'd better go now, I have to get Cleo's tea.'

There didn't seem to be any point in pushing it, so I made to leave.

'Bye, Cleo.' I waved to the toddling girl, who was over by the window again, banging a fist on the pane and watching the rain drizzle down.

'Dith ... dith ... dith...' she said to herself.

I don't know why Lucy was worried about the kid. I could understand every word she said.

It was dithing it down outside.

CHAPTER FIVE

It was dark and well stormy by the time I got to the Aurora Corona Rest Home, and the residents were probably battened down for the night. I parked Armstrong on the road and walked down the short drive to the impressive Gothic porch around the front door. That at least had a light showing. At first I thought the rest of the building was in total darkness, but as I crunched gravel and got closer, I could see they used extra-thick curtains, maybe leftovers from the blackout. They'd help deaden the screams.

I got wet again, as the rain had set in in stair-rods. The interior of Armstrong was beginning to smell of wet dogs, and that just added to my bad mood. Since lunchtime, I'd done nothing except be in the company of women, hanging around in pubs or crawling through traffic. I was getting hungry and frustrated because I hadn't been able to enjoy any of it.

There was a printed card fixed above the doorbell, which told me I had about ten minutes before visiting times were up. I pressed it, and there was a buzz and a click and the door opened an inch by itself. I shook the rain out of my hair and wiped my feet on the doormat, then stepped into the porch and tried the inner door. That opened into a hallway with a huge open staircase, almost certainly pinched from an older house, and a reception desk.

If it hadn't been so quiet, it could have been Paddington station during a commuter cull. The hallway and various passages off it were full of visitors helping pyjama-ed relatives in and out of chairs, plumping cushions for them or fetching magazines from a well-stocked rack, or encouraging them to that last little drop of cocoa from what seemed to be a standard-issue purple mug. None of the wrinklies – sorry, shouldn't be ageist – looked remotely grateful or pleased to see their visitors, and the feeling was probably mutual. They needed something to stimulate them, even I could see that, to dispel the overwhelming atmosphere of gloom.

I thought about leaving a few of Simon's visiting cards around, or suggesting they all get together and build a glider in the loft, but then I saw the frosty-eyed Matron in a blue uniform and matching hair rinse clocking me from behind the desk.

I was on borrowed time. Better turn on the blag.

'Good evening, Matron,' I beamed, walking straight towards her. 'I hope you don't mind me arriving without an appointment like this, but I understood you had an open door policy.'

She looked as if she didn't know what I was talking about, which was okay. That made two of us.

'I am right, aren't I?' I pressed on. 'You do encourage potential residents to call in and inspect at any time, don't you?'

'Well, actually–' she began.

'Of course, it's not for myself.' Big joke, smile, show the good teeth to full effect. 'It's my grandmother.'

'Your grandmother?'

'A marvellous lady. Eighty-seven going on 55, as we say in the family.'

'She's...?'

'Yes, you've guessed. She's just getting too much for my sister to handle, and what with me being abroad so much... Even with Concorde, I'm away for long periods nowadays.' Steady on, don't overdo it. 'So I thought I'd strike while the iron was hot, so to speak, and we were just passing, and so here we are.'

'Your grandmother's here?'

'Well, outside in a taxi, actually. She has her things with her–'

'I'm sorry, but this is highly–'

'And we've been recommended to you by one of your staff, I believe. A Miss Zania, is it? She gets on very well with my grandmother; in fact, she's one of the few young people she'll actually listen to when–'

'Sorry, we don't have... Oh, you must mean Zaria.'

'Zaria?' I played dumb, having been cut off in mid-flow.

'Zaria Inhadi. She's one of our staff nurses. Or rather...'

Behind me, I heard one of the elderly male residents say to his visitor: 'Oh God, it's her.' Then another toothless male voice said loudly: 'Quick, son, stand in front of me, she's coming.'

I sneaked a glance to my left, but all I could see was a rather attractive young nurse wheeling a chair-ridden, white-haired old dear down the corridor towards us.

'I'm sorry?' I concentrated on the Matron. It was important not to give her thinking time. 'You were saying ... about Nurse Zaria?'

'I'm afraid she's not here any more. She gave her notice in and left yesterday. She had family problems. It was very sudden.'

'Good lord. My grandmother will be most disappointed. Zaria was one of the few people who could control her when she had the moods.'

'Well, there's nothing I can do about that,' she said stiffly. 'And it is certainly most unusual just to turn up on the doorstep like this, Mr...?'

'Prentice,' I said off the top of my head.

Behind me, one of the men seated in the hall whispered urgently: 'For God's sake stand in front of me, son.' I still couldn't see what the problem was, but the whole hallway area had gone suspiciously quiet. The pretty nurse with her wheel-chaired lady was nearer, and I could read 'Sally' on her white uniform badge.

'I really don't see how we can accommodate your dear grandmother at such short notice...' Matron plugged on. Then I realised most of the visitors and all the residents were watching me, and I turned my head from side to side to see why I was getting that uncomfortable my-flies-must-be-open feeling.

As 'Sally' came level, we made eye contact and I smiled politely at her. The rubber wheels of the chair she was pushing squeaked on the tiled floor as she passed behind me, and then I felt a hand on my inner left thigh.

I think my eyes bulged and my buttocks clenched in reflex, but there was a fair amount of surprise there, as I could see both of Sally's hands on the handles of the wheelchair. I knew what she was doing but I couldn't work out how.

Then the hand got higher and the grip tighter and suddenly Sally was not looking at me but at the old lady in the chair and saying sharply: 'Mrs Cody! Stop that!'

I got a quick squeeze and then the hand withdrew.

As she went by, the old dear cackled loudly and yelled: 'Did you see the arse on that, young Sally? Eh?'

The Matron flushed.

'Mr Prentice, I'm so sorry...'

'Don't worry about it,' I said generously. 'I think my grandmother would fit in very well here.'

I meant it as well, even though I knew she'd miss the hang-gliding.

The next morning, I was a day older, no wiser and put in a bad mood right from the off because I was dragged from the Land of Nod kicking and screaming (well, grunting and stumbling actually) by the Celtic Twilight hammering on my door.

I'd christened the new residents of the flat above that just in case they ever decided to form a folk-singing duet and needed a stage name. From the first moment I'd seen Inverness Doogie and his Welsh wife, Miranda, I'd had them down as a sort of suicidal Sonny and Cher.

Doogie was Scottish – well, he would be; nobody would admit to coming from Inverness if they weren't – and had absolutely no sense of humour. It was almost as if it had been surgically removed along with his appendix when he was a kid. On our first meeting, he had thought I was a removal man working for Frank and Salome who had gone on to higher things (mainly higher rates, mortgage repayments, so forth, so fifth). Things had got worse after that, when I'd met Miranda: as dark and austere as a Welsh mining valley and as much fun as chapel on Sunday. It was she who'd told me that Doogie was a commis chef at one of the better Park Lane hotels (and I'd said I hadn't realised his politics were important and she'd just looked at me) and that she was a journalist with one of the North London suburban weeklies. I'm sure she wrote everything from the 'What's On in Stoke Newington' column to the reports of the Council's planning committee meetings with equal sincerity, convinced she was helping to change the world. If she didn't change it, I suppose Doogie could always poison it.

Many a time I had wished that Frank and Salome were not so upwardly mobile and were back slumming it in Stuart Street. But short of a stock market crash, a hundred percent divorce rate and the legal profession starting to work for free, I couldn't see it. Frank had designs on being the first black High Court judge, and Salome actually enjoyed her job in the City, as well as prospered from it. The other factor against a return was that I reckoned it only a matter of time before they stopped being Dinks (double income, no kids) and became Whannies ('We have a nanny').

An early morning call from Doogie and Miranda left a lot to be desired, especially as

104

it was not yet nine o'clock. I fought off the duvet and padded to the door, grabbing a towel from the bathroom to wrap around my waist and avoiding a cunning ankle-tap trip-and-throw move from Springsteen. He'd been practising it while I'd been away.

Doogie's idea of knocking on a door was to impersonate a heavy machine-gun, and I'd never heard him run out of ammunition. The only way to stop him was to open it.

'Good morning, sir,' I said cheerfully. 'Do you mind if I ask you something? Do you actually read your Bible? Do you know that the answer to all your questions, all your problems, is actually contained within its glorious covers? There you can find hope. There–'

Doogie held up a finger.

'Ahm knocking on *your* door,' he said slowly.

I hit my forehead with the heel of my hand.

'So you are. I'm sorry. Force of habit.'

Behind him, the dark and diminutive Miranda rolled her dark eyes to the ceiling and shook her head.

'Just give him the message,' she said wearily.

'A friend of yours called Bunny rang last night and told you not to forget that you're playing at Christopher's place this morning,' said Doogie, then nodded to himself, pleased that he'd remembered his lines.

'Thanks. I hadn't forgotten.'

I had, but I had no intention of giving Miranda the impression I was disorganised. I grabbed at my towel just before it slipped.

'C'mon, Doogie, let's get to work,' she said, starting down the stairs. 'Before he starts rehearsal.'

Doogie raised his eyebrows, then his shoulders and then the corners of his mouth, and set off after her.

'Rehearsal?' I shouted after them. 'Don't know the meaning of the word.'

But as soon as I had the door shut, I began to ransack the flat for the sheet music I keep for special occasions such as Christmas, *bar mitzvahs,* weddings and so on.

In the bottom of the hi-fl cabinet I found, sandwiched between an old Ramones LP and the new Tommy Smith, the few printed sheets I possess. In there were 'Santa Claus Is Coming to Town', 'So This Is Christmas' and, of course, 'Do They Know It's Christmas?'

I love the traditional carols, don't you?

I had a feeling that this jam session on the back of a truck with Bunny was going to end in tears, even before I left the house. If Bunny had organised it, it usually did. But even I couldn't blame him for the phone ringing just as I was at the front door.

It was a police person telling me that the

inquest on Billy Tuckett would be at ten o'clock the next day at Queen's Road mortuary, where there was a Coroner's Court. Detective-Sergeant Prentice had specifically requested my presence and left instructions that I was to go to Queen's Road and not Whipps Cross Hospital mortuary. It appeared that the roof Billy had fallen off was in one coroner's jurisdiction, but where he'd landed was in another's. Billy never could do anything right.

I said I'd be there, and no, I didn't need fetching. Me being carted off with the sirens going would just about put my street cred in overdraft.

This close to Christmas, the wild West End was a militarised zone for private transport, even taxis. So I bus-hopped into the City and took the Central Line as far as Bond Street. I had my trumpet case on my knee and half a carriage to myself, so I pulled out a paperback of Gore Vidal's latest essays and read the one where he thinks he gets confused with Anthony Burgess. Funny, that; one's so much taller than the other.

I emerged on to Oxford Street, where the decorations festooned the streetlamps and even the Wimpy bars had spray-snowed their windows. The crowds weaved around the barrow boys selling Christmas wrapping paper and ribbon and those party-popper things that go bang and send streamers of shredded Hong Kong daily newspapers across the room. (Not the other sort that contain amyl nitrate, are marketed – legally, so far – as 'liquid incense' and can be bought in the sex shops on Tottenham Court Road for £5.95. Or so they tell me.)

I had a back pocket full of readies, as I planned on doing some Christmas shopping while up West and I had no intention of joining the Christmas Eve rush to the lingerie departments of the big stores, so the first thing was to get away from the temptation of the HMV shop. I did that by averting my eyes and crossing the road quickly, almost tripping over a chestnut-seller at the entrance to St Christopher's Place.

I knew a self-employed barman by the name of Kenny who, the Christmas before, had thought up the wicked scheme of telling the chestnut-roasters that they had to be licensed street vendors. He even ran up some fake City of Westminster chestnut licences, and it would have been a laugh, but he tried to charge for them. They'd ganged up on Kenny, and afterwards he looked as if the mean streets had come up to meet him face first. Never mess with anybody who really does know how to roast nuts.

Martin had almost certainly made the rendezvous first, because he was keen. And because he was a good trombonist, I was quite happy to rescue him from Chase,

Bunny's tuba playing friend. Let's face it, I'd rescue Martin Bormann from Chase, the one man I know whose conversation makes Mogadon an upper.

'Wotcha, Marty. Hello, Chase,' I said, spreading the smile thinner as I went. I'm not a racist, but (have you noticed, there's always a 'but'?) I hate tuba-players. 'Any sign of a truck?'

'Not yet,' said Martin, all eager, 'but we're early.'

I looked at my watch: one minute to 11.00. All over London, the bolts on pub doors were tensing themselves for their daily bid for freedom.

We were roughly in the middle of St Christopher's Place, which isn't a 'place' in the French sense, just an alley that cuts between Oxford and Wigmore Streets. It has a fair cross-section of shops selling fashion, books, military models and bathroom smellies. There were also places to eat if you fancied (a) a very expensive hamburger, (b) authentic Austrian cuisine, if you didn't mind the creaking of lederhosen as you ate, or (c) high quality Japanese food, some of it dead before it got to the table, if you had all day.

Because we were standing outside the Japanese restaurant, I told Chase to go in and order some takeaways for about two o'clock, while Martin and I would scout either end of the Place for Bunny's truck.

He looked suspicious at first, and so did the Japanese waiters as they helped him pull his tuba case through the very narrow doorway. By the time he'd got inside, I'd taken Martin's arm and we were down the alley outside the Pontefract Castle just as the doors opened.

'Bit early isn't it?' asked Martin, reaching for his wallet.

'Iron rations,' I said, tapping my nose.

I ordered two coffees with rum at the bar – Watson's Trawlerman's rum is the best, if you can get it, as drunk by Scottish fisher-men – and while that was coming, I emptied the pockets of my parka. Now unless you're a skinhead of the old school, or have been time-warped for 20 years, parkas are not exactly in when it comes to neat threads. If, however, you need deep pockets, a fleece lining and a hood, because you know you could freeze your butt off on the back of a truck, they're the business. If the parka also has USS Ticonderoga printed across the left breast and you won it in a backgammon game on San Francisco's Pier 39, then you have enough kudos to carry it off.

I pulled out some money and laid it on the bar, followed by a pair of black leather driving gloves with the tops of the three middle fingers cut off the right hand, a tube of mint-flavoured lip salve and a metal hip-flask engraved with the words: 'I am not a diabetic; in case of accidents, please rush me to the nearest public house.' Gross, I know, but it came in handy.

'Can I have four brandies and two shots of ginger wine to put in here, please?' I asked the barman, who didn't bat an eyelid.

Martin peered over the top of his coffee.

'What do you call that?'

'What?'

'Brandy and Stone's ginger.'

'It's a Brandy Mac, the best thing for keeping out the cold. And it's gonna get chilly out there.'

'I hadn't thought of that,' he said, looking down at his sports jacket, shirt and tie. (He wasn't senior enough at the BBC to wear a suit.)

'You'll need some of this too,' I said, holding up the lip salve. 'There's a chemist's round the corner.'

'Good idea,' he nodded.

In the days before Aids, I'd have thought nothing of offering it to him, but nowadays you didn't even have to mention it. I suppose it's the same for people who used to pass joints around at parties.

I'd just finished filling the hip flask when it went dark in the bar as a truck pulled up at the traffic lights outside. I turned to look through the windows. It was a flat-backed Bedford, a homemade job by the look of it, with bits of a drum kit and an ancient upright piano waving around dangerously. I saw Chase hump his tuba case over the tailboard and climb in after it, just as Dod climbed out.

The lights changed and the truck pulled off with Chase trying to keep his balance and looking thoroughly bemused. The pub door opened and Dod stalked in.

'Pint of Bass, please,' I ordered, so that it was half-pulled before he got to the bar.

'Mornin', Angel,' he said gruffly, and nodded down at Martin. 'Anybody else here?'

'Just Chase,' I said. 'You passed him on the way in.'

Dod reached out a ham of a hand for his beer.

'He was rabbit-rabbit about a Chinese restaurant or sumfink. Said they didn't do takeaway. What's he on about?'

He got the glass to his lips and conversation ceased for about 8.3 seconds.

'Can't think, Dod. What's the traffic like?'

'Bumper to arse all round the block. The truck won't be back for ages.'

'Time for another, then?' asked Martin.

He was catching on.

It was after noon by the time we actually got sorted, much to the annoyance of the lady from the public relations company who had hired us.

There was a delay while the truck-driver –

a guy called Ali who was almost as big as Dod and who had a library edition of *The Satanic Verses* on his dashboard – strung banners down the side of the truck saying: 'All your presents in one Place – St Christopher's.' Then we had to tie Trippy to the piano. We had to do this because some chucklehead had provided him with a typist's chair on castors, and every time the truck turned left he did a circuit of the flat-back, sending everybody else flying. He thought it a gas, but we secured his chair by a double strand of rope running right round the piano. Fortunately, Dod and Chase had been provided with camping stools, and although Dod's creaked a bit under his weight, it did mean they stayed roughly in the same place.

I took up my position near Dod, as it was preferable to having my ear down the muzzle of Chase's tuba, and Martin was told to hang over the back of the truck as best he could. (Ever wondered where the expression 'tailgate trombone' came from?)

Bunny, with his clarinet, had a sort of roving commission, which in his case meant roving among the three promo girls dressed in red mini skirts, fake fur jackets and hoods, black fishnet tights and white boots, who would be dishing out leaflets advertising the shops.

It was quite a crush, but the first circuit – left on to Orchard Street and all the way

113

round Selfridges, then Oxford Street as far as Marylebone Lane and then Wigmore again – went off without serious injury. Then we stopped as one of the Santa Claus girls had to go to the loo, and anyway we'd forgotten the leaflets they were supposed to dish out.

One of the Santas turned out to be Kim on a moonlight from Simon's Boozebuster operation, but I promised not to tell. We were getting on famously by half-way round the second circuit, and Dod was digging into a case of canned lager he'd hidden under his stool, then Martin said wouldn't it be a good idea if we actually played something.

We looked at him, then at each other, and finally I got out the lip salve and said 'Okay, it's showtime!' and Kim said: 'Whatever do you mean?'

The day went downhill after that.

In a ramshackle sort of way, we actually put together a few decent tunes, though as is always the case with truck bands, or marching bands for that matter, quality loses out to volume. We did the Christmassy stuff and the old New Orleans favourites and, with Trippy playing the top of the truck cab with a pair of spare drum sticks, I got them organised into a version of Masekela's 'Don't Go Lose It', which lasted one and a half circuits. Then the PR lady appeared and told us we should be playing more sing-along.

Dod was half way through his case of lager, Kim had severely damaged my hip flask and Ali knew the route so well he was now reading *The Satanic Verses* while driving. I hoped that by knocking-off time I'd be able to say that I knew someone who had finished it. (Rule of Life No 7: no day is wasted.) We decided to grab some lunch on the hoof.

This involved a detour round to the McDonald's on Baker Street before the PR lady missed us. It also involved us in playing 'When the Saints' (which we'd resisted up to then) for the two policemen who caught us parked on a double yellow line. They let us off after our three Santa Clausesses mobbed them and asked to play with the red furry pandas they had clipped to the aerials of their radios, on condition we played 'Saints' until out of sight.

We were further delayed getting back on station by a detour for me to the south end of Duke Street. While the rest of the gang dived into the pub opposite to use the toilets, I called in at H R Higgins (Coffee-man) Ltd and bought six gift boxes of coffee (assorted) and two of tea (scented). That was my Christmas shopping sewn up. Who said it was stressful?

The PR lady had disappeared by the time we reached the Wigmore Street entrance to St Christopher's Place, which was probably just as well. Kim, well fortified with Brandy

Mac, was feeding cold Big Mac to Trippy while straddling his lap, his arms around her waist so he could still play. One of the other girls was sitting splay-legged, using Dod's drums as a windshield, trying to roll a joint using one of the advertising leaflets as a roach. Bunny was chatting up the other girl, Chase was still going oompah-oompah and Martin was desperately starting his ninth solo on 'Tiger Rag'.

I tapped Martin on the shoulder and signalled a cut by drawing a finger across my throat.

'C'mon, guys and gals, this is falling apart.'

'I agree,' said Dod, popping the ring pull on another can of lager.

'We've another 20 minutes to do,' said Bunny, untangling his identity bracelet from Santa Claus's fishnets. 'Or we don't get paid.'

Trippy hit a couple of bass chords, classic threatening music, and shouted: 'The crew be turning ugly, Cap'n.'

I suspected that Kim sitting on his lap like that had perked him up no end.

'Okay, troops,' I said. Why did it always have to be the trumpet-player? 'Three more times round the block doing the seasonal cheer bit, playing it dead straight. Then off to the pub to get rat-arsed.'

'Seems reasonable,' said Dod, like he'd seen Richard Widmark say it in a film once, really chill.

Martin and Chase nodded, Bunny buried his head into Santa's neck and Trippy yelled, 'A wise decision, Cap'n Smollett,' and struck up 'Jingle Bells' with us all joining in at some point or another.

On that circuit, I was vaguely conscious that there were more blue uniforms on the streets than normal, but then that was normal in the West End for the pre-Christmas rush. Not that it was any sort of crackdown on muggers or pickpockets, but in the week before the Season of Goodwill, the Marks and Spencer store on Orchard Street gets more bomb threats than the average American Embassy east of Cyprus. Parked somewhere nearby would be a couple of police vans with sniffer dogs, and cordoning off parts of the street had become so commonplace that the cops had left reels of white tape and tripods at strategic points just in case.

It was as we started our second run and we were at the lights at the corner of Portman Square, that I saw the cops had concentrated themselves on the traffic island in Baker Street.

As I just knew that everybody on the truck had a clear conscience, they couldn't possibly be interested in us, could they? Just in case, I bent down and told the joint-smoking Santa to get rid of it. She did so by lifting one of Chase's Doc Martens (the other was keeping time) and pushing the joint under it. Chase

117

looked horrified, but had to keep playing as he was backing Trippy's solo on 'So This Is Christmas' (which at one point, I'll swear, had drifted into 'Wabash Cannonball' – you had to be there).

Martin and I came back in together for a verse to give Bunny a lead in on his clarinet for three or four choruses, and he was good, but probably barely audible above the traffic. As I relaxed, I took a look around to see what was going down, just as we pulled away from the lights and turned left.

It sounds crazy to say I hadn't noticed it before, as we must have driven by ten or a dozen times, but you really don't notice that much when you're trying to keep your balance and play at the same time.

A fair crowd had gathered on the Wigmore Street-Portman Square corner, and at first you could have mistaken it for a queue out-side a sandwich shop, or even the post office just a bit further down the street. (People going there to post Christmas cards had been advised to take sleeping-bags.) But this crowd were not queuing for anything.

They were mostly women and they were outside a fur shop called Naamen's. One of them was dressed in a Bugs Bunny rabbit costume and was handing out leaflets. Two were unrolling a 30-foot banner, which read 'It takes 53 dumb animals to make this coat but only one to wear it.' You didn't have to be a genius to work out they weren't from the Lord's Day Observance Society.

As we came round On Wigmore one more time, it was clear even from a distance that the situation had flared up drastically. The traffic had jammed up, for one thing, and then we were treated to the sight of the guy in the rabbit costume (it must have been male, women don't run like that) tearing down the street carrying a sledgehammer, hotly pursued by two policemen trying to keep their helmets on.

'Far out,' breathed Trippy.

'Run, Roger!' yelled one of the girls.

'How about "Run Rabbit Run"?' suggested Martin, with a big grin.

I checked out what was happening ahead. The crowd outside Naamen's had spilled into Wigmore Street, stopping oncoming traffic, but the cops were trying to clear our lane. Women of all ages were shouting, and I clearly saw a handbag swung overarm. One policeman tripped over a litter-bin and sat down heavily in the gutter. He had a streak of red paint across the back of his uniform, so one at least had come armed with the essential spray can.

'Let's do "How Much is that Doggy in the Window",' I suggested, and took the lead before they could argue.

By the time we got level with the riot, we had quite a crowd of supporters on our side of the street singing along. I reckoned we were doing more damage to Naamen's image than the demonstrators.

Being higher than the policemen on the ground, I could see that most of the action was down to a half-a-dozen women wearing anoraks with the hoods up. They were the ones nipping in and out of the general ruck, tapping ankles, trying to spray-paint out the windows, and one of them even trying to set fire to a bunch of leaflets stuffed through Naamen's letter-box.

Through the window of the shop, I could see two or three salesgirls cowering behind a desk, trapped and frightened. It had been the same at university. I had always argued against sit-ins and 'direct action' against campus property, as it was always the poor bloody infantry – the cleaners, maintenance men and secretaries – who got the rough end of the pineapple, never the generals in command. All they got was embarrassed.

At the traffic lights, we got into the thick of it. One or two of the demonstrating ladies had sat down on the pavement (they should never have shown *Gandhi* on TV) and were singing 'The one with the waggerly tail...' with gusto.

About a dozen were still milling around, hurling themselves at the fur shop window, almost certainly bullet proof, the rest were arguing or wrestling with about ten policemen who were too busy to tell us to move on even when the lights changed.

A big, blond sergeant, minus helmet, had gone for the ringleaders in the anoraks and had two of them in headlocks, one under each arm. He was being waltzed around by his captives and he bellowed for help, but his colleagues had their own problems. From the other side of Portman Square, I heard a police siren, which meant that the cavalry was on its way, but with the traffic plugged solid it would take them a while.

A third, small, anoraked figure approached the sergeant from behind where his two captives were kicking their legs like the rear end of a pantomime horse on speed. This one stayed back, unzipped her anorak and from somewhere inside produced a silver metal can.

I got a good look at her, and the can. Mace in an aerosol, and probably not even ozone-friendly.

It sure as hell wasn't intended to be policeman-friendly.

She zipped up her anorak and began to work her way around to the sergeant's face. To do that, she had to step out into the road near the truck.

I stopped playing and tossed my trumpet to Kim, who had been showering our remaining advertising leaflets onto the melee. She was surprised but she caught it.

Then I leaned over the back of the truck, just avoiding a long, rasping glissando from Martin's slide, and grabbed the would-be mace maniac by the shoulders of her anorak.

She wasn't heavy, and although I'm no weight-training freak, I lifted her until her backside was balanced on the tailboard, and then it was just a matter of rolling her into the well of the truck, the back of her head making a satisfying thud as she landed.

'Trippy,' I shouted breathlessly, 'go!'

Trippy took his cue and banged the palm of his left hand on the top of the cab, and Ali must have put down his book – or got to a frightening bit – because he set off sharpish, left back towards Oxford Street.

I leaned over the girl, who was squirming like a landed fish trying to get her balance and stand up. She didn't resist when I took the can of mace from her hand and slipped it into my pocket. I doubt she actually noticed.

'Hello again, Lucy,' I smiled.

CHAPTER SIX

'I just get so ... so ... *angry*,' said Lucy with venom, 'I just don't know what comes over me.'

'Criminal damage, assaulting a policeman,

resisting arrest. Violation of probation orders, remand, young Cleo put in care... That's what could come over you.'

'Hey! No sermons, see, or I'm outa here!' She was almost shouting, but it was the week before Christmas and we were in the Three Tuns and there were at least six different parties going on, so nobody noticed.

'I'm sorry,' I said over the background roar.

'I just don't like being fucking sermonised, okay?'

'You got it.'

I had taken her to the Three Tuns, and told the others to meet us there, on the basis that it was the second nearest pub to the scene of the demo and the nearest one to Seymour Street police station. The last place the cops would look for her, if they were looking, which I doubted.

I had made Lucy take off her anorak so she looked a bit less like an urban guerrilla, even though the T-shirt she was wearing underneath – 'Rats Have Rights' – was a bit of a giveaway, or maybe I was just paranoid. We had managed to squash ourselves into a corner table with two pints of strong winterwarmer beer. I'd ordered it because brandy always makes me thirsty (noticed that?) and Lucy because she said she liked 'well-balanced, high gravity bitters.' Fair enough. I presumed it was politically correct. I mean, there's no meat in beer, is there? Or brandy, or whisky or wine for that matter, so we had common ground there at least. I had a sudden thought about the swimbladders of fish used to fine beer – to take the suspended proteins to the bottom of the cask and clarify the final product. I wondered if that counted. I decided not to mention them, just in case.

'I know what you're thinking,' she said, before I'd had a chance to say anything. (Rule of Life No 72: when a woman says she knows what you're thinking, make your mind a blank and recite the 12 times table, or the *Book of Genesis* or the Hong Kong telephone book if you know it, just in case.)

'It's just a bunch of crazy women making a spectacle of themselves when they should be home minding the kids.'

'No, I really don't think that,' I said, but I couldn't tell if she believed me. It happened to be true, though. I knew lots of males who were two bricks short of a wall who enjoyed making spectacles of themselves, and I'd certainly never trust them to mind kids.

She took a huge pull on her beer.

'Why did you pull me out of the protest?' she asked, steely-eyed. I wondered if this was the 64,000-dollar question.

'Somebody had to,' I shrugged, ducking it.

'You were just passing, eh?'

'As a matter of fact, I must have passed you three or four times without seeing you. Why, did you think I was following you?' She cocked her head in a 'maybe' sort of way. 'Then I was, if that's what you want to think. I had this brilliant idea to blend into the scenery just so I could keep an eye on you. I got half a dozen drunks and three women dressed as Mother Christmas and put them on a truck, and we drove round the West End on the busiest shopping day of the year playing loud jazz and bunging up the traffic. Naturally, nobody gave us a second look, and I had the traffic lights coordinated by computer so that we stopped near you just as Sergeant Plod, with perfect timing, gave you an excuse to mace him. Okay?'

She didn't say anything to that, just drank more beer and then came back with: 'So why the interest? Why the care and concern, why the drink and sociability?'

I wondered if she was talking to me for a minute. Down the bar, someone was trying to start a darts match, despite there being a mass of people between them and the board. It could end up like the Little Big Horn. Behind Lucy's head, an office party, obviously continued from lunchtime, was getting slowly and inevitably out of hand, and at least one guy from the Accounts Department (why is it always Accounts?) was not waving, but drowning in the typing pool. The Tuns was a good pub, but hardly a counselling centre.

'Yesterday, when I asked you about animal rights, you said you were out of it and clammed up good and proper. Today, you're ripping up the cobblestones and storming the Bastille to stop the fur trade. I was curious.'

She eyeballed me some more, then finished her beer in one gulp. 'Another?' I asked quickly, and walked off with her glass before she could reply.

I wanted to give her time to think over what harm it would do to tell me the truth. There was no way she'd respond to a third degree, so I was hoping she'd decide I was harmless. In fact, I gave her more thinking time than I'd bargained for, as the crush at the bar was worse than when we'd arrived. Somebody was muttering about a bomb scare at Marks and Spencer, which accounted for the influx. Most of the new customers were M & S staff.

I got Lucy another pint of the lethal winter ale, and for myself, a pint of Smithwick's alcohol-free beer, which looks and smells good enough to fool anyone. She was still sitting where I left her; that was a good sign.

'I didn't lie,' she said, cupping her hands around her glass. 'I was helping out some old friends from my women's group today, that was all. There's one hell of a difference between our protest here and the heavier stuff.'

'So explain,' I said, hoping she wouldn't

ask why.

She looked down into her beer.

'I've grown up a lot in the last two years,' she said quietly, and I silently agreed with her. Jumping probation and knowing where to get mace canisters – yeah, I knew people who had graduated from that particular school of life. Some of them were still on the streets. 'Sometimes your beliefs have to take a back seat in your life, otherwise they become obsessions to the exclusion of all else.'

It sounded as though she'd rehearsed that.

'You mean now you've got Cleo to think about...?'

She paused just long enough for me to realise that that was not what she had in mind at all. She'd been thinking about something, or somebody, else.

'Yes, yeah ... exactly,' she said, unsurely. 'I couldn't let – wouldn't let – the cause take over my life.'

'The animal cause?'

She nodded, sipping more beer. She had a head on her, I'll give her that. Two pints of winter headbanger is usually enough to stun an armadillo.

'So why today?'

'Like I said, to help out. The way to stop the fur trade is to alienate the customer. No market for furs equals no shops like that one, equals no fur trade, no species extinction. It's one of the longest-running fights we have, and we thought we were winning and we got lazy.'

'I don't follow,' I said, meaning it.

'We successfully politicised a generation of women – those now in their thirties.' She leaned forward as she became more enthusiastic. 'But it's a younger generation – the Yuppies, the Sloane Rangers, the rich whizzkids, women my age – who are seeing fur as a status symbol again. Money is God, fur means money. It's a women's problem and women have to solve it. We can't rely on television pictures of baby seals being clubbed to death; we've got to be there on the streets where the things are sold.'

'A lot of the stuff in that shop was labelled farmed fur, you know, and fake fur isn't the turn-off it once was, if it's marketed right.'

'Utter bollocks,' she said nastily. Fair enough, I can take the honest cut and thrust of intellectual debate.

'It's *never* okay to wear fake fur; it simply encourages aspirations to the real thing and creates a class division of real and fake. And some fakes are no better than wild species. Have you seen any cats in north Germany recently? Do you know how much a cat pelt is worth in some parts of Europe?'

I hadn't and I didn't And I didn't give it a moment's real consideration. Honest, Springsteen.

'And even if they really are fakes –
synthetic fur–' she was on a roll now '– it's
made from petrochemicals, and they're
non-biodegradable and therefore damaging
to the environment.'

Hell's teeth, they had you all ways.

'And don't give me any crap about hunting
and fur-trading helping to preserve the
primitive economies and lifestyles of Eskimos
and Bantu bloody tribesmen or whatever.'

'Okay, I won't,' I said, but she didn't hear
me.

'You create a cash market for polar bear
fur and the Eskimo spends it on booze. You
offer cash for leopard skins and the Czechs
sell more rifles in Africa.'

I held up my hands in surrender.

'I'm convinced, I'm convinced. I'm
bowled over by the logic and impressed with
the religious zeal.'

She blinked at that; something she did so
rarely that it was noticeable. What had I said?

'I don't apologise,' she said moodily. 'And
okay, I get carried away, like today when the
pigs wade in and start throwing their weight
about.'

Rats had rights, but pigs didn't, it seemed,
but I kept that to myself.

'But, don't you see, if it wasn't for women
passively accepting fur as fashion status,
there wouldn't be a problem. It's up to
women to change attitudes, and if our protest

makes one woman think, then it's a victory. We've got to do it, all of us. Women, that is. It's a women's issue, not an animals issue.'

'And that's not the heavy stuff?' I prompted.

'Oh no, I've pulled back from that. *That* can take over your life.'

'Stuff like breaking into research laboratories?'

This time, I hid my face in my glass.

'How...?' She drew back her hands from the table and put them on her lap. The body linguists would have had a field day. 'How did you know I'd been put on probation?'

At last, the 64,000-dollar question; but she stayed cool enough. 'I asked a policeman. Sorry, I shouldn't be flip. A policeman told me – in passing.'

'In passing what? Have you told them where I live?'

'Have they raided the house yet? Have they sent in the SWAT teams?' What on earth had she done that was so terrible? She hadn't thought twice about trying to mace the police sergeant earlier. 'Whatever they want you for, they won't get you through me. What are you, anyway? The mastermind behind the Surrey Red Brigade?'

That got to her. She didn't like being reminded of her nice, safe, middle-class upbringing. She mumbled something into her beer, the last few drops of it. It was almost worth getting her another to see if she could stand up afterwards.

'Pardon?'

'Sussex. I said I was from Sussex originally. Not Surrey.'

'Close enough,' I smiled. 'Look, Lucy, I don't think the police have got you on their Ten Most Wanted list. As far as I can see, your name cropped up simply as an explanation for why Billy Tuckett was trying to get into the house in Dwyer Street.'

'Poor Billy,' was all she said.

'Poor Billy right enough,' I said, coming on strongly. 'Maybe it was poor, frightened Billy. Something had scared him enough to make him go running across rooftops in the early hours of the morning. He wasn't high and he wasn't drunk and he wasn't delivering chocolates to his lady-love. I think he was scared shitless to be up there.'

Lucy's eyes widened and she pointed a finger at her own chest.

'But it's nothing to do with me. I wasn't there.'

'Billy thought you were. Maybe he thought he could hide there with you.'

'Hide from what?'

'Action Against Animal Abuse.'

She let her mouth fall open.

'You heard,' I pressed. 'They'd been raiding the school at the end of Dwyer Street.'

'The kiddies' zoo,' she said quietly.

'Except it was closed for Christmas and the animals had gone on their holidays.'

'A soft target.'

'What?'

'It would have been classed as a soft target. You hit places like that: small schools, charities, private houses and private institutions that can't afford to either repair the damage or introduce security precautions.'

'Nice logic. Make friends; influence people.'

'Do you know how many animals are used, quite unnecessarily, in school biology classes? Have you ever–?'

I shook my head and regretted not slipping a large vodka into my alcohol-free beer.

'Okay, okay, now I'm giving the sermon. I'm not apologising.'

'Why break the habits of a lifetime?'

'If only you knew how much of my life I did spend saying sorry.'

I kept a straight face somehow. It wasn't her fault; she was sincere enough. It was just that people saying things like that reminded me of one of my all-time favourite cartoons, where Dr Watson is saying to Sherlock Holmes: 'But if you saw the conditions these Moriartys had to live in, you wouldn't be so quick to judge.'

She shivered, pulling herself together. 'I've got to go. I have to pick up Cleo from the creche.'

'The inquest on Billy is tomorrow,' I tried.

'So? It was nothing to do with me.' Her eyes were back to their natural shade of flint. 'Just what has it got to do with you?'

It was my turn to shrug. 'I was there when it happened. I happened to have met Billy once or twice before. That's two coincidences too many for the police. They hassle me, I hassle you.'

'You said you wouldn't tell anybody...'

'I won't unless it gets too uncomfortable not to.'

She swallowed hard. 'This is ridiculous. Billy alive wouldn't hurt a soul. Now he's causing grief when he's dead.'

'Not just to us.'

She looked puzzled.

'I was thinking of his parents.'

'Them too,' she said dismissively. I was going off her rapidly. 'But what's it going to cost me to stay out of it?'

'A name, a suggestion. Some idea of who Billy might have been with on his zoo liberation raid. Something I can barter with, with the cops.'

'There's no other way?'

'Fuck it, he's dead!' I said it too loudly and felt people looking at me. 'This is serious.' Quieter this time.

'There was a guy called Geoffrey Bell,' she said slowly. 'Lived in Romford, where Billy came from. Billy was very taken with him.

133

Under his spell, you might say. He was an animal activist.'

'A member of Action Against...?'

'I don't know. I never got in that deep. That's all I can think of. Look, I'm out of it and I want to stay out. You've got to believe me.'

I didn't, but I let it – and her – go. As she fought her way through the crowd to get to the door, I bet myself that there would be another house on the market in Highbury by the next night. And this time, she'd know not to ask anyone to store her furniture.

A mild uproar at the other end of the bar told me without looking that Bunny, the Mother Christmasses and the rest of the band had arrived and had walked into the middle of the darts match.

Kim fought her way through a dozen pairs of clutching hands to bring me another pint of something I hadn't asked for but wouldn't refuse. Seeing there were only two seats at the small table, she plumped down on my lap. Bunny and Martin wandered over with more drinks, but Dod never made it past the darts game. He was good and could win beer that way. Between the door and the bar, Trippy and the other two girls seemed to have disappeared, but nobody was offering to send search-parties. After all, the pub was crowded and it was nearly Christmas.

'What happened to Chase?' I asked.

'I can't think,' said Bunny innocently. 'We specifically told him we'd meet in the Marlborough Head.'

'But this is the Three Tuns,' said Kim.

'*Really?* I'll be damned.'

I reached around Kim to get at my beer. Very closely round her. Like I said, the pub was crowded.

'I'm glad you guys made it,' I said truthfully. 'I'm feeling starved of intelligent conversation.'

'Your off-the-street pick up disappeared, then?' asked Kim, pretending to soothe my brow and being anything but soothing in the process.

'I've got to hand it to you, Angel, I'd never thought of that technique,' said Bunny with genuine admiration.

'What technique?'

'Just cruising down the street, see one you fancy and literally pick her off the sidewalk – wallop, in the back of the truck.' He mimed the action. 'Just like landing a salmon.'

'He's being serious, isn't he?' whispered Kim in my ear.

'I'm afraid so. Oh God, what have I done?'

It was around 6.00 when the party broke up in disarray. The shops were still open – it was more or less late night every night this time of year – I remember that. And I remember somebody saying that my trumpet and the

135

coffee and tea I'd got as Christmas presents were all stashed in Dod's van. Dod agreed with that, but couldn't quite remember where he'd left the van.

Martin said it was in the National Car Park across the road, about 20 yards from the front door of the pub, and Dod said 'Oh, yeah,' and reluctantly gave up his place in the darts game, slipping at least three five-pound notes and some coins into his pocket and not bothering to thank the guys he'd played.

Trippy had already gone – to see a man about a dog, down Tottenham Court Road, he said – and Bunny had found the other two Mother Christmasses. They'd got changed in the Ladies and given their outfits to Kim, who was still wearing hers, as she'd borrowed them from Simon's wardrobe.

I asked her where she lived and she said Tower Hamlets, so I offered her a lift in the van. She said that was probably out of Dod's way. As he lived in Bethnal Green, it was, but so was Hackney.

Bunny, Martin and the other two girls decided to go for a meal in a Swedish restaurant Bunny said he knew in Lisson Grove, the Dead Zone between the Edgware Road and Lord's Cricket Ground. I suspect Bunny probably meant that he once knew a Swedish waitress, but I let it pass. They managed to flag a taxi, and they piled in amid a lot of shouting and general drunken bonhomie.

The cabbie's expression told anyone interested that Christmas was probably not his favourite time of year.

We found Dod's van in the NCP and I explained to Kim that, as he had only one passenger seat, the two of us had better travel in the cold and bare, unheated back along with Dod's drum kit.

Kim said, but wait a minute, there was a pile of blankets in the back (which Dod used to cushion his full kit on long runs) and we could lay those out and maybe cuddle up for warmth.

I said that was a brilliant idea, and by the time we were out of the car park and in the thick of the traffic, I was asking her what she was doing later. She said there couldn't be a later as she was on duty with the Samaritans at 9.00, so it would have to be now.

I remember thinking that there seemed to be one hell of a lot of buttons on the average Mother Christmas costume. But fortunately the traffic was heavy and it took ages to reach Bethnal Green.

Dod dropped me in Hackney, two streets away from Stuart Street so I could call in the Chinese take-away on the way. I got the distinct impression that he wasn't actually too keen on slowing down so I could get out, let alone stop. But he did. Anyone would have thought I'd lowered the resale value of the van or something.

I had a Tsingtao beer by the neck while chatting to Esmonde (don't ask), the proprietor of the Last Emperor, and picking my meal by numbers from the menu nailed to the counter and covered in drunk-proof plastic.

Esmonde was a really interesting guy – I've said that even when sober. He was a movie nut, and the take-away had in its time been called the Yangtze Incident, the World of Suzy Wong (copyright difficulties) and Enter the Dragon (raided by the Drugs Squad). It was known, I'm ashamed to say, as Aladdin's by the locals who patronised it.

I picked out a selection, deciding on even numbers only because it seemed like a sensible thing to do at the time. To prove, yet again, that he was a good salesman as well as a good cook, Esmonde did me a special offer on a small bottle of rice wine, which he persuaded me I just had to try.

Sometimes they see me coming. And what's more, they telephone each other to say I'm on the way.

I certainly felt that way as I staggered into Stuart Street and up to the steps of No 9.

At first I thought they were muggers, but then there were only two of them and it was the middle of the street. Corners are the favourite spots, even at night – fewer windows and more places to run. They were also

Indian or Pakistani, not black or white or a mixture. Not that, I'm sure, India or Pakistan couldn't put a mugging team in the next Olympics if they wanted to, but it was unusual. The dead giveaway, though, was that they were both way beyond Juvenile Court status and they were both wearing suits.

And they weren't out to mug just anyone passing. Oh no; they were after me.

They must have been waiting in a car, as neither wore an overcoat and both were suddenly there smack in front of me, blocking the pavement, tantalisingly close to home.

Even in my befuddled state, I could see they meant trouble. It wouldn't be a fair fight either; there's no such thing, as far as I'm concerned. If just one of them had sent one of their grandmothers, *and* I could have come out of the sun, *and* if I could have had a silenced chainsaw, then maybe it would have been fair. But then, thinking about Mrs Cody at Zaria's rest home, I still wouldn't have put money on me.

Zaria. That must be it. They were her brothers or cousins or similar, just trying to find out where she was. Like me. There was absolutely no reason why I shouldn't be straight arrow and honest with them.

'You Angel?' said one, the older one, who wore a black pointy beard but no moustache.

'I'm sorry, who?'

'Angel,' he repeated.

139

'Sorry, never heard of him.' I shook my head and edged closer to the steps of No 9.

'It is. I've seen him here,' said the other one, without taking his eyes off me.

'Yes, I live here,' I said, looking nervously from one to the other. 'My name is Goodson, Flat One. I don't quite know what this is all about, but I'm sure I've never seen either of you two gentlemen...'

When in doubt, keep talking. But it wasn't going to work.

'Sunil wants to see you,' said spiky beard.

Sunil?

'About some stolen property,' said the other, who, I'd decided by this time, had shifty eyes. 'Missing from his home.' And dandruff.

I had got my back almost round to the steps by this time, but I knew I'd never get my parka open and the front door key out unless I had an edge.

'You're coming with us. Now.' And as he said it, Shifty-Eyes-With-Dandruff (and I'll throw in bad breath) put out a hand for my arm.

I had my trumpet case in my left hand and my Esmonde special take-away in a paper carrier and my coffee in a Higgins' bag in my right. What the hell. I could always get another horn out of hock, and Esmonde stayed open to 1.00 am.

I smiled broadly at Pointy-Beard and yelled

'Catch!' as I threw the bags up in the air in front of his face. I do believe he almost tried to catch them, but I was too busy by then, swinging up the trumpet case and trying to use it as a battering-ram into Shifty-Eyes' midriff, or private parts if I was lucky.

I wasn't. He grabbed the end of the case before it hit him and stepped backwards using my momentum to take me forward and off balance, then he shoved back. He was stronger than he looked, and I stumbled back into his partner. Both of us went down and rolled off the hard, wet pavement into the gutter, but it was me who cracked the back of his head en route and me who got a boot in the stomach that even my US Navy parka did little to cushion.

I had the good sense to let go of the trumpet case and try and keep rolling out of range. Then my head hit something else and I realised it was one of Armstrong's rear tyres. I had just time to think what a help he was being when another boot landed in my guts and I gasped for air. When I found some, it had a strange smell – of sweet and sour sauce – and it seemed to be very moist.

If Esmonde ever asked me how I enjoyed the evening's 'specials,' I could always say I'd found them warm and soft; comfortable to land on.

I grabbed Shifty-Eyes' foot as it landed again and hung on. Pointy-Beard was somewhere underneath me and was trying to roll me out from under Armstrong. We probably presented quite an obscene picture, and suddenly we seemed to have an audience.

I heard the pounding of rapid footsteps and I knew straight away that it wasn't a policeman (they wear rubber soles these days), and then somebody yelled, 'Hey, you!'

Actually, it could have been 'See, you!' – and I've even told people since that it was 'See you, Jimmy' – but then and there, lying flat on my back looking up at Shifty-Eyes and still holding his foot, all I really registered was that the 'you' came out as just 'U.' It was the war cry of the Scottish male in full flight.

And I do mean flight.

Inverness Doogie was actually in mid-air when I realised it was him. Instantly. I also realised I was going to be okay. In fact, I was going to win a fight without landing a punch. (My kinda fight.)

Doogie went straight for Shifty-Eyes' face with his forehead, launching himself like an American footballer going over the opposition for a touchdown. Shifty-Eyes couldn't do much about it, as I was hanging on to his foot. The impact was sickeningly loud, even to me. God knows what it felt like from the inside. I let go of his foot and he just kept going.

By this time, Pointy-Beard was out from

under me and on his knees. Doogie allowed himself a small smile of satisfaction as Shifty-Eyes hit the road, then he turned and grabbed Pointy-Beard's tie. That was all he did. He didn't physically touch him, just grabbed his tie.

Then he ran down Stuart Street.

Pointy-Beard never did make it to his feet. He just followed Doogie as best he could on his knees. Well, he had to really; the alternative was strangulation.

Doogie left him about 20 yards away, then walked back to me, dusting his hands off as he came.

'You okay, son?' he asked, helping me up.

'Think so,' I said, checking the pockets of my parka, which gave off the odour of Hoy Sin sauce mixed with Mocha-Mysore coffee (filter-ground).

There seemed to be Chinese food everywhere. I kicked a pile of rice off the pavement in the general direction of Shifty-Eyes, who was beginning to moan, his hands clasped to his face.

'Is he?' I nodded, and Doogie took a pace forward and looked down. 'He's fine. I saw his eye move.'

Well, that was all right then.

Pointy-Beard was trying to stand and loosen the knot (by now probably no bigger than a square centimetre) in his tie. He was doing fine too.

143

'Ah nivver could stand someone with a beard but no moustache,' said Doogie.

'I know what you mean,' I said admiringly. 'They're usually religious nutters.'

'Or sociologists,' mused Doogie.

I suddenly felt we had a lot in common and maybe I'd misjudged him.

Miranda appeared in the doorway of No 9 and said, 'Are you coming in now, darling?' like other wives would say, 'Had a nice day at the office, dear?'

'Aye. We're finished here, my numptious one,' said Doogie.

Numptious? I realised we were still worlds apart.

'You coming in for a nightcap?' he asked.

Maybe not that far after all.

'Sure. Got a microwave?'

He looked affronted.

'Ahm a chef,' he said proudly. 'Ah don't need...'

I held up the intact bottle of rice wine I'd finally recovered from the depths of my parka.

'Thirty seconds on defrost?' he said professionally.

'Let's do it.'

CHAPTER SEVEN

Rule of Life No 77: if you should ever have to attend an inquest or similar official/judicial function: make sure you don't have a hangover.

Rule of Life No 76: sometimes there are exceptions.

To be honest, it was relatively painless. But then, so would be nuclear fusion in the state I was in.

I turned up at Queen's Road mortuary, parked Armstrong on a single yellow line, and followed the signs to the Coroner's Court.

Like a dutiful citizen, I checked in with the usher, and he looked at his clipboard and said there would be about a 15-minute wait, so why didn't I take a seat? I did, and soon learned to distrust ushers as a species. He was telling everybody who turned up that there would be a 15-minute wait: even two guys I knew who were self-employed window-cleaners looking for a contract.

Then Prentice took the seat next to me in the corridor and I just knew the day wouldn't get any better whatever the weather forecast.

'Hello, there, Roy,' he shouted loudly. Well, maybe he didn't actually shout; it just felt that way as my brain recoiled on its springs. But he was loud. 'How y'a doing?'

I tried to inch away from him, but there wasn't another seat to move to.

'Surviving. Just.'

'Any news for me?'

Why was he talking so loudly? I realised that the previous night's rice wine, followed by Doogie's steak cooked in Glenfiddich and then more Glenfiddich, had left my cranial suspension system shot to pieces, but he was definitely going over the top.

'Being a bit ... obvious ... aren't we, Sergeant?' I whispered.

He leaned towards me and whispered: 'Just in case there are any of Billy's animal friends here.' He stroked the side of his nose with a forefinger, then winked.

'You bastard! You're setting me up.'

Instinctively I looked around the corridor to try and spot the lurking animal activist. Not a likely-looking suspect in sight, but then they don't all wear T-shirts like Lucy had.

Prentice came over all innocent.

'But I thought you were more than happy to help clear up the unfortunate Billy's death. Incidentally–' he patted me on the knee '–we're calling it the Infenestration of Leytonstone back at the shop. Get it?'

'Oh, highly droll,' I said sarkily. 'I'm

surprised you haven't had the window-frame shipped off to the Black Museum.'

'Ah-ha,' he started confidently, 'that would happen only if it had been a *defenestration*. A murder. If he'd been thrown *out* of a window.'

'I know what it means,' I snapped. Then, a bit more politely: 'Or is that a subtle hint that you really believe it was an accident?'

He plunged his hands into his leather jacket pockets and crossed his feet, dead casual.

'Gotta be honest, Roy, there's not a sniff of anybody else being on that roof or near that window.'

Like they say in the movies: it was quiet. Too quiet.

'Except you, of course.'

'So you're on my case now, eh?'

'Now and for the foreseeable future, old son.'

He was pleasant about it, I'll give him that. But should I let myself be intimidated this way? He had nothing on me. I did the noble thing.

'How about a deal?' I suggested.

'I'm all ears,' he said, totally unfazed.

'I have a name,' I offered.

'I know, Fitzroy, and it's a corker!'

'My, but we must have got up on the right side of the interrogation cell this morning.'

He held out his hands in surrender.

'Okay, okay. It's serious now. What's the name?'

'What's the deal?' It was my turn to lay back.

He narrowed his eyes. 'What do you want?'

'Out of this. No tricky questions, no suspicion, no "helping with enquiries", no more court appearances, no officialdom of any kind.'

'Difficult...' he drawled.

'Bullshit,' I said.

'Okay, can be done; will be done. I'll see the Coroner's Clerk before we start. Now who've you dug up?'

I smiled. Beamed, actually.

'Let's wait until the hearing's over, shall we?'

His eyes had gone to positive slits by now. He straightened himself up.

'I've been checking on you, Angel,' he started, quietly but firmly. 'No regular job, but doesn't draw social security or benefits from the unemployment office–' I knew that was a con for a start, as the cops rarely liaised with the Social Security people, let alone with the income tax ferrets, thank God '–and yet no known criminal source of income. Background sketchy, certainly no criminal record. Educated – oh, yes. University, well we know that – you were there with Billy. Haven't gone much further back, but I'd lay odds on a comfortable, middle-class up-

148

bringing; don't know for sure, though. Definitely a perennial student who never grew up. Never accepted responsibility. No wife, no kids, no mortgage repayments. Probably no income tax, no nine-to-five routine.'

He paused, but it wasn't just for effect.

'Lucky little bleeder, aren't you?'

'Jealous?' I asked innocently.

'Damn right.'

I spotted Billy's mum as soon as I entered the court. Apart from extra weight, the years had not been unkind, although she wouldn't get away with lying about her dress size for too much longer. She sat quietly through the proceedings, which the Coroner conducted in a dull monotone, occasionally sniffing into a balled-up frilly handkerchief firmly gripped in her right hand. In her left hand she held the arm of – I presumed – Mr Tuckett, a short, wide, ruddy-faced man with white sideburns. He could have modelled John Bull for a Victorian Toby jug painter.

Unfortunately, Mrs Tuckett spotted me, and I saw recognition click into place in her mind before I had to stand up and do my bit.

That went quickly enough, with no tricky questions. I presumed that Prentice had had a word in somebody's shell-like, or maybe nobody was very interested. Certainly the various court officials who came and went didn't seem interested. And once Hatchard, the CID man who'd come round to Dwyer Street on the night in question, had done his bit and told the Coroner twice that he didn't suspect foul play, then most people seemed satisfied, and I could get back to enjoying my hangover.

I didn't exactly try to sneak out of the Court; funnily enough, most Courts aren't designed with that in mind. Let's just say I tried to leave with the minimum of fuss.

My big mistake was pausing for that half-minute too long to hold the door open for the redheaded girl. I had only just noticed her – so I must have been taking things seriously – but she was worth waiting to be polite to. Her black, suede-look high-heels put her a good three inches taller than me, and a grey checked suit and crisp white shirt offset with a thin red bow tie, and the fake leather document wallet she clutched, gave her a professional air.

She also wore large, red-frame glasses, although she wore them on top of her head, as if to keep in place the shock of ginger-red red hair that she'd rubber-banded into a pony tail down most of the length of her back. As she passed me, I caught a whiff of a clean, peachy perfume – the sort of scent women buy for themselves. She didn't even notice me. You can't win 'em all; but one or two now and then would be nice. It might almost be worth coming to Court again.

Then it was too late to escape, and Mrs Tuckett was between me and the daylight at the end of the corridor. But that did mean she was also between me and Prentice, who was hovering trying to cut off my retreat as well, so maybe it's true what they say about every silver lining having a cloud.

'It's Roy, isn't it, luv? That's what they said, wasn't it?' she gushed as she closed on me. I took a lungful of her perfume: the sort men buy for women because they like the ads or they can pronounce the name. 'I'd like to thank you for coming.'

I hadn't realised it was a party, but I didn't say it. After all, I can be sensitive to other people's feelings. And anyway, I was giving away at least 50 pounds. (Rule of Life No 131: if you ever really have to fight, pick on someone two weight divisions lower. At least two.)

'It was the least I could do,' I said weakly as she brushed her lips against my cheek.

'You do remember me, don't you, luv?' she pleaded, searching for eye contact I was trying to avoid.

Behind her, Mr Tuckett sighed loudly. He'd realised a long time ago that he'd married a woman who cuddled complete strangers in the street and probably had a season ticket for West Ham in her handbag.

Behind him, Prentice looked at the ceiling and squirmed with pleasure as Mrs T put an

151

armlock on me and began to walk us both down the corridor.

'It's Bernice, Billy's mum,' she sniffed. 'You looked after Billy at university for me – and now this happens.'

She shook her head sadly. I shook mine in wonderment. Where did she get all this from?

'I ... er ... didn't exactly keep in touch, you know, Mrs Tuckett,' I said lamely.

Her grip tightened. 'I know how it is, luv. You have your own life to lead. Are you married? Children?'

I shook my head.

'Neither was Billy,' she ploughed on. 'He was an only child, you know.'

She said *that* over her shoulder. Mr Tuckett exhaled noisily and said: 'I'll go get the car,' and left us in the entrance hall. Over Mrs T's head, Prentice hopped from one foot to the other, making 'get rid of her' movements with his eyebrows.

'He never had many friends, you know. I hoped that university would bring him out of his shell, but he kept himself to himself.'

I remembered something Bunny had said.

'Did Billy have a car, Bernice?'

'No, that was his father's one big disappointment in him.' Just the one big disappointment? I'd have thought that was a good track record.

'We bought him one, of course, for his twenty-first birthday, but he would never learn to drive. He used to say it polluted the environment. Even with this unleaded petrol we have nowadays, he said it was too late for the ozone layer, or whatever it is.' She paused. 'Though he had been a bit more interested in driving recently. Kept bringing the subject up, when he was home.'

She dabbed at a watery eye.

'Why do you ask, Roy?'

I could feel Prentice hovering. He wanted to know why as well. 'It's just something one of the lads said the other night. Somebody who was with us at university. We were–' I thought up a good lie quickly; they're the best ones '–remembering all the times we had when we were students. Somebody mentioned that Billy used to ride a bike.'

Bernice forced a smile. 'A ten-speed mountain bike,' she said proudly. 'He asked for one last Christmas and I insisted, even though Barry – Mr Tuckett – thought it a bit childish.'

My God: Barry, Bernice and Billy. Happy Families.

'You don't think so, do you?'

'Heck, no,' I said generously. 'They're very fashionable in the City now. People go utter mega on them.'

Well, they did during the Underground strikes, and I honestly did know a young brat-race type who went to work in the West End on a unicycle. But then, he was in

153

advertising, so you had to make allowances.

'Billy went everywhere on it, even had a name for it.'

'Really?' How ridiculous.

'Larry, he called it. I don't know why.'

'Did he live at home, Bernice?'

'Well, we always kept his room for him, and he could come and go as he pleased. He went away a lot, with his work, but he's been back with us for the last year or so, off and on.'

Prentice was frowning at me, wondering where this was all going. I did too. Pretty soon I'd be putting in a claim for ten percent of his salary.

'What sort of work did Billy do, Bernice? I don't remember him saying anything about a job.'

'Oh, it was always charity work or his campaigning. He was involved in all the things like Greenpeace, cruel sports, protection of birds, that sort of thing. Animal mad he was. Mr Tuckett thought it was all to get at him, but Billy was very sincere about it. Barry knew there was never much chance of Billy going into the family business, and he was disappointed, but he's not a vindictive man. He let Billy get on with his life.'

At that point, a new, bright red Mercedes estate car eased up to the Court steps. Mr Tuckett was at the wheel, and obviously the family business was doing okay.

'Will you be coming to the funeral? It'll be

a quiet do,' Bernice said softly. 'We've had to wait for today before we could fix anything.'

'If you've something to write on, I'll give you a phone number and you can let me know the arrangements.' I could always get Fenella or somebody to answer the phone, and I wasn't in the phone book, so I figured that if I chickened out, I could block her.

She rummaged around in a handbag as big as my trumpet case and eventually found a length of till receipt from a grocery store. From the length of it, she must have had a truck waiting outside the check-out.

As I scribbled the Stuart Street number, Mr Tuckett honked the horn of the Mercedes. Bernice flapped a hand at him in dismissal, so casually that her jewellery hardly rattled.

'I've just had a thought, Roy, though I know it's an imposition,' she said, cheering visibly. Under other circumstances, I'd have had a snappy answer for her.

I just said 'Yes?' and as I dropped the pen she'd handed me back into her bag, I noticed that she carried at least two fat rolls of ten-pound notes secured with circular gold clips shaped like salamanders, or maybe alligators. I didn't get that good a look.

'If you're not doing anything, would you come back to the house with us now? You can stay for lunch.' I must have looked worried. Behind her, Prentice certainly did.

'It's just... Look, I know it's asking a lot, but I can't bring myself to go through Billy's things. In his room. Barry wants it done, but I won't let him. He won't know what to keep and would probably just throw out everything. And I want to keep a few things to remind me of Billy. Would you do it? Now? Strike while the iron's hot, sort of thing, now we've had the idea? You know what I mean.'

She managed to open her eyes even wider; wide enough to give a suicidal Spaniel decent competition. How could I resist?

Prentice was nodding encouragement.

'Well ... if you think I can be any use...'

'Oh, thank you, Roy, you're an angel.'

She hugged me, not realising what she'd said.

'As long as you can give me a lift back here this afternoon,' I said, establishing some ground rules. I wasn't in the adopt-an-orphan business.

'Of course, of course.'

Mr Tuckett hooted again.

'Come on, before the old man loses his rag.'

She frog-marched me down to the street, leaving Prentice holding the door open.

He made as if to say something, but I just beamed at him and he had to let it go.

As we approached the Mercedes, Bernice said:

'Was that a friend of yours? Do you want

to ask him along?'

'Never seen him before,' I said.

Some of the people I know regard Hackney as the sticks and half expect to see herds of grazing wildebeest when they come to visit me. In their book, Leytonstone would therefore be real bandit country, and Romford, once you'd convinced them that it wasn't actually off the edge of the map, was probably the Twilight Zone.

Barry Tuckett drove smoothly and quietly, not contributing to the conversation in the back seat, which wasn't really a conversation but Bernice's potted biography of Billy. By the time we got to Romford, she'd said an awful lot but I wasn't any wiser.

The Mercedes slid to a halt outside a fair-sized, 1930s detached house set back from the road by a small garden that had thoughtfully been concreted over. There was a sundial on a plinth in the middle of it, which was quite tasteful, and three faded concrete gnomes, which were anything but. From their expressions, they were wondering where all the grass had gone as well.

Mr Tuckett muttered something about having to get back to work, and Bernice said that would be fine, as she could drop me back in her car. She patted him on the shoulder, and he drove off as she plumbed her bag for a ring of keys that wouldn't have looked out of place at Balmoral.

The house had been furnished with a lot of money badly spent in a mixture of styles. There were also no books anywhere and no immediate evidence of a sound system. I'd noticed two separate burglar alarm circuits on the way in, but I didn't spot anything that wasn't instantly replaceable and therefore over-insurable.

I told myself not to be such a snob.

Bernice said she would show me Billy's room and leave me to it while she made lunch, and did I fancy a drink? I said a large mug of strong, sweet tea would do the job and she agreed, adding that it was the best thing 'after a shock.' I hadn't been thinking of stress or shock, I'd been nursing a hangover. The adrenalin of going to a Court had kept it at bay so far, but now I could feel the walls closing in again.

Billy's bedroom looked more like a student's room than his pad at university ever had. The posters on the walls were all reproductions of newspaper adverts showing battery farm conditions or dogs and rabbits with various electrodes attached to them. Under one of these someone had added, in pencil, 'An Animal Auschwitz?'

There was a desk overloaded with papers and two freestanding bookcases, though they held few books. Most of the space was taken up with piles of pamphlets and hand-outs.

I pulled out the stool that Billy must have sat at the desk on, and began to rifle through things in no particular order.

It all made depressing reading. One four-pager told me that around 500 million animals were killed for food in the UK each year. It made no mention of fish, so I supposed that while 'meat is murder,' fish eating is justifiable homicide. Nearly four million animals were used each year for experiments, 80 percent of which were rodents, which gave the activists a problem, as rats don't have good PR potential. (It's their naked tails. Can you think of a sympathetic animal with a hairless tail? Especially one that moves quickly?) There were hand-outs on 'cruelty free' cosmetics, positively promoting cosmetic companies who did not drip shampoo into rabbits' eyes in what I knew was called the Draize Test for irritancy. And there must have been a hundred copies of a pamphlet on the campaign against street trading in animals. I remembered reading about the protests over Club Row just north of Spitalfields' market, where a street market in animals had been held since Victorian times. Those particular Victorian values had been shot down about 1983. One up to the libbers.

There were books – Peter Singer's, which had popularised the term 'animal liberation,' and Robert Sharpe's *The Cruel Deception*. And there were photocopies of press coverage of the famous 1982 march on the Porton Down chemical defence establishment and on the activities of the Hunt Saboteurs Association, including the famous quote from one master of fox hounds advocating that horse-whipping a saboteur was, like beating his wife, a private matter.

Maybe it was true that the Devil got all the best lines.

In all of it, there was a marked absence of anything actually written by Billy. Perhaps he had just been a delivery boy.

In the top drawer of the desk, I found some more photocopies, and these had at least some notes scribbled in red ink in the margins.

There were four sheets paperclipped together. The top two were extracts from the Animals (Scientific Procedures) Act 1986, the Government legislation that established that animal experiment projects, the researcher involved and the premises where it would happen, all required licences. Certain sections had been underlined in angry, wavy red lines, including one that read: '... anything done for the purpose of, or liable to result in, the birth or hatching of a protected animal...' But there wasn't enough in the extract for me to get the context.

The other two sheets were copies of short press reports – one from an unidentified newspaper and the other from some sort of scientific magazine – about a Professor Brian Bamforth. Actually, the reports concerned various research grants won by Professor Bamforth, and though the reason for the grants was there in black and white, it didn't make much sense to me. I could understand the term 'genetic engineering' – well, as long as nobody asked me to speak for a minute without hesitation or deviation – and I recognised 'DNA,' which was said to be the basic stuff of life. I had friends who thought tequila was.

On both these pages, in red, at top right, was the word 'Transgenic' followed by two or three exclamation marks. That didn't mean much either. Lower down, one reference to Professor Bamforth had his name circled in red, and a red line led off to the margin and another hand-drawn red circle. In that was a plus sign, followed by 'GB, P & L,' and the 'L' had been underlined twice. There was also the notation of a date, the 31st of the 12th month. New Year's Eve, in about ten days' time.

I heard Bernice coming just in time to fold the photocopies and stuff them inside my jacket. By the time she'd elbowed the door open with two steaming mugs of tea, I was reading the first thing that had come to hand.

'I thought for a minute you could have been Billy sitting there,' she said as she put the tea down on the desk. 'But I'd be kidding myself.'

I looked at her with a new respect.

'Billy used to sit there all hunched over,' she went on, holding her right arm up to demonstrate. 'Like he was doing an exam and didn't want anybody to crib the answers from him.'

She gave me a little 'that's-all' smile and looked around the room. Then came back to me.

'You interested in filming too?' she asked, before putting her mug in front of her face.

I looked at what I was supposed to be reading. It was the instruction manual for a Minolta autofocus video camera. I'd seen them in the shops marked down, as a Christmas offer, to around 900 quid. I tended to regard them with some scepticism. People who bought amateur video-making equipment, however good it was (and the Minolta stuff is state of the art), usually had little of interest to actually film. It was people like me, with no money for such things, who led the interesting lives. Well, that's how I rationalize it.

Still, it was a growing market and there was money to be made there somewhere by somebody. I knew a guy who made a fortune out of CB radio when it became legal in Britain. Not out of the radio sets themselves, mind you, but – about a month after legalisation – he flogged cassette tapes

162

on 'How to keep a conversation going on CB,' with a follow-up manual listing good 'handles' (mostly pinched from *Lord of the Rings)* for Citizen Banders with absolutely no imagination. I thought he was conning me when he told me his plan. He now lives in Jersey. I don't.

'Oh ... er ... well, I've never been able to afford gear like this,' I said sheepishly. 'Was Billy keen?'

'Seemed to be. All of a sudden, like. He asked for that camera for his birthday this year.' She looked around the room and frowned. 'We never saw anything he videoed on it, and it doesn't seem to be here. He probably loaned it to somebody.'

I knew people who would borrow a video camera, especially if they were throwing a particular kind of party. But I didn't think Billy knew them.

'Lunch won't be long,' said Bernice, sitting down on the edge of Billy's bed and letting a hand stray over the duvet. 'I've put the oven chips in.' She looked towards the window.

'Worried about the neighbours?' I asked.

She knew what I meant. We'd arrived and Mr Tuckett had driven off and within minutes I could be seen, from the street, through the open curtains, upstairs in a bedroom. And now she could too.

'Sod 'em,' she smiled. 'They pay enough

rates. Something to gossip about is extra.'

I smiled politely and scalded my mouth on the tea.

'Is there anything worth keeping?' she asked.

'I have to say, there's nothing personal here that I can see.' It was true. No family photographs, no girlfriend evidence, no souvenir ticket stubs from plays or concerts or similar. Just animals.

'We weren't that close,' she said softly, and looked down at the floor.

If I'd been standing, I'd have shuffled my feet.

'You must think we're a funny family, Roy,' she said, not looking up.

'And why should I do that, eh?' My God, she should see some of my lot.

'I'm not crying,' she said. 'I feel I ought to cry more than I have. It's expected, isn't it? Billy, our only child, dead. All those years together... All the sacrifices... Oh, bugger it. Who am I trying to kid?'

Yourself, Bernice. But I kept it zipped.

She sniffed loudly and looked at me.

'Billy was a disappointment to his father. They've had nothing to do with each other for damn near 20 years. And I suppose I've always sided with Barry. I had to. It was him I married, after all. Billy went his own way. Don't get me wrong, Roy. It's not that we didn't get on together, it's just we had nothing in common. He was like a stranger. And now he's gone, and it ... it really hasn't made that much difference.'

I moved towards her and sat on the bed and put an arm round her. It wasn't that my shoulders are broader than anyone else's or that I have the most understanding nature in the world. I was just the one who was there.

'We just ... we just didn't love him, Roy,' she breathed. 'Is that really bad?'

'It happens, Mrs T, more than you'd think.' I gave her a squeeze. 'Are those chips done yet?'

'Five minutes,' she said, standing up. 'How do you like your steak?'

We ate in the kitchen, though if my steak had been much bigger, we would have had to move into the garage as well.

'We've a bottle of wine somewhere,' said Bernice, 'if you fancy it.'

The spirit was willing, but the flesh was still recovering. And I was eating steak for the second time in less than 15 hours. How could I do that after what I'd read in Billy's bedroom? Aw hell, this cow was past saving.

'No, thanks,' I said with noble restraint. 'I'll be driving again this afternoon.'

'I've got some of those no-alcohol lagers in the fridge, if you'd prefer,' she said enthusiastically.

'That'll do fine.'

She left her plate, eager to please. Eager to do something.

Mothers. Who'd have 'em?

'Where exactly was Billy living?' I asked when we were munching again.

'Here,' she said, forking chips. 'Well, as much as he ever did. He would sleep here maybe one night in five. The rest of the time, he'd stay with one of his friends when they were out campaigning for the animals.'

'Anyone in particular?'

'Mostly his friend Peter, in Islington.' She saw my next question coming. 'No, I don't know what his last name is. The police asked me that as well. And I don't know exactly where he lived either. Billy used to take his bicycle up to town on the train. Did I tell you he even used to have a name for it? Larry. He used to call it Larry. Have you ever... Oh, I have told you that, haven't I?'

'Is it still here?'

'No. He took it with him when he went to see Peter last Friday. It's not that I mind. Maybe Peter has a use for it.'

'You've never met this chap Peter?' I was perking up under the influence of what seemed like half a ton of protein.

'Not really. Saw him once. Well, I saw his van really, once when he came to pick up Billy when they were going off somewhere for the weekend. They used to travel around a lot, handing out leaflets and things. I remembered the van because it was just like the ones Barry bought for the business, except it was red, not white.'

'Did Billy take the camera with him as well?' I asked to keep her talking, but I was thinking of the scribble on the photocopies I'd found.

'P & L' couldn't be Peter and Larry, could they? A mountain bike called Larry? And there was 'GB' as well.

'Oh, I haven't seen that for over a month.' Bernice speared her last chip. 'He probably lent it to Geoffrey.'

'Geoffrey?'

'Geoffrey Bell. Used to be a great friend of Billy's until he moved away, but Billy still used to go and see him.'

'You know Geoffrey Bell?'

'Of course I do. He used to be the vicar.'

After lunch, Bernice and I armed ourselves with black plastic dustbin liners and we made a concerted attack on Billy's room. I found nothing else of interest, but Bernice turned up a couple of old school exercise books of Billy's and decided to keep them in remembrance. The piles of pamphlets and the hand-outs went in the bin. The books and clothes we put into boxes for Oxfam.

She thanked me every five minutes or so until we'd finished. Then she got a brand new Ford Fiesta out of the garage and drove me back to where I'd left Armstrong in Leytonstone.

Before we left Romford, though, she made a minor detour to see Mr Tuckett at work. In fact, she wanted to get me 'a little something' for my trouble from the shop we parked outside.

The little something was a nine-pound leg of lamb, and it came in a plastic carrier bag that bore the same legend as the shopfront and the two white Escort vans parked at the side: 'B. TUCKETI – FAMILY BUTCHER.'

CHAPTER EIGHT

Back at Stuart Street, I cemented my new-found friendship with Doogie and Miranda by presenting them with the leg of lamb. Let's face it, not even with Springsteen's help could I munch through that alone. It might have come in handy frozen, as a weapon in case Pointy-Beard and Shifty-Eyes turned up again, but then I now had Doogie on side. Lisabeth, from the middle flat, was in danger of losing her unpaid job as my unofficial bodyguard.

Miranda even managed a smile, revelling in the fact that someone apart from herself appreciated Doogie, if only for his street-fighting qualities. I tried to look pleased when she told me that Prentice had been ringing at half-hourly intervals since mid-afternoon and had left a multiple-choice list of numbers where I could get him that evening.

But first, I had my own problems to sort.

It took me ages to get Iris, the landlady of the Duke of Wellington, to answer the phone. It couldn't have been because the pub was busy; it was more likely she'd just forgotten where the phone was. But eventually she did.

'Hello, Iris, it's Mac. Mac Maclean. I called in the other day to see if there was a package for me. Remember?'

'Oh yes,' she said vaguely, sounding as if she'd got her valium tablets on optic.

'Has there been anything?'

'Through the post?'

'Yes.'

'For you?'

'Yes.'

'Not through the post, luvvy.'

'Has anything come by carrier pigeon, then?' I snapped, regretting it immediately.

'There's no need to adopt that tone of voice. This place isn't run just for your benefit, you know. I've had enough of men just thinking they can ride roughshod over...'

'Look, I'm really truly sorry, Iris, but this is important.'

I smiled my best smile down the line. 'Did somebody leave something for me?'

Well...' She paused to consider if I was sorry enough. 'She didn't actually leave anything, but she had a parcel with her.'

'Who had, Iris?'

'The girl who came yesterday.'

'What girl, Iris?' I asked patiently.

'The foreign one. More than a tint of the tarbrush there, if you ask me.'

I hadn't, but never mind.

'I think she fancies you, Mac. She kept calling you "Angel" all the time.'

'Did she leave the package, Iris?'

'What? No, she took it with her.'

'Any message?'

'No, she just went when I said you didn't actually live here. Though the way some people treat this place, I might as well be running...'

'Thanks a bunch, Iris.'

I hung up and rested my forehead against the wall in despair. Then Fenella tapped me on the shoulder and I almost had a heart attack.

Our communal phone is on the hallway wall by the front door. Fenella, Lisabeth's younger, slimmer room-mate, had sneaked down the stairs from their flat without making a sound. I suspected she was taking lessons from Springsteen.

'Oooh, sorry, Angel. Did I make you jump?'

'It's your natural static electricity, Binky, my dear. You just gave me a shock. Has anybody ever suggested plugging you into the National Grid?'

'Is that rude?' she asked, frowning.

'Only if you want it be,' I said wearily. For some reason, Fenella thought most of what I said to her was rude. 'Now, what can I do for you?'

She thought about that one for a second, then decided to give me the benefit of the doubt.

'I've a message for you.'

I held up a hand. 'I know. From a guy called Prentice.'

'Well, actually, no, Mr Clever Boots, so there,' she pouted.

'A girl? A girl called Zaria?' Although I'd no idea how she'd got the number.

'Zaria. What an unusual name. Quite nice, though.'

'What did she say, Binky?' I didn't actually take her by her shoulders and shake her, but it was close.

'Oh, it wasn't her. I just said I thought it a nice name. Why are you grinding your teeth? No, it was Mr Tomlin…'

I squeezed the bridge of my nose with forefinger and thumb. It didn't seem to ease the pressure.

'Who is Mr Tomlin, Fenella?'

'The man who lives down the street at No 23. He has Siamese cats.'

'So?'

'So he said that if he caught Springsteen in his back garden again, he would heave a half-brick at him. You don't think he would, do you? I can't stand people who are cruel to animals.'

Me neither, but it seemed to be open season on Angels.

I tried the Aurora Corona Rest Home again, because I couldn't think of anywhere else. But this time I asked for Nurse Sally, the hyperactive Mrs Cody's minder.

The woman who answered said she thought Sally had gone off duty but would put me through to the staff quarters. Then a younger female voice with a thick Irish accent came on.

'Sally's gone out, oim afraid. Yer've just missed her.'

'Sally used to be good mates with Zaria, didn't she?' I tried, as I didn't have anything to lose.

'Zaria? The one who left this week?'

'Yeah, that's right.'

'Maybe she was, I don't know. I've only been here a month meself, and I'm on nights for the extra money. Even when I'm on days, I haven't the cash to go gallivanting up West every night.'

'Sally goes up West, does she?' I oozed innocence.

(Rule of Life No 83: approached in the

right way, anyone will tell you anything, and it will usually be true.)

'Sure she does. She goes window-shopping up Oxford Street, then meets her cronies in that dreadful French Pub in Soho.'

She said it like it was somewhere south-east of Sodom.

'Well, give her my regards when you see her.'

'I surely will,' she said, and I hung up before she could ask my name.

It wasn't much, but it was something to go on. Whatever it was I'd taken from Sunil's house – and I'd only done it as a favour to him, after all – he couldn't have said anything to Nassim about it. If he had, my furniture would have been out on the street by now and Springsteen and I would have been queuing down the night shelter. But whatever it was, he didn't think twice about sending his heavies to see me. Maybe I should go and meet him and explain. Maybe there was a Santa Claus after all.

I rang Prentice, as I couldn't think how to put it off any longer, and got him at the second number he'd left. While it was ringing, Lisabeth appeared on the stairs and said, very pointedly I thought: 'You are logging all those calls in the book, aren't you?'

'Of course,' I lied, and cursed to myself for not remembering to put a pencil behind my ear like I normally do when I use the phone.

173

Prentice came on, and I said who I was.

'You have a name for me,' he said. 'I was getting worried we'd have to send out a search-party.'

'Call off the dogs, I have three names for you, and two facts.'

'Oh, we have *facts* as well? I'm impressed.'

I hate sarcastic policemen. I think they all take a course in it during basic training. Prentice must have been near the top of the class.

'First, you tell me you've called off the dogs.'

'What do you mean?'

'I give you the names and that's it. Good-bye. Don't call me; I won't call you. Okay?'

He paused just long enough to make me feel uncomfortable, then said: 'Very well.'

'Got a pencil?' In the hope that he hadn't, I went straight on. 'First thing, I think you can cross Lucy Scarrott off your hit list. I don't think Billy has even seen her in over a year.'

'Did Mrs Tuckett tell you that?'

'Not exactly. I don't think Mrs T had any idea what Billy was up to. Now, the names. Firstly, there's a Peter. A friend of Billy's, and Billy used to stay with him some nights.'

'Gay?'

'I've no idea and never thought to ask. But here's fact one: Peter drives a red Ford Escort van and lives in Islington. Actually, that's two for the price of one, come to think of it.'

'Get on with it.'

'Okay, name two is Geoffrey Bell. The *Reverend* Geoffrey Bell, would you believe. Until last year, a vicar in Romford.'

'Rector,' said Prentice.

'What?'

'He's a rector, not a vicar, and he is currently incumbent in–' I heard paper rustle as if he was turning pages '–the parish of West Elsworth near Cambridge. I wondered if he'd turn up again.'

'If you knew all this–' I started angrily.

'I didn't know it, I just have a good memory. And I wouldn't miss having you on the payroll for anything, Angel.'

'Payroll? What payroll?'

'I was speaking figuratively.'

I might have known.

'Okay, well I'll just confirm that Bell is definitely worth a look. And that's from stuff in Billy's room and also his mum, who thinks the sun shines out of his rector.'

'Now, now...'

'Last one, and then it's bye-bye. Professor Brian Bamforth is the name, and the fact is a date. New Year's Eve.'

That shut him up completely.

'Prentice? You still there?'

'Yes. Fucking hell, you save the best till last, don't you? Fucking hell,' he said again, slowly.

'I hope they do,' I said. And hung up.

He rang back, of course. In fact, I hadn't
even got to the first stair before the phone
went. And I had to answer it. Lisabeth would
have appeared to cut off my retreat if I
hadn't.

And I had to give Prentice full marks for
cheek when I did.

'Listen, Roy–' so it was 'Roy' now? '–I've
been thinking.'

And you've had all the time in the world it
takes to dial seven digits.

'If you could make contact with Bell, it
might give us an in we've never been able–'

'Hold it! No way, José. I've said it once
and I'll say it again: it's bye-bye.'

'Now wait a minute. Think about it. You
could say you were a friend of Billy's and–'

'Bye-bye.'

This time, after I'd hung up, I laid the
phone down at an angle to the receiver tits
so he'd get an engaged tone if he tried again.

It was an old trick. But I'd never done it to
a policeman before.

It felt strangely satisfying.

It was still early, not yet eight o'clock.

Back in Flat 3, I changed out of my court
appearance gear and into civilian clothes. In
other words, I took off my tie and trans-
ferred money, keys and a pack of Piccadilly

176

No 1 cigarettes (only three gone in a week; I was winning) from my one, half-respectable navy blue blazer into my fur-lined leather bomber jacket.

I found Springsteen sitting on the draining-board gazing out of the kitchen window, which I have to open for him so he can come and go as he likes. I'd built a cat flap in the flat door so he could get into the rest of the house and one more in the back door so that he could get out into the square yard of concrete that our landlord Nassim called our patio. But he still liked to use the window, maybe just to maintain the impression that we mere humans were here to serve him.

He was gazing up at the stars, probably communing with the mother ship and receiving new instructions. There was a full dish of cat food on the kitchen floor.

'No appetite, huh?' I asked him. 'Been pigging out down at Mr Tomlin's, I suppose?'

He didn't even curl a lip in my direction, and he didn't howl when I playfully cuffed him behind the ear. (Well, he does it to me.) Perhaps he was off-colour.

'You're in charge,' I said, and turned the light off on him.

Everybody knows the French Pub, or at least they say they know it if you prompt them with 'You know, the one in Dean Street,' though it's not in many of the guide books. Thank goodness.

Let's face it, there wouldn't be room for any tourists, so why advertise?

After about 30 years with a genuine French landlord who only sold beer in half-pints, among his other idiosyncrasies, the brewery bowed to public opinion and renamed the place the French Pub. It had officially been called the York Minster, or similar, but that had been too *passé* for Soho's artist colony. Nowadays, most of that set had moved on one way or another, though the odd one still dropped in occasionally. Today, the French was the place to be seen in. No-one went there to enjoy themselves.

I parked Armstrong on Soho Square and hoofed it round the corner into Dean Street, keeping an eye out for the fly-posters to see if anyone interesting was playing in the vicinity.

Once in the French, I elbowed my way through the crush to the bar and ordered a lager. I didn't get any say in the matter of how big or which brand it was, but the barmaid smiled sweetly and said *'Merci'* when I paid her, because they all pretend to be French even if they aren't.

I scouted the surrounding faces over the top of my glass. There were no world-famous painters or film stars, but a lot of people trying to look like them. I did spot an up-and-coming bass guitarist I'd once played

with, and in one corner, drinking champagne, was the author of what was supposed
to be the definitive guide to the beers of the
world. Apart from him, I was pretty sure I
was the oldest person there.

I treated myself to a cigarette and did
another scan.

Nothing. No sign of Nurse Sally or anyone
looking remotely like her. Then I felt a
pressure on my arm, and a soft female voice
asked me for a light.

She was dressed in funereal punk: all black
and chains. The tight wool mini just wider
than the belt that held it up, ended where the
ripped black tights began. She also wore
black, spiky, button-up ankle boots, a baggy
black cardigan and enough stainless steel
jewellery to make a dinner service. Her face
was a white powder mask with black eye
make-up and black lip gloss. She offered a
black Balkan Sobranie for the light I offered,
and only then looked up from under the
wide-brimmed black hat she wore.

'Thanks.' She blew smoke at me. 'Glad to
see you've recovered from being goosed by
Mrs Cody. We call her Buffalo Belle.'

I did a quick triple-take, and having made
sure there wasn't a ventriloquist anywhere, I
said:

'Sally?'

She nodded.

'I didn't recognise you,' I said stupidly.

'I should bleedin' well hope not. This is my night off.' She stared at me and then flicked ash with a black fingernail.

'Aren't you gonna buy me a drink?'

'Sure. What'll it be? Guinness and a twist?' I asked, eyeing her outfit.

'What's the twist?'

'I put a vodka in it.'

'Sounds good.'

As I fought for bar space to order the drinks, I looked over my shoulder and caught her making hand signals to a bunch of her friends camped on the stairs leading up to the Ladies toilets. The message was clear enough; she'd bet the others she could con a free drink out of me, probably not letting on that she'd seen me before. I didn't mind; I'd done it myself in the past and probably will again.

But I had no intention of getting suckered by the rest of her crew. I scanned them once just to make sure Zaria wasn't among them, and was pretty sure she wasn't. It was difficult to tell as, in their search for an individual expression of fashion, they had adopted what virtually amounted to a black uniform. Only the blue and yellow vegetable dyes in their hair distinguished them.

I poured a single measure of vodka into the half-pint of Guinness without disturbing the head, and handed it to Sally, leaning over so I could get close to her ear. There were two upside-down crucifixes hanging from it.

'I was hoping to run into you,' I said. 'One of your fellow guards at the maximum security twilight home said you came here.'

'Bet you wouldn't have recognised me,' she said, sipping her drink and leaving a trail of creamy white on her lip gloss.

'I've said so. When you go off duty you really go.'

'It's such a relief to get out of the starched uniform and the black stockings,' she said loudly, so that the crowd around us could hear.

I raised my lager, shaking the glass slightly as it came up.

'Oh, I do like it when you talk dirty,' I said, equally loudly.

She laughed. 'I'll never forget the expression on your face when you felt Mrs Cody feeling you. You were a real rabbit-in-the-headlights job.'

'Only because I couldn't work out how you were doing it,' I said, and she laughed some more and asked if I wanted to join her friends.

'Not tonight, I've got to run. Listen, I wanted to ask you if you'd seen Zaria. You know, Zaria who used to work with you.'

She thought for a second. 'Are you the guy with the taxi?'

'That's me.'

'Yeah, she mentioned you.'

'Have you seen her since she left?'

'Nope. You looking for her?'

'Yeah, and more to the point, she's looking for me.' A flash of disbelief crossed her eyeliner. 'Straight up, she is, but she doesn't know where I live. Have you any idea where I can find her?'

Sally shook her head as she drank. I didn't believe her for a minute, but I didn't see what I could do.

'If she does get in touch, will you give her my number?'

'Only if I can keep it if she doesn't.'

I considered this for a while. 'Fair enough.'

I ripped the top from my packet of cigarettes and borrowed a pencil from one of the barmaids to scribble the address and number of the house in Stuart Street. Sally took the strip of paper and stuffed it down the front of her skirt. Nobody in the pub turned a hair.

'It'll be safe there,' she smiled sweetly.

I was probably still thinking about that as I got back to Armstrong in Soho Square, which is why I reacted so slowly when the white Ford Capri screeched alongside Armstrong's parking place and nosed into the kerb so I couldn't move him.

I was still fumbling the key in the driver's door as the two Pakistanis – one of them Pointy-Beard but the other a new one on me – piled out of the Capri towards me.

I whipped the key out and turned to run

through the Square, only to find Shifty-Eyes standing blocking the pavement. And this time he had a knife.

They didn't say much and, to be fair, they didn't even touch me more than was necessary. Pointy-Beard simply said that Sunil wanted to see me when he'd finished eating and we were going to meet him at Shazam's and did I know it. I said yes automatically – it's just about the best Pakistani restaurant in town. And then they made their big mistake; they let me drive Armstrong.

Shifty-Eyes and Pointy-Beard were in the back, of course, the third cousin having disappeared with the Capri. And they kept the glass panel wide open and Shifty-Eyes sat on the jump seat, twisted round so he could keep the knife blade resting on my right ear. If I braked sharply, I could go to a New Year's Eve party as Van Gogh.

The restaurant we were heading for was in the block opposite Harrods on the Brompton Road. Normally a short hop by cab from Soho, via Piccadilly and Hyde Park Corner, but there was plenty of traffic around, thanks to late-night Christmas shopping and the social life of the Sloane Rangers, as we neared Knightsbridge. That cut our speed some and gave me thinking time, but the traffic seemed to consist entirely of black cabs and VW Golfs full of party-hoppers.

Cabs. Of course.

If I was lucky with the traffic, I had an idea. What did these guys in the back know? Just because there were two of them and they had a knife at my ear, they thought I was their prisoner. As we rounded Hyde Park Corner, I looked in the rear-view mirror, then the wing mirror, and I estimated I had them outnumbered about five to one.

Shifty-Eyes must have sensed something.

'You just drive carefully, unnerstand?'

'Sure,' I said, cool as I could.

'You nervous?' He asked, and stropped the knife blade gently up and down the skin behind my ear.

''Course not,' I blagged. 'Don't everybody's ears sweat?'

He didn't get that straight off, and I didn't give him time to think about it.

For the first time in my life, I accelerated to catch a red light at the intersection with Brompton Road, steering Armstrong right down the middle of the two lanes, blocking both.

Before I'd hit the handbrake, another cab had honked me, and in the mirror I could see four more pulling up behind me and two across the road at the other side of the lights.

I hit the door handle and did a dip and shuffle so that my head was below the knife slash arc and made an undignified but unscathed exit, taking the keys with me.

Then I started shouting before Shifty and

Pointy could react.

'Now look you two, I'm having none of that in the back of my cab! I paid good money for this vehicle, and I won't have the likes of you doing what you're doing! It's disgusting! There ought to be a law against it! There probably is a law against it! So you can just get out right now and catch a bus or walk or whatever you want, but I'm not having you doing that in the back of my cab! This is my living, you know. Hanging's too good for the likes of you!'

By this time, I'd walked round the front of the cab and even slapped Armstrong's bonnet to make a point. There were hoots coming from the back of the other black cabs stuck behind me. The lights had changed to green but nobody was going anywhere unless I moved.

Shifty and Pointy just sat there, sinking lower under the window level.

Then first one, then another and finally eight cabbies all wandered over to see what the fuss was. And when the first said, 'You having trouble with these two ponces, mate?' I knew I had it made.

It's better to be lucky than good.

But on the way home, the prospect of a day or so out of sight seemed a prudent thing to consider.

I had no intention of trying to explain the

whereabouts of Sunil's goods to Sunil or his henchmen until I'd made contact with Zaria, and if she didn't come across soon, there was a good chance she'd find me hanging from a Christmas tree by the neck. Sunil had sent three of them tonight, and if he kept that rate up they'd need a double-decker bus to follow me by Christmas Eve.

Checking all the time that there was no-one on my tail, I reviewed the situation to the sound of a bootleg tape of Sade singing jazz in cabaret.

On the minus side, they knew what I looked like, where I lived and what I drove.

On the plus side, I didn't think they'd jump me at Stuart Street as long as Doogie was there.

That was it as far as the upside. And Doogie had a job to go to.

But then I hadn't. I could just take off. Disappear until they got bored or Zaria finally showed up.

Back at Stuart Street, I found Fenella and Lisabeth and Miranda and Doogie busy decorating the staircase with brightly coloured tinsel streamers, which had clumps of real holly tied into them every 18 inches or so. The holly, being the sort of holly that is sold on street corners in London at this time of year, must have cost a fortune, and it didn't have berries on. (They fetched a premium price in the West End stores.) Still, as a festive substitute for barbed wire, it was pretty effective. Even the mysterious Mr Goodson had a cut-out paper sign saying MERRY XMAS across his door. I suspected that Fenella had bullied him into it.

'There you are, Angel,' boomed Lisabeth from five steps up. She was doing what she was best at: supervising.

'You haven't forgotten you're responsible for getting the tree, have you?'

'Of course not,' I smiled as I lied. 'Hello, Binky.'

I said that only to annoy her, as Fenella was leaning over the staircase banister to fix some tinsel with double-sided tape, and one more inch and she needn't have bothered wearing a skirt at all.

Lisabeth followed my eye-line and reached to pull down Binky's creeping hemline. Fenella smiled between blushes.

'We were thinking of having the party on New Year's Eve,' said Miranda, spraying fake snow from an ozone-friendly aerosol onto a twig of holly.

'Oh good,' I said, squeezing up the stairs behind Lisabeth.

What party?

'Well, you see, Doogie's got to work on Christmas Day – at the hotel.'

'Sure. Er ... fine. Whatever. It's okay by me.'

'Oh good. We were worried in case you couldn't get the band together.'

Band? What had I promised the night before?

'I'll have to see, of course, but I should think the lads will come if we get plenty beer in.'

'Aye, that's a pre-requisite,' said Doogie, who was doing something unspeakable to a metal coat-hanger. It looked as if he was weight-training, then I realised he was bending them into circles so they could be covered in coloured paper and turned into Christmas wreaths. That had always struck me as pretty morbid, but this was the season of goodwill to all men. Even Scotsmen.

'Have yer decided which lager we'll be having?' Doogie asked.

Pardon?

'It'll be a surprise,' I smiled. 'A cheeky little brew, but you'll be amused by its pretension.'

'Och, weel, that's all right then.'

I had made it to the door of my flat.

'Doogie, did I promise to do my special punch as well?' I asked, as I fumbled my keys out.

'Sure yer did,' grinned Doogie, damaging another hanger. 'Both sorts, the white and the red. You're not chickening out, are you?'

The wire hanger twisted into a figure eight in his hands.

'No, Doogie, just checking.'

As soon as I had the door closed and my

jacket off, I found a road atlas and turned to the Cambridge area.

It wasn't just Sunil who had convinced me that the rest of the week would be better spent out of town.

Just where the fuck was West Elsworth?

CHAPTER NINE

When I take Armstrong on long journeys – which these days means anything over about 20 miles from Big Ben – I always use my mystery tapes to keep me awake and amused. The idea is that you create a tape or two of things you think you might like, but in no particular order and never more than two tracks from the same source. Then you forget about them for a couple of years and suddenly, half way down a motorway somewhere you say, 'Hey, I remember this,' and you perk up and pay more attention to driving. Well, that's my theory anyway.

I was having reservations about the theory before I'd hit the M11 the next morning. Pavarotti belting out 'Nessum dorma' had been a great start to the morning, followed by Sipho Mabuse's 'Taxi Driver' and then Paul Simon's 'Me and Julio'. But then the tape had run into Earth, Wind and Fire, and

I shrugged it off by thinking I must have been drunk when I put that on. And then it moved into some early Bryan Ferry, and I reckoned I must have been drunk and very young when I recorded that. If it didn't get better, I'd be getting paranoid about policemen pulling me over and planting Richard Clayderman tapes in the glove compartment as evidence.

But then, I could always say I was on police business, and it would be sort of true.

I had phoned Prentice before leaving, and he'd got all excited about 'having me on the payroll,' as he put it. To be fair, he had offered 'reasonable expenses,' but I'd just mumbled about that. I had it in mind that I might need a favour from him rather than a few notes in the back pocket for fuel, if Zaria didn't touch base with me soon.

'Keep your ears open for any clues to the other cell members,' Prentice had said enthusiastically. 'They normally work in units of four, five at maximum. If Bell is one and this Peter – we're running a trace on him – is another, there'll be one more to identify; and don't forget, they'll be one short.'

'Are you suggesting I volunteer to take Billy's place?' I'd asked.

'Far be it from me to...'

'Good, 'cos you can file that one away in the Department of Daft Ideas. Right now.'

'Okay, okay, just a thought. For God's sake

get me some more on Professor Bamforth though; that's important.'

'Just who is the guy?'

'I can't explain now; haven't time. Just trust me.'

Trust me. The second most popular phrase in the *Police Community Phrase Book* after 'You're nicked, sunshine.'

'Is there anything you can tell me about this guy Bell?'

'Youngish, radical, on the fringe of everything from Greenpeaceing to bomb-banning. We've picked up whispers of his animal rights activities, but nothing definite. Clever, certainly. Done his initial God Squad stint in Romford, then moved out to Cambridgeshire about a year ago.' Prentice had paused, as if measuring his words. 'He's what you might call a good example of muscular Christianity.'

Then he'd burst out laughing, and I was really worried.

West Elsworth was to the west of Cambridge and, I presumed, to the west of East Elsworth, if there was such a place.

I had the big-scale road map out by this time, and I'd worked out that I had to turn off the Bedford road just after Caxton Gibbet. There really is a gibbet there – a place where they used to hang people – and there used to be a pub, but it seems to be permanently being redeveloped as a motel or something these days. That left just a big roundabout and a couple of petrol stations. If there was a village called Caxton, I'd never found it, but the gibbet at the side of the road was a well-known landmark.

A single lane road with no markings off to the right was signposted 'W Elsworth,' and half way down it, I found a pub, but of the village itself there was no sign.

Still, gift horses with their mouths open – for the sale of intoxicating liquor on or off the premises – should not be ignored.

I was the only customer in the snug bar. Perhaps because it was the sort of pub that had a snug (although indistinguishable from its lounge and its public bars), I shouldn't have been surprised at that.

The landlord was a surly, diminutive south Londoner. Almost certainly an ex-brick-layer, or my name isn't what it says on my driving licence. He was delighted to serve me a pint of bitter, which was as close as he would come to cleaning the pumps and pipes that week, and reluctant, until pressed, to assemble a ploughman's lunch for me.

I quizzed him over the village, which he said was another mile down the road in a dip so you couldn't see it (Cambridgeshire isn't totally flat, despite the legends that the giants Gog and Magog played pool on it). He made a point of saying that the first thing I'd see would be the church bell-tower, which gave me an intro into the subject of the local vicar. Sorry, rector.

That set him off on an obviously-well-ridden high horse, and I got the saga of how he'd helped out the new rector every way a human Christian soul could, including offering the use of his valuable premises – this was a free house, his own business – for a harvest festival in traditional style. Well then, stone him, if the new poncy rector didn't turn up after they'd spent *ages* decorating the place with corn sheaves and antique agricultural implements, only to say he wouldn't conduct a service for poachers! And just because some of the locals – who actually were poachers – had added a few snared rabbits and a coupla brace of pheasants to make the tableau more realistic.

What was worse, the new rector – Mr Geoffrey Bloody Ding Dong Bell – was now thick as thieves with the landlord of The Five Bells in the village, a brewery-owned pub that attracted all the youngsters in the area, had live music on Saturdays, did meals – including bleedin' vegetarian pasties, would I believe? – and stayed open until 3.00 on Sundays just to keep in well with the church goers!

I nodded and muttered sympathetically until I'd finished my two slices of (white) bread and a piece of cheese I'll swear had fang marks. Then I left the unfinished majority of my pint and picked up my jacket.

'Which way did you say The Five Bells was?' I asked ever so politely.

But he didn't look pleased.

Actually, I knew where The Five Bells would be – opposite the church. Any pub with 'Bells' in the name usually referred to the number of bells in the local church tower. After the Reformation, the landlords of many a country inn found it prudent not to show their Catholic sympathies – the Catholic church having owned most of them prior to Henry VIII getting the hump over his divorce – so they changed their names from things like The Virgin Mary to The King's Head. Some of them kept a link with the church, though, by coded references such as 'Bells' or just by calling themselves The Angel – and why not? It's a perfectly good name.

I know stuff like that because I keep my eyes open and have time to think these things through. Frightening, isn't it?

I didn't go in to The Five Bells, but I parked Armstrong slap bang outside it and wandered casually over to the church across the road, which a fading signboard told me was called St Michael and All Angels. It must have been fate.

The church was locked, of course. Sadly, most of them have to be these days; there are some pretty dishonest people around. But I reckoned that by the time I'd strolled leisurely back to Armstrong, the village jungle drums would have beaten out the fact that I was there.

I got half way back across the road before their first remote probe picked me up.

She was about 13, trying to look 15, sensibly dressed in a long kilt skirt and a duffle coat, and she was riding a ladies' bicycle with a wicker carrying basket on the handlebars. She could have done commercials for sensible English maidenhood.

The brakes on her bike squealed as she stopped and balanced, one foot on the road.

'Hello. Are you looking for somebody? Can I help?'

Now if someone had come up to me and said that in London, they would have been muggers or Mormons. But out here it seemed perfectly normal, until I remembered that there are more murders per head out in the Fenlands of East Anglia than there are in London and Glasgow on a Saturday night put together. It's something to do with the wind coming in straight from the Urals.

'The vicar actually,' I said, having checked her out just in case she had an axe in the basket. 'Sorry, rector.'

She smiled a smile it was worth being British for, but also betrayed her own emotions.

'Oh, Geoffrey won't be back until 11

minutes past three.'

It came out dreamily, and I wondered if the Reverend Bell knew he had a fan club. Women have spoken of me in the same breathy way, but they've usually responded to the treatment.

'That's pretty specific. I'm impressed. What time does he take Evensong? Twenty-six minutes past six?'

She put her head on one side and narrowed her eyes.

'He'll be on the bus from Cambridge, which gets here at 11 minutes past,' she said as if talking to a smaller, stupid brother. 'We only have one bus in the afternoons, and it's always on time. But you can wait in the rectory; that's never locked.'

She got off the bike and wheeled it between us.

'It's just the other side of the church,' she said. 'My name's Stephanie, by the way.'

'That's a nice name,' I said, wishing I'd thought of something better, but then I remembered how old she was and didn't feel so bad about the cliché. 'Known Geoffrey long?'

'Since he came here,' she said enthusiastically. 'He's really livened things up. It was Deadsville, Arizona before he came. I suppose you've come for the hunt.'

'Er...Well, I...'

She nodded her head knowingly.

'That's okay, I know I'm not supposed to

know about stuff like that.'

'Well...' I said, trying to give the impression that I knew what the fuck she was talking about, but it wasn't me who'd made up the stupid rules.

'What is it about you lot?' she asked, but it was to herself more than me. She wasn't interested in eye-contact or serious answers. 'Do you have to be a black belt or something before you can get involved?'

'Oh yeah, fifth dan at least,' I said, not knowing word one what I was agreeing to.

'You're being patronising, but I get the message,' she said seriously.

Good. Would you mind explaining it to me?

'Aren't you even going to ask how I knew you were one of them?' And this time she looked at me.

'I suppose I'd better,' I said, keeping a straight face.

'We're here, by the way.' She stopped wheeling the bike and pointed to a detached Victorian villa that, if the light had been better, wouldn't have looked out of place on the cover of a Henry James novel. 'Just go in and find the kitchen. Geoffrey will be along at–'

'Eleven minutes past three.'

Stephanie made to mount her bicycle.

'You never told me,' I said, 'how you knew.'

'Coming here in a London taxi,' she yelled over her shoulder as she pedalled off. 'Why do you lot have to be so fucking obvious?'

I found the kitchen of the rectory easily enough, still wondering about how they didn't make schoolgirls like they used to. Then I thought how stupid that was. It wasn't that there was any difference in them, it was me who was too old. And that just made me irritable.

I had time, if Stephanie was right about the local stagecoach, to suss the rectory good and proper. So I did. I didn't know what I might find, so when I found nothing of interest, I wasn't disappointed. One thing did strike me, though, and while I can't claim to be any sort of authority on 19th Century vicarages, it seemed odd to me that the largest downstairs room in the house – maybe a ballroom at some point – was completely bare of furnishings and fittings. It was a huge room running down the side of the house with French windows giving out on to the garden. And there was absolutely nothing in it, apart from light bulbs.

I had no better luck upstairs, not even in a bedroom that had been converted into a study. There was nothing of note there except what you might expect to find in the way of books and back copies of the parish magazine. Not so much as a sniff of an anti-vivisectionist tract.

The bathroom wall cabinet was more interesting, with a variety of shampoos and facial scrubs from the Body Shop. They all declared that they weren't tested on animals, so that could have been significant, but then again, I used most of them. What was more interesting was the thought that there certainly wasn't a Body Shop in West Elsworth.

Did the good Reverend Bell buy his cosmetics in London, perhaps?

Big deal, if that was the sum total of my investigation. I didn't, at the time, pay much attention to the three different brands of condom there were in the bathroom cupboard. Well, to be honest, I did wish I'd been the person to market an 'Extra Large' brand. (It was no different to a regular sheath, it just sold more. That's marketing.) But that was a passing thought. The rector's sex life was his own business. Back in the kitchen, I put the kettle on and found a catering-size tin of instant coffee and a choice of up to three dozen mugs of assorted design. I tried to put some significance behind that and came up with, the fact that the rector must entertain Stephanie and the rest of the youth club once a week.

That couldn't have anything to do with the condoms in the bathroom, could it? No, of course not. My imagination was running away with me.

I heard the unmistakable sound of a bus in the road outside and checked my Seastar. Eleven minutes past three. Good. The watch was right.

I made myself comfortable with my mug of coffee and had a last check over my appearance. I was wearing entirely man-made materials or cotton, and I thought the Lynx 'Roar of Disapproval' T-shirt was a masterstroke, given the dedication that required in December. I hoped that the 'Stop the Bloody Whaling' Greenpeace sticker I'd put on the back bumper of Armstrong had been noticed too.

I had my story straight and was ready to go.

I hadn't expected there to be two of them.

And I hadn't expected one of them to be a luscious redhead. Especially not the one I'd last seen in Leytonstone, with me holding the door open so she could leave Billy Tuckett's inquest.

Plan A went out of the rectory window straight away, closely followed by Plans B to E. There was little to fall back on except the truth. Or some of it.

'Hello there. My name's–'

'Angel,' said the redhead.

Ah well, there went Plan F. It hadn't been much of a plan anyway.

'Can we help you?' asked Geoffrey Bell tightly. He looked down at the coffee cup, and his expression said that there was a thin line between open house Christian hospitality and breaking and entering.

I stood up, turned on the smile and held out a hand.

'Roy Angel. I hope you don't mind me making myself at home, but a charming young lady called Stephanie found me wandering in the village and brought me here. She said you wouldn't mind.' Then, to the redhead: 'I'm sorry – I didn't realise we'd met...'

The rector shook my hand and didn't take his eyes off me for a second. He was taller than me, about my age, with jet black hair slicked back with hair gel. If you'd substituted the anorak, jeans, black shirt and dog collar for a Giorgio Armani imitation and red braces, he could have been an extra in *Wall Street*.

He didn't say anything to me, but to the girl behind him, he said softly: 'Lara...?'

The redhead had lost a couple of inches due to her trainers rather than the high heels I'd last seen her in. In fact, all the trappings of power-dressing had gone, her anorak and jeans matching Bell's almost as a uniform, and her hair plaited and secured over her right shoulder with a rubber band. She was still strikingly pretty.

'Mr Angel was at the inquest on poor Billy Tuckett. You remember, Geoffrey, I was telling you about it. Mr Angel saw the accident when poor Billy died.' Her accent was as English as her complexion.

Bell was still holding my hand, and I felt his grip spasm.

I got a feel of what Prentice had called 'muscular Christianity' in no uncertain terms.

'I didn't actually see the accident,' I said quickly. 'I just had the misfortune to find the body, and I had to identify it.'

'You knew Billy?' asked Bell, finally dropping my hand.

'Yes, that's the bizarre thing about it all. Billy and I go back to university days, but I hadn't actually seen him for ages until he suddenly drops in on a house I'm sitting for a friend of a friend. I'm sorry if that sounds crude, but it was a bit of a shock.'

'You said you were sitting a house?' Bell pulled out a kitchen chair and straddled it. Maybe this was the modern Anglican version of the confessional.

'Yes, house-sitting. Living in somebody's house while they're away.' I sat down and faced him across the table. 'It's quite common in London nowadays. It's supposed to deter burglars.'

'So you were there by chance?'

'Totally. Though funnily enough, I'd been thinking about Billy lately.'

'And why was that?'

The redhead Bell had called Lara pulled out a third chair and sat on the edge, resting her hands on the table. She curled her hands up when she saw me looking at them. She was a nail-biter and a self-conscious one at that.

'I'd seen Billy a few weeks before. Not to talk to. He was riding his pushbike through the City and I was in a traffic jam,' I lied in answer to her. 'That reminded me of some of the things we used to get up to as students.'

'You drive, then?' asked Bell, and it seemed such an odd question it almost threw me.

'Yes, sure. In fact I used to drive the Students' Union van when Billy and I took people on demos.'

I thought that was pretty good considering I was making this up as I went along.

'Demonstrations?' quizzed the Rector.

'Peaceful ones,' I said quickly. 'We were protesting about the animal markets in the East End. They've been shut down now, thank God.' I pretended surprise. 'Oh, sorry, Reverend, I didn't...'

Bell allowed himself a smile.

'That's quite all right.' He glanced at the girl, then back to me. 'Lara and I share the same views Billy had on animal welfare. I regard the humane and decent treatment of the animals we share this planet with as a prerequisite of Christian behaviour. And I've read of the street markets in animals in places like Club Row. People call them pets, but they are no more than slaves. Good

203

riddance to them.'

'But what brings you here?' Lara asked, cutting in as if she wanted to stop Bell before he got fully launched on his lecture.

'Billy's mum actually. You must have seen her at the inquest.'

Lara showed worry at that. She was a good natural actress, but not that good.

'Yes...' she said cautiously.

'Were you called to the inquest?' I pushed innocently. 'I don't remember you...'

'No, I was there just to see what had happened to Billy.'

'I asked Lara to go,' said Bell, 'on my behalf. I was unable to go myself and had always felt ... an affection ... for Billy. I knew him from my previous parish.'

'In Romford,' I said, and he nodded. 'Yes, Mrs Tuckett said Billy thought very highly of you. And that's why she asked me to come and see you.'

'Mrs Tuckett did?'

He was on guard now.

'Yes, about a video camera Billy had.'

'Camera?'

He was positively rigid in his chair.

'It's missing and she thought he might have left it with you. It's only that if he did, she's quite happy with that. If it has gone to a good cause, she'll be well pleased.'

Bell relaxed visibly. Lara's expression hadn't changed.

'As a matter of fact, he did leave it here. And I suppose Mrs Tuckett must have it returned if she wants, but I think I can say it is being used in a very good cause. Don't you, Lara?'

'Absolutely,' said the redhead, deadpan.

'In fact,' said Bell, 'we'll show you what Billy was working on with it. But first, how about a biscuit with your coffee?'

Yes, she said, it was like the Lara in *Doctor Zhivago,* and if only she had a penny for every time anyone said that... I knew how she felt.

The Reverend Bell busied himself finding biscuits and making a pot of tea. Did I want another coffee? No, thanks, one cup of instant a week was my limit.

'It must be nice living here in the country,' I tried. 'I envy you.'

She looked at me as if I'd just suggested something obscene – and doing it in public.

'Finchley's quite near Hampstead Heath, but I'd hardly call it rural,' she said without any trace of humour.

'Lara comes up here at weekends to help with the youth club and other activities,' said Bell.

I'll bet, my expression must have said, as he went on: 'And stays over at The Five Bells so that the village gossips have one less thing to occupy their tiny minds, though most of them seem to be hooked up to the television most of the day. Do you know there are now four hours of Australian soap-operas on the box each day?'

'Geoffrey's just written an editorial in the parish magazine on the subject,' said Lara, but I couldn't tell if she was being sarky or not.

'Don't you find this a bit of a backwater after Romford?' I asked as he strained tea into china mugs emblazoned with adverts for the Guide Dogs for the Blind organisation.

'A lot of people would say Romford was the backwater,' he said evenly. 'It's different, certainly, and certain of the church authorities would say I was out of the way here, and therefore safer.'

He sat down at the table again and pushed a packet of chocolate biscuits towards me.

'Safer?'

'Less of a potential embarrassment, shall we say. Oh, I know I'm not long for the Church. My views on certain issues do not conform with how the Church defines pastoral care. But I intend to stick to them, and I have the support of some good friends–' he couldn't stop himself glancing at Lara, who remained stone-faced, watching me '–if not of my parishioners. It was quite a clever move by my Bishop, sending me here.'

I wasn't sure if this was some sort of test question or not. 'I'm sorry, I don't follow.'

'My support for a more humane philosophy towards animals is sometimes seen by others as taking precedence over concern for my flock.' He permitted himself a wry smile. 'And they might have a point. So, what better way of making me restrain my campaigning instincts than to set me down here in a community where most of the population works in either the local abattoir, one of two battery farms, or even in the university's animal research laboratory. And for recreation, it's a toss-up between fox-hunting and poaching around here. My Bishop is convinced that within two years I will have alienated every section of the local community and be forced to resign. He's probably right.'

'But, Geoffrey, you've done marvellous work with the young people,' said Lara right on cue. They worked well together.

'But the youth club members won't have much say in the matter when the crunch comes. Still, life must go on – hopefully. And that reminds me, we have a disco tonight for the under-15s.' He said it in a tone that implied that the over-15s would all be down the pub. 'And I'm not sure we have a disc jockey.'

'Something wrong with Wayne?' asked Lara, ignoring me for a moment.

'No, nothing wrong with Wayne, but Wayne's wife's expecting twins, and today is supposed to be the day. Excuse me while I phone up for a progress report.'

He stood up.

'Poor Wayne. About to become a father again, and not yet 21,' he said, shaking his head.

'And he's not even a good disc jockey,' said Lara seriously.

'I know,' said Bell sadly, 'but it's his one ambition to become good enough to go on the road with his mobile disco and pack in his job as a farm labourer. Back in a minute.'

He left the kitchen and got to work on the phone in the hallway.

'Do you help with the discos?' I smiled at Lara now we were alone.

'No. I help out with some of the other activities.'

She gathered up the mugs from the table and made to wash them in the sink.

'So what do you do back in the wilds of Finchley?' I asked, reaching for a drying cloth and turning up the charm volume a notch or two.

'I'm a secretary,' she said, looking straight ahead out of the kitchen window into the rapidly darkening night. 'What did you expect?'

'I didn't expect anything in particular. Don't you want to be a secretary?'

'I'm actually a very good secretary,' she said, her voice hardening. 'Good enough to have negotiated my own flexitime contract so I can have three-and-a-half-day weekends.'

She was proud of that, too. It hadn't occurred to me to wonder what she was doing in deepest Cambridgeshire on a Friday afternoon. I forget that most people have to work for a living.

The Reverend Bell reappeared.

'Good news for Wayne, but bad news for us,' he announced. 'He'll be spending the night in the maternity hospital while we try and run a disco without a disc jockey.'

He ran the fingers of both hands up and back through his hair, just like he'd seen Michael Douglas do it.

It was time to ingratiate myself.

'Rector, I think I might be able to help.'

'Good heavens, a London taxi!'

Which, if you think about it, was quite an appropriate reaction from a man of the cloth, even for a beast like the black cab which is much maligned by everyone from archbishops downwards.

'Are you a cabbie?' asked Bell, rubbing his hands together in enthusiasm.

'No, I'm not a musher,' I said, using the technical term. 'The cab is de-licensed, but I find it very useful in getting around London.'

I decided not to say anything about him being called Armstrong. You can tell a vicar just so much.

I opened the door and let Lara and Bell into the back, then I climbed, into the driving seat and got Armstrong wound up. With a minimum of movement – and I am good at it – I flicked a cassette into the tape-deck where the old fare meter used to be, turned on the amp and selected the rear speakers. They got Sipho Mabuse's 'Celebration' in all four earholes which, if not exactly up-to-the-minute-top-of-the-charts stuff, was at least politically correct.

They loved every minute of the drive to the farm cottage where Wayne – West Elsworth's Mr Music – lived when he wasn't being an expectant father. I'd swear that Bell would have waved if he'd seen any of his parishioners, not that they would have seen him now it was dark. And because I'd deliberately put on the passenger light, I could see in the mirror that even the Ice Maiden's features cracked into a smile as they swayed to the music and chatted frantically to each other.

I couldn't hear what they said, of course, as anyone who has ever tried to talk to a real London cab-driver will testify, and the music didn't help. But at least it gave me a few minutes to observe them and think.

The impression I got in Armstrong was that they were like kids in a sweet shop. Maybe it was as simple as that. Bell had gone to Cambridge to meet Lara and come back on the bus. Neither of them had cars. And Bell had asked me early on if I drove or not. Maybe they couldn't. Billy hadn't been able to.

It was a tenuous link but a nagging one, and it had cropped up before. Was it possible that these two, and Billy, had been members of Action Against Animal Abuse, the only urban terrorist movement to travel by the No 13 bus?

I felt a hand on my shoulder.

'Anywhere here'll do, driver,' said Bell, and roared with laughter.

As we piled out he said: 'I'm sorry, I just couldn't resist it.'

'That'll be two pounds forty, guv,' I replied with a smile, and his face fell. 'I can't resist it, either.'

Lara remained unamused by the exchange.

Bell led the way not to the cottage we'd stopped outside, but to the ramshackle wooden garage at its side. He reached up and took a Yale key from the narrow lintel across the double doors and slotted it into the lock. Amid all the other junk that accumulates in garages (I sometimes think they're sold complete with contents), wrapped in a big sheet of plastic, was Wayne's disco gear.

It was very much the standard beginner's kit: a twin turntable desk with built-in amp and tape-deck, control panel, mike socket and two 150-watt speakers. There were also four columns of flashing lights, which would cue into the bass and treble outputs. Wayne hadn't made it to the auto remix with synthesiser and laser beam stage yet. On each piece of equipment was the word 'FENMAN' in the sort of stick-on letters that usually spell 'DUNROAMIN' on the front doors of bungalows.

'Wayne calls himself the Flying Fenman,' said Bell. 'Can you fly this stuff?'

'All the way to the moon, Alice,' I said, but neither of them got it. 'I'll check my pilot's licence, but it looks easy enough unless he's rewired it for any particular reason. Where are his records?'

Bell did a double-take.

'Er... Probably in the back of his van at the hospital. I never thought...'

'Now that could be a problem.'

'I've got my record collection back at the rectory,' he said hopefully. 'In fact, I haven't unpacked them since I moved here.'

'Can't you use the tapes from your taxi?' asked Lara.

'If the deck works, yeah, that's an idea. Where does all this stuff have to go?'

'The Parish Room,' said Bell. 'It's what passes for a village hall here. It's next to The Five Bells.'

I'd seen it on my way into the village and just assumed it was a bottle store for the pub. Still, what it lacked in architectural stature, it made up for in location.

We packed the Flying Fenman into Armstrong, the speakers and lights going in the luggage space (where normal vehicles have passenger seats) and the turntable unit lying across the floor in the back.

The Parish Room was as cold and uninviting inside as it looked from the road. It took us five minutes to find a power socket and a further 20 to untangle cables and connect the speakers and lights. I set the turntables on a trestle-table as near to the push-bar fire exit door as I dared. If the local teeny-boppers didn't like the music, I wanted an escape route.

Bell sent Lara back over to the rectory to get his record collection, and she returned with a cardboard box that said on the side that it had once contained tins of baked beans. A quick scan through Bell's collection of LPs made me think we'd have had a better evening with the beans. The music was mostly folksy female imitations of the Carly Simon, Janis Ian vintage, plus a well worn copy of Mike Oldfield's *Tubular Bells*, which he may have bought because of the pun on his name but was probably there because it's obligatory for anyone who had a stereo before 1980.

I tried the system out with a tape from the collection I keep in Armstrong. The one with no details on the cover except the word 'Loud' in red ink. Gerry Rafferty belted out, shaking the speakers, flashing the synchronised lights and rattling the aluminium windowframes of the hall.

'Okay, kids,' I yelled, 'Let's boogie till we puke!'

But fortunately they didn't hear me, or the rector would have looked even more worried than he did already.

CHAPTER TEN

'I don't remember Wayne playing the disco quite so loudly,' Bell had said over an early dinner. That was probably because Wayne wanted to work in the village again, I thought, but said nothing.

'We're vegetarians,' Lara had said, warming up three tins of mushroom soup.

'I've already turned down nine invitations to Christmas dinner,' said Bell. 'In Romford, people would at least try and do a nut cutlet or a vegetable curry, but out here they just stare at you and pretend they haven't heard right.'

'It must be difficult,' I sympathised. 'I always say to people, why is it unusual not to eat meat? I mean, you don't eat the flesh of any meat-eating animal, do you?'

Bell considered this seriously. It was an argument Lisabeth had put to me once when I'd had a few drinks and made some crack about her vegetarianism. I hoped I was remembering it right.

'Think about it. Humans only eat meat from animals that eat grain or grass or similar. Cows, sheep, pig, chicken, duck...'

'I think you'll find some exceptions – unpleasant ones – but it's an interesting idea.' Bell said it like he was already considering it for the next week's sermon.

They hadn't actually asked me if I was a veggie or a vegan, and I'd accepted Bell's invitation to food and a bed for the night in return for offering to run the disco. He repeated how grateful he was for my standing in for Wayne, as both he and Lara had other plans. He didn't specify what they were, nor did he mention showing me Billy's video gear again, but now I had time to snoop around myself.

Just after seven, the front door of the rectory opened and two young girls came in without knocking. They both wore long, belted raincoats and carried small torches. I had forgotten that they didn't run to street lights out here on the tundra.

Despite the overdone eye make-up, I recognised the first one.

'Hello, Stephanie,' said the rector. 'Hello, Amy.'

'Hello, Geoffrey,' said Stephanie, ignoring Lara and looking at me.

'This is Roy, he's standing in for Wayne tonight,' said Bell, and Stephanie rolled her

215

eyes up until the whites showed. 'Stephie and Amy here, they take the admission money and run the bar.'

My expression must have betrayed me. 'It's a non-alcoholic bar,' said Bell quickly. 'Alcohol-free lager, cola, crisps, that sort of thing. Let's go across.'

I grabbed my coat from the back of a chair. 'See you later?' I asked Lara.

'Perhaps. Depends what time we finish.' She was giving nothing away.

The rector led us over to the Parish Room again and unlocked the door and hit the light switch. There was a small kitchen and two toilets off in a side annexe, and I helped him set up another trestle-table and load it with boxes of crisps and cans of soft drinks from a padlocked pantry. He gave the keys to Stephanie, telling her to get more if she needed them and to make sure she locked the takings away at the end of the evening.

The two girls knew the score, and they went round the hall pulling curtains and setting out folding chairs down the side, leaving plenty of dancing space. Then they set up a card table near the door and opened an empty cashbox. They did all this with their coats firmly belted, which I thought was a bit odd. It was no sauna in there, but it wasn't that cold. I thought country girls were tough and wrote love-letters to the milkman in the ice on the inside of their bedroom windows in the morning.

I got the Flying Fenman warmed up and tested the lights with a Bob Marley tape. The two girls looked mildly interested, and with the light show going, they flicked off half the lights at the main switch. I suspected that all the lights would go as soon as the rector did.

'I'll leave you to it,' said the rector. 'If you have any problems, I'm across at the rectory, and don't hesitate come and get me or send Stephie or Amy.'

'No problems,' I promised.

'I'll pop back for ten-thirty; that's closing time.'

'Okay. Leave everything to me.'

He turned so the girls couldn't hear him.

'I feel I have to say this, Roy, but take it in the spirit it's given.' Here it came. 'You're in charge here, and you'll be the only adult, so you'll be responsible.'

For what?

'Like I said, Geoffrey, no problems.'

He smiled, wished us all a good rave-up and left.

Okay, so he was a vicar and he had to play it straight, but there was no need to make any big deal out of playing music for a bunch of harmless adolescents, was there?

Stephanie waited until the door had closed after him, then she produced a pair of high-heeled shoes, one from each pocket

217

of her raincoat, and dropped them on the floor, then kicked off her sensible school-issue flatties. Amy did likewise and they both stepped into their new shoes as if they'd rehearsed. They both took off their raincoats in the same, choreographed way. Underneath, Stephie was wearing a brown suede mini skirt and matching halter. The gap in the middle was vaguely covered by a cowgirl-style fringe from the halter. Amy – the elder of the two unless my eyes deceived me – wore a red lurex tube that ended just as the fishnet tights started to cover her legs.

I realised why they didn't need central heating in the Parish Room.

By 8.00, the joint was jumping and I was a hit.

I knew I was, because Stephie told me so as she brought me another alcohol-free lager in a plastic cup. (Not half bad if cut with vodka from the quarter-bottle I keep in Armstrong's glove compartment for emergencies.)

'I don't know any of this stuff you're playing,' she shouted into my ear, 'but Wayne only does about four records an hour 'cos he talks so much. Tries to be the big DJ and all that crap. You just keep it rolling.'

She was half-sitting on my knee by this stage, showing off to her friends that she had influence over the disc jockey.

If she got much closer she could prove

grounds for assault to the magistrates as well.

I didn't want to let on that I had just about exhausted my supply of music already. My taste and the taste of the audience diverged in both style and content quite radically. The rector's taste split from everybody about ten years ago, but I had been able to use one of his Paul McCartney LPs by announcing it as a remix. They seemed to swallow that. Maybe some of them had even read about the Beatles in history lessons at school.

I flipped through the rector's box of records one more time, to make sure I hadn't missed anything, and found I had. The only record less than ten years old was Simply Red's *Men and Women* LP. That might have a couple of tracks familiar to the more ancient among the audience, say the 14-year-olds, as it was less than three years old.

'Wayne had hundreds of records,' Stephie was yelling.

'I go for quality not quantity,' I shouted back.

I wondered if she'd have been impressed by the time, as a student, I ran a disco with one Rolling Stones LP and the soundtrack from *A Clockwork Orange*. I decided not to boast. She'd have been about two at the time.

I had the LP out of its cover, balanced between thumb and middle finger, when I noticed the writing on the sleeve. I had to hold it closer to one of the disco's traffic light set-ups to read what it said. Alongside the list of tracks for side one had been added, next to the listing for Cole Porter's 'Ev'ry Time We Say Goodbye', the words: 'Even if we cry a little, it's for the best. Love, Lucy.' And then there were two little crosses signifying kisses.

Interesting. I filed it away mentally and decided to play the whole of side one.

There was no indication of how long the side lasted, but I reckoned I had 15 to 20 minutes in which to have a snoop around outside, which was another reason I'd set up the disco close to the fire exit. It wasn't much and I would have preferred a longer record that I knew better. But you just can't trust the recording companies these days. Some of them actually extend the gaps between tracks so you can't fit a whole LP on one side of a C90 cassette. There's no trust left in the world.

I cued up the record and turned to tell Stephanie what I was doing. Her face was buried in the plastic cup she'd brought me, which was half-and-half non-alcoholic lager and vodka.

'That's not bad,' she said, slamming the empty cup down and wiping her mouth with the back of a hand. 'I've never had one of those before.'

Well, there you are: no day is wasted.

'Listen, I'm putting the whole of this side

on, okay.' She nodded. 'And I'm nipping out to my car for a minute. If there's any problem, just cut the amp here–' I showed her the amplifier power on/off switch '–and I'll hear it.'

'Sure,' she said, standing up. Then she leaned over to see what the record was. 'Oh, not that! Geoffrey's always playing it when he's by himself.'

I wondered how she knew, if he was always by himself, but I let it go. She said she'd get some more drinks in and, as I sneaked out of the fire door, having locked the bar up so I could get back in, I watched her pour herself an alcohol-free lager at the refreshment table.

She pulled a face at the first sip, then tried another. Then she sniffed the contents of the plastic cup and finally held the can up to see if she could see why it didn't taste the same as mine. I decided it was a good time not to be there.

I had a torch in the back of Armstrong and, though it wouldn't have been as suspicious as it would in London, because all after-dark pedestrians used them here, I left it there. I reasoned that I could say I'd got lost in the dark should anybody catch me where I wasn't supposed to be.

It wasn't far back to the vicarage – sorry, rectory – even when cutting across a piece of what I classed as waste ground but the locals probably called a field, to come at it from the back garden. On the way, I saw a couple of torch-holding revellers heading towards The Five Bells, and I wondered if they needed the torches when they left at chucking-out time.

The rectory, or at least its ground floor, was lit up almost as brightly as the pub; in particular, the large room at the back with no furniture and the French windows. I eased my way towards the windows, fearful of stepping in anything unspeakable, which was always a hazard out here in the back-woods, keeping one ear open for the muted hum of the disco working on auto-pilot.

Hugging the rectory wall, I could hear other muffled sounds from inside, but couldn't make them out. I sneaked a look in through the French windows, pretty confident that I wouldn't be seen unless someone was looking straight at me.

Nobody was. They were all looking at the Reverend Bell, though it took me a few seconds to recognise him.

He, and the other dozen or so people in the room, were dressed in judo gear, the full pyjama suit outfits with belt sashes, some coloured but mostly white. All except Bell and another man – and most of the others seemed to be women – were seated in lotus positions on the bare floor in an oval. In the middle, Bell was saying something I couldn't hear and turning to each of – I suppose it was a class – in turn. Then the man with him took up a defensive fighting stance just like a kid would do coming out of his first Kung Fu movie, sideways on to reduce the size of the target he offered. (Even I knew that, and my idea of self-defence is a pre-emptive strike, preferably nuclear.)

Bell's assistant, if that's what he was, fixed his arms in an outstretched position and settled his legs bending at the knees, but made no other move. Bell disappeared from my line of vision for a second and reappeared with a roof tile, one of the old red, ridged sort called treble tiles, which were probably common as muck around there but fetched a pound a time among the shadier landscape gardeners operating in Hampstead these days.

The assistant took the tile in his outstretched hands and braced himself. Bell took a big pace backwards and then his right foot came up and smashed the tile to smithereens. It seemed that before the pieces had tinkled to the floor, he had landed with both feet together and his forehead touching the now empty hands of his assistant in a formalised bow.

The class didn't applaud or cheer or anything, they just lowered their heads and put their hands out in front of them, fingers splayed and tensed almost as if they were arthritic. The assistant was now centre stage and, as he tensed himself, Bell appeared with a block of inch-thick timber, maybe a foot square. The assistant looked at it as Bell offered it, then drove his forehead into it, splitting it cleanly in two.

He didn't even shake his head. Maybe it really didn't hurt him. Well, he couldn't have any brain in there, otherwise he wouldn't have done such a thing.

I was about to change position to see if I could identify Lara in there when I sensed something behind me. If it was one of the Karate Kids, I wasn't sure I wanted to see it coming, but I turned anyway.

Stephanie was standing about five feet away, hands on her hips, head on one side, her right high-heeled shoe tapping impatiently on the grass.

'I told you you needed a black belt before they'd talk to you round here,' she said primly. Then, accusing: 'And another thing.'

'Yes, what?' I made flapping motions with my hands to try and keep her voice down.

'We've run out of vodka.'

I got her back inside the disco just as the record finished, and I was able to slot in a tape to cover me while I charged out again, this time to The Five Bells.

The landlord gave me a funny look when I asked for a treble vodka, but it was a busy

Friday night and he was not going to argue. As nonchalantly as I could, I sidled towards the Gents, and there I poured the contents of the glass into the empty quarter bottle I'd rescued from the disco's deck, where Stephanie had left it. Then I filled the bottle with water from the washbasin tap and screwed the top back on. I hid the bottle in my jacket pocket and left the glass on the bar as I pushed through the crowd.

Sneaking back through the fire door again, I got a very revealing view of Stephanie leaning right across the turntable deck trying to talk above the music to a pretty blonde girl with glasses.

I pushed by Stephie's proffered backside and fumbled for another record. She grabbed at my shoulder and yelled into my ear.

'Manderley wants you to play something by Bros!'

Manderley? As if the poor kid hadn't enough problems without being a Bros fan.

'Sorry – got none,' I shouted back, and Stephie leaned over again to yell in Manderley's ear. I got the distinct impression what she actually told her was 'Piss off!' but I couldn't be sure.

I got another record going and cued up my Armstrong wildtrack tape. Most of the audience were past caring what was being played, as long as it kept going. Only about a third were dancing; the rest were getting down to some serious petting in the chairs around the wall.

I liberated a couple of chairs and sat Stephie in one. She didn't mind. She'd already found the bottle of vodka and was adding liberal splashes to a plastic cup of coke.

'Okay, supersleuth, you seem to know all about it. What gives with the martial arts set-up?'

There was no good reason why she should tell me anything. I could have threatened to tell on her for drinking under age, I suppose. And I could have really frightened her by telling her there was no Santa Claus.

'It's not martial arts,' she said, and when she saw my look of disbelief she put on a fake resigned expression and began to explain it to me.

'It's Kateda. That's what they do. It isn't a martial art because there's no combat involved. It comes from Tibet and is based on control of breathing. In yoga, you breathe to relax, but in Kateda you breathe to get control of your muscles, and you can therefore harness your reflexes.'

'And it's not violent?'

'Well, of course it can be, but it is only used in self-defence.' Oh yeah? 'There are no attacking moves, only defensive ones.'

She knew her stuff, which I suspected had been picked up listening at keyholes as she followed the good rector around.

'And Bell – Geoffrey – teaches this Kateda?'

'Yes, he's run classes since he came here, but he says I'm too young. He won't take anyone under ... 18.' She had been about to say '16,' and even in the flickering strobe lighting I could tell she was blushing. 'But I think it's because of my father. He's in the local Hunt, you see.'

Then, because I was obviously moronic, she added: 'Foxhunt.'

'So he's the local squire, is he?'

I'd better be careful; there could be horse-whippings talked about if one messed with Stephie.

'He's a builder, actually,' she said, as primly as she could above the music. 'Foxhunting is no longer the prerequisite of the landed rich, you know.'

I wondered where she'd heard that.

'You mentioned the "hunt" when I first met you this afternoon. What did you mean?'

'I assumed you were one of Geoffrey's animal-lovers. They always start to appear from the woodwork when there's a meet in the offing.'

'A what?' I thought for a minute she'd said 'meat.'

'Boxing Day Meet.'

'What's that?'

'Boxing Day? It's the day after Christmas Day,' she giggled, thinking either she or the vodka had made a joke.

'What meet?'

'The local hunt always meets on Boxing Day morning near the Caxton Gibbet. Loadsapeople turn out to watch. My dad says it helps them work off the turkey and Christmas pud.'

'And what does Geoffrey do?'

'I expect he'll have his student friends there demonstrating like he did during the spring. They have banners and stuff and make a lot of noise trying to distract the hounds. Bloody childish if you ask me.'

I nodded sympathetically.

'Geoffrey makes a bit of a spectacle of himself, does he?'

'Yes.' In front of Daddy too.

'And you thought I was one of them? A hunt saboteur?'

She leaned forward and screwed up her face.

'I couldn't give a fiddler's fuck if you were.'

I bet myself she hadn't heard that in the vestry after choir practice. Oh, I don't know, though.

She reached for the vodka bottle, which she'd put under her chair, but I beat her to it. It was already half-empty.

'Hey!' she grabbed at my hand but missed. 'Don't you tell me I've had enough,' she said.

'I wasn't going to. I was going to tell you it was your round.'

The Reverend Bell arrived just after 10.00, and I knew he was in the Parish Room before I saw him, from the way the glow of several distant cigarettes suddenly vanished and from the number of young ladies who hastened to the loo, adjusting their clothing.

Things were pretty well under control, in fact. The last bus connecting neighbouring villages had gone at 10.00, so quite a lot of the kids had had to leave before then, allowing for the obligatory 15-minute fare-well sessions with boy/girlfriends. Stephanie had sulked off for a final dance and I'd made a start on packing things up. With luck, we'd hit The Five Bells half an hour before closing.

No such luck.

'Everything okay?' asked the rector, flashing a weak smile. His hair was slicked down from a shower and he was wearing jeans and a Lynx sweatshirt in the same 'Roar of Disapproval' series (against fur trading) as my T-shirt.

'Sure. Last waltz just about to start.'

I phased the volume down so we didn't actually need semaphore to communicate.

'Good. I'll help you clear up. Lara's over at the rectory setting up the video. I'd like you to see what we are using it for.'

I feigned an oh-yes-I'd-forgotten-about-that expression and cued up the last track of side one of the Simply Red LP.

Stephanie and Amy appeared wearing their long coats and flat shoes and began to clear away empty cans and crisp packets as Bell started to fold away some of the chairs down one side of the hall.

'Last record, folks,' I announced into the microphone. 'And a real beauty to charm you on your way. This one's even older than me.'

I flicked the turntable release and 'Ev'ry Time We Say Goodbye' wafted out through the speakers.

Stephie gave me a filthy look, then rolled her eyes to the roof and giggled something at Amy.

The Reverend Bell just gave me the filthy look.

He'd stopped dead in his tracks with an armful of folded chairs and his head had whipped round.

I was swaying gently, singing along and the picture of innocence and determined to avoid eye contact with him.

It wasn't easy. Even from that distance, the killer look he flashed me was mighty venomous, though it lasted maybe two seconds before he went back to picking up chairs.

For two seconds, though, I had an insight into what a treble tile or a block of timber might feel like in their last moments before their atomic structure was reorganised.

I hadn't seen a television on my snooping tour of the rectory, or a video recorder, or Billy's Minolta video camera or a collection of about two hundred video cassettes and an old, but professional, editing machine.

That's because I hadn't looked in the cellar, and that was because I'd walked by the door under the staircase at least six times thinking it was a cupboard.

There were also lights down there; professional spots with metal flaps and sheets of greaseproof paper clothes-pegged over them to filter or direct shadow. And there was a desk, like a newsreader would use, surrounded on three sides by sheets of plywood on exhibition stands. In effect, they had a homemade film studio.

Lara seemed to be in charge.

She was wearing a pale blue tracksuit and trainers, and she too was not long out of the shower. She held a hardbacked shorthand notebook and a pencil with which she occasionally tapped her teeth. It seemed like a habit to stop her biting her fingernails.

'This is – was – very much Billy's project,' she said, ignoring my 'Hello again!'

She selected a cassette from the main collection and added it to a pile of about a dozen near the video recorder, then she turned the TV on and inserted the first tape.

'Billy collected these excerpts from everywhere he could,' she said as the video clicked

231

in and onto the screen came the closing credits of *Hill Street Blues*.

'Not this,' Lara said seriously. 'Watch the commercials.'

The first was an ad for a facial cold cream, which I must have seen a thousand times but still couldn't tell you the name of the product. At the end, in the bottom left of the frame, the words 'Cruelty Free' came up in small white letters. The commercial finished and the tape went blank, then a hand-lettered caption came up: 'Cruelty Free? But still tested on animals.'

Lara stopped the machine, ejected the cassette and fed in another. This time it was for a shampoo, and the ad agency had used lush green tropical locations, mountain streams and exotic flora and fauna, partly to give a really natural feel to the thing but partly to justify a two-week shooting schedule in Tobago.

There was another homemade caption after this one: 'The Draize Test.'

'That's where they drip shampoo into the eye, isn't it? To test for irritancy.'

'That's right,' said Bell, impressed. 'And totally unnecessary. They know what produces the irritation. Why not stick to the substances we already know about?'

'Because it stifles innovation?' I said, like I was quoting from something.

'That's what they say,' Lara chipped in

bitterly, not taking her eyes from the screen.

The next tape featured a washing powder, the one after, an eyeliner, then a make-up remover, then a baby's bubble bath. They weren't all TV commercials; some were poster sites and some had been clipped from magazines, mounted and videoed. They weren't all aimed at, or blaming, just women either. There were shaving soap and after-shave commercials, each with a caption along the lines of: 'Tested on 93 Bunny Rabbits Before Macho Man Dare Use It!'

'Billy's project was all about replacing animals in cosmetic testing,' said Bell.

'With humans?' I asked stupidly.

'Of course. He would make video compilations, and the idea was to show them to young people who would volunteer to be...'

'Guinea pigs?'

That went down like a lead balloon.

'...product testers. Even if they weren't taken up because the cosmetic companies knew the tests were dangerous, the bad publicity would hit their sales.'

'He collected 147 examples,' said Lara, reading from the notebook.

I stretched my neck and looked at pencilled squiggles on the page she held open.

'Shorthand?' She nodded. 'Pitman's?' It was too elaborate for T-line, the shorthand most journalists use these days.

'Gregg's,' she said. 'But I can do Pitman

and T-line. I told you, I'm a very good secretary.'

I was impressed.

'Lara can do most things she puts her mind to,' said Bell cheerfully. 'Do you want to see more?'

'No. It will only make me angry.' I kept a straight face at Bell but could feel Lara watching me. 'I'll tell Mrs Tuckett that you're putting Billy's gear to good use. I'm sure it's what he would have wanted.'

'Thank you.' Bell bowed slightly. 'And thank you for your help tonight. Lara and I are involved in teaching night classes that go towards raising funds for this and other projects.'

'You mean like the hunt saboteurs?' I tried.

Bell stood up and folded his arms. Lara stared at me.

'Why do you say that, Roy?'

'It's no secret there's a big Boxing Day meet at Caxton Gibbet, is it?'

'No,' he said slowly. 'It's a well-known – some would say – social occasion. And I will be there, certainly, lodging a peaceful pro-test, much to the dismay of some of my nominal congregation. But we're not mem-bers of the hunt saboteurs. Good heavens, some of them are known to the police.'

He flashed an impish look at Lara, who checked back the temptation to frown at him.

'Are you interested in coming along, Roy?'

she said softly.

'I could be.'

'You could give me a lift from London if you did.'

She was looking straight at me, almost daring me to guess what she was thinking.

'Yes, of course, that would be a great help,' Bell said quietly, almost to himself.

'Well then, why not? Let's join the country set! Where do I pick you up?'

'Can I give you a ring?' she came back quickly.

'Okay,' I said, more cheerfully than I felt. I could always get Lisabeth or Fenella to field the call if I got cold feet.

I gave her the Stuart Street number and she wrote it in the shorthand book, then she closed it and stood.

'I'd better get across to the Bells, Geoffrey,' she said. 'It's way past closing.'

It was too, dammit.

'And I've got a sermon to write,' said Bell.

'I suppose this is a busy time of year for you,' I said, just making small talk, but Lara's ears pricked up as if she was checking for double meanings.

'Actually,' Bell said with a smile, 'my diary always seems fullest around the Easter weekend.'

'Oh yeah. Sorry,' I said goofily.

We trooped upstairs and Lara pulled on an anorak in the hallway.

'Can I walk you to the pub?' I suggested, in the hope that the landlord might be serving 'afters.'

'No, thanks, I'm fine. Good night.'

She turned and went and Bell closed the door after her.

'Lara's one of the few people who really can take care of themselves, you know,' said Bell. 'Nothing seems daunting to her.'

He sighed. So did I. Their relationship was, to me, more confusing than ever.

'Would you like me to ferry the disco gear back to Wayne's in the morning?' I offered.

'No. Wayne's picking me up early. I have to go with him to the maternity ward and talk about christenings with the new mum. It's part of the job. He can pick it up himself. Now if you'll excuse me, I have some paperwork to catch up on. I've made you up a camp bed in the bedroom at the top of the stairs. Bathroom is next door.'

So that was it, was it? No nightcap, no offering to share a last naughty cigarette. No, maybe not.

'I may be gone by the time you get up,' he said, making for his study. 'But you know where the kitchen is.'

'If I don't catch you tomorrow, what about Boxing Day?'

'Oh, don't worry,' he said, flicking the study light on. 'Lara will sort you out.'

And I'm sure there was a glint in his eye as

he said it.

'Well, good night then.'

I started up the stairs and then the phone rang. Bell came out into the hallway to answer it but kept his back to me. At the top of the stairs, I paused to do a bit of earwigging.

'Hello, Mrs Munson. Yes, I know it is late, but what is the matter?'

Pause.

'Well, I'm sure Stephanie didn't mean to be so rude. I can't think what could have come over her. What did you say Manderley was asking for...?'

I decided it was probably a good time to go to bed after all.

I used the bathroom carefully. I rarely stray far from base without a spare toothbrush, but I didn't want Bell to hear me as it might look as if I'd planned to stay over. I had no wish to make a man who could unroof a building with his bare hands suspicious.

There was a camp bed in the room and a table lamp that had been left on the floor beside it. Apart from that, nothing. Not even a book. After half an hour, I cracked and got my emergency packet of Gold Flake out of the inside pocket of my jacket and smoked one leaning out of the window like a naughty schoolboy.

It was so long since I'd had a whole

cigarette, it went straight to my head and I slept like a log.

The sound of the front door slamming woke me next morning, and my Tissot Seastar told me it was 7.30. My eyes told me it wasn't even properly light yet, and it wouldn't have taken much to persuade me to go back to sleep.

But I got out of bed and dressed rapidly as soon as my body registered how low room temperature was. Those 19th Century vicars had to be tough, and you could understand why they had large families.

I sauntered downstairs and into the kitchen and put the kettle on. While it boiled, I looked out of the window across a field to the Parish Room. There was an old Bedford van with its lights on parked outside, and I could make out 'FLYING FEN-MAN' in day-glo orange down the side. Bell and a younger guy I presumed to be Wayne loaded up the disco and climbed aboard.

I gave the van a good two minutes to make sure they weren't coming back to the rectory. Then I put boiling water from the kettle onto a tea-bag in a mug and let it brew while I tiptoed down into the cellar.

There was nothing there that hadn't been there the night before and, to be honest, I didn't know really what I was looking for. I fingered through a few VHS cassettes, checking the wording on the title edge. Most were handwritten, some typed; different handwriting, different typewriters. They'd probably been sent in by the faithful from different parts of the country. Some had notations like 'Anglia TV News – 15 January' others just said 'Hare Coursing'. All the tapes were mixed up, some 30-minute ones, some 60, mostly 180-minutes, the most common type. They were all different brands too.

Except for one pile of four stashed behind the front rank. These were all expensive, top-of-the-range TDK tapes and they didn't have hand-written titles, just a cross in red ink on the spine.

I took one at random. It had been used and the little plastic tag removed so that you didn't record over it by mistake. (A square of black insulating tape over the hole makes them usable again.)

I removed the tape from its box and peeled off the spine label with just the red cross on it, transferring it to an old 180 tape that had a 1988 date pencilled on it. Then I put the TDK tape in the old box and – let's not mince words – nicked it.

I got home to Hackney just after 11.00 and went straight to Lisabeth's lair to ask if there had been any message from Zaria. There hadn't

'You haven't shaved,' said Fenella, appear-

239

ing behind Lisabeth.

'He always looks like that in the morning,' said Lisabeth, who had the knack of talking about men as if they were dead or at least not present.

'Don't be chopsy,' I said, 'and come and help me get the Christmas tree.'

'Oooh goodeee,' Fenella squealed, and was withered on the spot. 'Where is it?'

'In the back of Armstrong.'

Out on the street, getting the thing out of Armstrong seemed much more difficult than getting it in.

'It's not very big,' said Lisabeth.

'Big enough,' I said defensively. I'd had to use the wing mirrors all the way from that damned Forestry Commission plantation near Cambridge because the rear-view one was out of action.

'And it's got bare patches,' moaned Fenella.

Well, I'd had to get a grip somewhere.

'And there's no roots,' cried Lisabeth. 'You have to have roots or the needles will drop. It looks as if they've been hacked off with a penknife.'

There was no pleasing some people, and I bet neither of them would think to give me a new penknife for Christmas.

CHAPTER ELEVEN

'Are you sure there were no messages?' I asked again as Fenella and I manoeuvred the Christmas tree, under Lisabeth's detailed direction, first to the landing near my flat, then back downstairs again into the hallway, where I knew all along it would end up.

'It would have looked more impressive near your bedroom if it had been bigger,' mused Lisabeth.

I gave Fenella a slow double-take at that and she blushed, but I honestly never said a word.

'That Mr Tomlin collared me in the street and asked after you,' said a voice behind us.

I twisted around to see Doogie and Miranda emerging from their flat for their Saturday shopping expedition.

'Who?' I asked Miranda as she came down the stairs behind us.

'Mr Tomlin, from No 23. Just wanted to know if you were in.'

'Friend of yours? Owes you money?' grinned Doogie.

'I've never met the man,' I said honestly. I was bemused but not worried.

'I told you he was looking for you,' said

Fenella from somewhere at the other end of the tree.

'Well he's still looking for you,' said Miranda. Then, to Doogie: 'Come on, snuggles, we've got our Christmas shopping to do.'

'Snuggles' blushed slightly and followed his beloved out on to the street, heading for the bus stop to take them up West.

Lisabeth decreed that we did the tree decorations *now* and began to produce boxes of tinsel and even a string of cheap tree lights shaped like small plastic candles.

'I want to put the angel on the top,' said Fenella with a twinkle in her eye.

'As long as I don't have to watch,' I said.

We stuck the tree upright in an old waste-paper basket and Lisabeth selected the appropriate site behind the front door. If we'd put it where she wanted it originally, as I pointed out, the reclusive and slightly weird Mr Goodson wouldn't have been able to get out of his flat.

The problem was the tree leaned at an angle of about 30 degrees. What we needed, said Lisabeth, was some sand to hold the trunk in place. I pointed out that we were in Hackney and not on Brighton beach, and she pointed out that there were such things as builders' merchants even in Hackney and open on Saturday mornings. So I had to point out that they didn't sell it by the bucketful and how about if I ventured out to the back yard and liberated a couple of half bricks from the crumbling back wall to use as wedges?

They seemed to do the trick, as long as nobody actually leaned on the damn thing, and Fenella set to with a will, draping the branches in tinsel and streamers of coloured paper. Lisabeth said she had some aerosol spray snow (almost certainly not ozone-friendly) in her room and she'd fetch her cards. Each year she kept any Christmas card she received and the following year she'd cut out the pictures, thread them on to cotton and hang them on the tree.

Even though the tree wasn't of the scale of those given by Norway to Trafalgar Square every year, Fenella was having trouble reaching the top branches. So I got her a chair to stand on and she was on it, making a right song and dance about keeping her balance, and I was checking the power plug on the tree lights when I heard the key go in the front door lock.

As we never ever saw Mr Goodson at weekends, I assumed it was Doogie and Miranda returning early from their shopping trip. Very early. Too early, if I'd had time to think about it.

I didn't even turn around. I just felt a whiff of cold air on the back of my neck, and the next thing I knew, something had exploded in the middle of my back and I was pitching forward into the Christmas tree.

I hit the tree, the tree hit Fenella. She screamed and fell off the chair, clutching at the tree for support that wasn't there. I had armfuls of tree as well, and between us we pulled the whole thing loose, flipping the wedging bricks onto the floor, which I promptly fell over.

Fenella, the tree and I ended up on the floor, and somehow my head ended up between her legs. Now that wasn't quite as bad as it sounds, as at least I was on my back and looking towards Fenella's feet. And the doorway.

Shifty-Eyes and Pointy-Beard had got new suits for Christmas.

Pointy had also got a new cricket bat, or maybe it was for his son who one day would lead the Pakistan cricket team out onto the cricket field to knock seven bells out of England. Why not? Everybody else does.

It didn't take me long to associate the shooting pain in the small of my back with the business end of the bat, but it didn't seem worth commenting on. Through Shifty's legs, I could see a big BMW parked at the kerb. There was somebody in the back. I took a wild guess.

'Sunil?' I hissed. Christ, my back did hurt, and Fenella squirming and squealing under me didn't help.

Shifty moved closer and looked down at me.

'We waited till your wild man friend had gone. You've got nobody to help you now.'

There was a deep growling noise from above me. I tilted my head back deeper into Fenella's legs and could see – upside down – Lisabeth standing outside her flat door, about eight steps up. She had a can of spray snow in one hand and a pair of very sharp kitchen scissors, for cutting Sellotape, in the other. She didn't say anything, she just stared at the two invaders who had put Fenella into such an undignified and compromising position with A Man; and even I count as such some days.

She started down the steps, shaking the aerosol slowly and giving the scissors an experimental snap.

The pain in my back seemed to ease. I smiled up at Shifty and Pointy.

'You haven't met my other friends, have you?'

Of course Lisabeth had been very brave; we all agreed on that, even Lisabeth. And it hadn't really been her fault that Shifty's hand was bleeding so much. After all, he was the one who put his hands in front of his genitals and got in the way of the scissors, so he'd really only himself to blame. And then we'd laughed at how she'd sprayed fake snow into Pointy's face so that his beard looked like a stick-on Colonel Sanders disguise. And again, when we remembered how he'd walked into the edge of the open door and almost knocked himself out because he couldn't see and the more he rubbed his eyes the worse it got. And then I spoilt it all by just mentioning that I thought maybe she had gone a wincy bit too far when she had marched up to the parked BMW and spray-snowed the back passenger window.

Lisabeth had burst into tears and locked herself in her bathroom.

'It's just delayed reaction,' I told Fenella. 'She'll calm down.'

'After about two days and four pounds of chocolate,' said Fenella drily.

'You're the expert,' I admitted, 'but why not give her one of her Christmas presents in advance?'

Fenella was genuinely shocked. More shocked than when she fell off the chair, or when I landed between her legs or when Lisabeth beat up our visitors.

'*Before* Christmas Day?'

'It was just a thought.'

I left her thinking about it and said I'd clear up the mess in the hall and reset the tree. It was a good excuse to get out of there before either of them asked why Pointy-Beard and Shifty-Eyes were after me.

Or how they came to have a key for our front door.

There is a certain school of thought that says that any half-decent policeman is always on duty at a football match on Saturday afternoons. The theory is that they either want to get to see the game free or they're the sort of copper who goes looking for a punch-up with the hooligan element. In either case, they are the sort of cop you know where you stand with.

I don't necessarily go along with this. Prentice, for instance, was at his desk when I rang, and offered to come straight away, and he seemed to be a half-decent copper. At least I hoped he was, as I was going to need him.

Now that Sunil's boys had a key, they could drop in any time, and God knows what might happen if both Doogie and Lisabeth were out and I wasn't.

By the time he arrived, I had restored order to our festive decorations (okay, so the tree wasn't exactly upright and most of the decorations were on one side only) and was tucking into lunch while listening to a bad quality pirate tape of a Chaka Khan concert, which an American friend had sent me.

I had defrosted and reheated a mass of frozen chilli, but Prentice said he'd had a sandwich though I wasn't to stop on his account.

'I'll have a crisp, though,' he said, helping himself.

'They're tortilla chips actually.'

He pulled a face. 'I'm impressed. Mexican beer too.'

'If you weren't on duty, I'd offer you one,' I beamed, pouring the last of the Dos Equis into my glass.

'Gee, thanks. Still, I'm glad to see you're still eating meat. They haven't converted you yet, then?'

I shook my head and, between spoonfuls, I gave him a resume of my adventures in darkest Cambridgeshire.

'So you've got yourself an in on this Boxing Day hunt? That's good.'

'If I should want to go, yes. And always assuming Lara contacts me.'

'You could just turn up.'

'Suspicious. Me hanging around.'

'I thought you'd be used to that by now.'

Cheeky devil.

'Coffee?'

'Yeah, okay.' He picked up the video I'd taken from the rectory. 'You seen this?'

'No, but several like it. I'm guessing that that one is a compilation tape. What Billy would have called a master tape, full of extracts from real TV shows and some of their homemade video stuff. There were four top quality tapes among all the others. I reckoned people sent them in from all over the country. You know, concerned people.'

'I spend my life dealing with concerned people. Can I put this on?' He nodded towards my video recorder. Springsteen was asleep on top of the television.

'Sure, but if there's anything nasty on there involving cats, turn the volume down. Springsteen's a sensitive soul.'

I busied myself in the kitchen until the coffee had filtered. That reminded me that I'd have to go back to Mr Higgins the Coffee Man, as the presents I'd bought had been scattered over the street outside and washed away by the rain since then.

I poured out two mugs and returned to find Prentice glued to the TV screen.

'What's this?' I asked, thinking for a second that he'd flipped channels and we were watching the Saturday afternoon movie. In this case, an early Technicolor war film with buildings exploding left, right and centre.

He didn't answer, but pressed the remote control and the volume came up. Over the explosions came a dull commentary talking about 'effective blast range' and 'thermal diffusion' and other stuff I couldn't understand.

Prentice said: 'Now why do you think the Reverend Bell, or maybe your friend Billy Tuckett, or both, needed an army training video on the use of plastic explosives?'

And for the life of me, I couldn't think of a good answer.

Like on a TV game show, the second round of questioning got harder.

I went over every nuance of everything Bell had said to me, and I definitely could not remember anything about plastic explosives, arms caches or thermonuclear devices. And no, there had been no mention of Professor Brian Bamforth and who the hell was the guy anyway?

'He's one of the country's leading experts on transgenics,' said Prentice sharply. 'Does that mean anything to you?'

'Yes,' I said emphatically. 'Well, not a lot, to be honest.'

I'd seen it written in Billy's notes, but the references hadn't meant much.

'A transgenic organism, or animal for that matter, is one whose genetic composition does not exist in nature. You know what DNA is?'

'It's the double helix – the stuff of life – genetic structure. Are we talking genetic manipulation here? New species of animals? A super race of ... say, cats...?'

Stuff of life? The stuff of nightmares.

'Relax. There's nothing weird about genetic engineering. They probably genetically engineer the yeast in that beer you drank. There's nothing wrong with isolating genes and improving them in things like crops, for instance, or in getting rid of bacterial diseases. But what gets people freaked about transgenics is the technology of taking genes from one species and injecting them at embryo stage into animals of a different species.'

'Hey, man, you're talking fucking Frankenstein here.'

'That's what they all say. Look, I'm no scientist and maybe I put it badly. It's not like selective breeding, it's creating entirely new genetic formations that don't exist as yet.'

'And no doubt there will be failures along the way.'

'It happens, but it's very tightly controlled. Professor Bamforth himself is up for the Advisory Committee for Genetic Manipulation.'

'So he's a target?'

'Absolutely, and this is prime time. Or do I mean open season?' He smiled thinly.

'What, the season of peace on earth and goodwill to all transgenic cross-breeds?'

'Christmas, Easter, the Bank Holidays, they're the favourite times for the activists. They have the spare time and their targets are low on security. Look at that school on Dwyer Street.'

'That's hardly a military establishment,' I observed.

'Okay then, the famous attack on the Royal College of Surgeons' research farm in Kent back in '84. That was turned over on a Bank Holiday.'

I'd had enough of this.

'Come on, Sergeant, I know some of the animal libbers are two bricks short of a wall, but if they hurt *people* they'll alienate themselves from any public sympathy. And you can always get sympathy by showing how badly treated the fluffy bunny-wunnies in the laboratories are!'

'I hear what you're saying, Roy–' (Rule of Life No 279: people who say, 'I hear what you're saying,' really mean they didn't want you to raise the subject in the first place) – 'but we're not dealing with sit-down demonstrators or protest marchers any more.

'You've seen how well-organised the anti-hunting lot are now, and the anti-factory farming faction have organised Animal Investigation Units to carry out daytime inspections of farms. The fanatics, though, they've gone for the arson and sledgehammer technique. That's what we call it: A and S. But it looks as if some are going beyond that. Do you know what the guy on that video was talking about?'

'Explosives.'

'Semtex H. The best of the new generation of plastics.'

'That's the stuff the dogs at the airport can't detect, isn't it?'

'The very same. The Czechs manufacturer it, and the Government's been pressing them to add something in so it can be sniffed out.'

'Any particular flavour?'

'It's not funny.' He frowned at me.

'Oh, come on. Where is a country vicar and–' I almost said 'and a legal secretary' but stopped myself – 'a backwoods parson, where does he put his hands on Semtex H?'

'Stranger things have happened. That's why I want you to keep your eyes open on Boxing Day.'

'You think they're going to blow up a fox-hunt?'

'Don't piss about; of course not. That hunt meet is a target for the hunt saboteurs, we know that. Oh, they'll cause trouble and so will the bloody huntsmen; they're just as bad as each other. There'll be a punch-up, no doubt, and pictures in the newspapers the next day. But think. It's perfect cover for the real loonies to get together.'

'And you'll have your informers in there as well, won't you?'

He shrugged that one off.

'Even better if we have you as well. Keep an eye on those not getting involved in the direct action. The real loonies are quite para-noid, you know. They're convinced we photograph everybody and have stacks of computer time to trace their movements. Most of them won't even learn to drive because they think we use the driving licence computer against them.'

Interesting. They should do what I do –

don't rely on just one licence.

'Anyone with a record of any sort,' Prentice went on, 'even a parking ticket, is regarded as a liability. That's what makes it so difficult to track the bastards down. They're all clean.'

'Until they blow someone up?'

'No. Until they get nicked.'

I broke my fast for the second time in 24 hours and lit a cigarette.

'If I do this for you – and it's a big "if," mind you – then you've got to do something for me.'

'That depends,' he said firmly. I reckoned it was the best I could hope for.

'I want you to locate somebody for me,' I said, then added quickly: 'Without knowing why. It's personal.'

'And totally innocent?'

'Not likely, not if I find her!' I gave him a real male chauvinist leer and a wink, hoping I wasn't overdoing it.

'Who is she?' he sighed, reaching for his notebook.

On his way out, he stopped in the hall and looked at the Christmas tree.

'It's crooked,' he said.

'Naw, it's genetically engineered that way for houses with dodgy foundations.'

I made a list of things I had to do. High up on it were: find Zaria (with or without Prentice's help), avoid Sunil, buy more Christmas presents, organise some musicians for a New Year's Eve party (the rods I make for my own back...) and stock up with booze for it, and restock the larder, which was getting rather bare.

I put the domestic shopping to the top of the list. After all, this was the last Saturday before Christmas and British housewives are always convinced that the shops will never open again, so they rape the supermarket shelves as if stocking up for a siege.

I made a couple of phone calls about getting some booze in for the party, and ended up mostly leaving messages as most people were out and about. Then, not able to put it off any longer, I zipped round the corner to Mrs Patel's delicatessen and piled up some essential provisions. Cat food, cat snack biscuits, cat litter, and food for me. And all the time, peeping around corners watching for pointed (white) beards, cricket bats and BMWs with snowed-out windows.

I got back to No 9 and shut the door with such a sense of relief that I celebrated by opening a bottle of tequila I'd been saving as an emergency Christmas present in case I found I'd forgotten anyone. Truth was, just then, I couldn't think of a more deserving cause.

Springsteen wanted feeding, which is a bit like saying Springsteen was still breathing normally, so I opened a tin of something that was definitely not cruelty free as far as some other animal was concerned, and he buried his face in it. I left all my shopping on the kitchen work surface after cutting a slice of orange for my drink and wondering for the millionth time why we couldn't get decent fruit from politically acceptable regimes. Then I flicked on the CD for some music and tore up the rest of the list of things to do.

I know I dozed off before the football results came on the TV because I normally tune in. Not that I'm a fan of football, but it sometimes helps to know what everybody else in the pub is talking about.

And when I was rudely awakened by Fenella hammering on the door, it was about half past 6.00.

'Why was your door bolted?' she asked as I scratched my head and tried to shake the sleep from my eyes, thinking that she had a point as she normally charges straight in these days.

'Pass.'

'What?'

'Too difficult. Next question.'

'You went out.'

She said it like I should be on the steps of the guillotine already. 'Yes, I did.' I stepped back into the kitchen and waved a hand at my shopping.

'Ugh! All that *meat!*'

I took a deep breath.

'Look, what's up, Binky?' Then I had a bad thought. 'It's not Lisabeth, is it? Is she okay?'

'She's fine. I did what you suggested.'

What I suggested? I had another bad thought.

'I gave her one of her pressies,' Fenella explained, and looked puzzled as I exhaled loudly in relief.

'So what's happening?'

'I didn't hear you come back.' And she'd been worried about me. I almost put my arms round her until I remembered Lisabeth and the aerosol and the scissors. And then she went on: 'And I took a phone call for you.'

I was awake.

'A girl? A woman? Female?'

'Yes. She's coming over here at seven. She'd got your number but she said she'd forgotten your address. So I told her.' She put her head on one side. 'Was that all right?'

'Brill, Binky darling. I could kiss you. Absolutely ace.'

'Oh good,' she said in what for her was a sarcastic tone. 'I'm glad I've done something right. She sounded ever so nice.'

I smiled, but to myself at that, knowing both Fenella's ultra-middle-class upbringing and sexual preferences.

'Oh, I doubt if you and Zaria would have much in common,' I said gently.

'Zaria? No. This one was called Lara. I'm sure of that.' Oh shit.

I turned the shower on and let it warm up while I stashed the shopping and tidied the flat. Everything that was meat or could have contained meat went straight into the freezer. Surely she wouldn't look in there. Did I know the sort of woman who checked out refrigerators? Yes. I wondered how she felt about butter, and played safe and threw that in the freezer too. Milk? The hell with it, I'd risk that.

What else?

Within five minutes, the fridge contained an ancient tub of margarine, some mushrooms, a clove of garlic, some celery, some politically dubious grapes and some right-wing Chardonnay (Australian – no sweat), about a gallon of bottled or canned beer and a bottle of tequila.

I checked my bookcases and, apart from the cookbooks, which I took and hid under the bed, I felt there was nothing that actually screamed out that I was a carnivorous crypto-fascist. Aside from the fact that the freezer door bulged at the seams and was in danger of pinging open, it was the best I could do. I dropped clothes as I ran to the bathroom.

When the doorbell rang, I was almost dressed and I had almost zipped up my jeans when I remembered the leather jacket I'd left draped over the Habitat sofa-bed. The doorbell had gone again before I'd thrown that under the bed as well, and if I didn't move it, Fenella would get there first.

She already had and was saying 'Ah yes, I spoke to you on the telephone earlier' as I appeared on the landing.

'Lara! What a surprise,' I said loudly, hoping she hadn't noticed I'd forgotten shoes and socks. 'I didn't know you knew where to find me.'

Fenella glared at me, so I turned up the volume on my smile.

'You were out when I called,' said Lara, looking at Fenella, which I thought was pretty tactless, 'so I just thought I'd drop round.'

'Why not? Come on up.'

No matter how badly dressed or off-guard, you always have the advantage if you are higher than somebody else, and I could see it rankled with Lara to the extent that she forgot about Fenella, who disappeared, unwanted and unthanked, into her lair after giving me the sort of look that could come in useful if we ever decided to strip the paint off the staircase.

'You'll have to take me as you find me,' I said, which, in normal circumstances, is not a bad line.

'That's fine,' she said, walking by me.

She was wearing a blue denim trouser suit, with medium-heel sandals that made her taller than me, and a stretchy white polo-necked shirt, with a single string of huge wooden beads around her neck. I bet myself that every stitch was man-made and that her underwear was all from Marks and Spencer, though no-one would offer odds on that if she was British and female.

'Come in, make yourself at home.' I waved her to a chair and I killed the CD set. 'It seems like only yesterday–'

'It was yesterday,' she said deadpan.

'I know. It was just something to say. You've rather taken me by surprise, I'm not ... it's just ... I'm not used to women coming calling on me.'

I hoped I wasn't overdoing it.

'I can't believe that,' she said. But I think she wanted to.

'Well, what I mean is calling here,' I said, not really sure where all this was going.

She looked around, her lush red hair swishing like a curtain so that she had to flick strands out of her eyes.

'Do you have a relationship with someone here?' she asked, businesslike.

'You might say I'm escaping from one.'

That was a pretty safe thing to say at any time.

'Then you won't mind if I ask you out, will you?' She forced a smile when she said it, and then screwed up her nose.

'Tonight?' I asked innocently, wondering why she looked as if she'd just found a bad smell.

'Why not? There's a new restaurant I've been meaning to...'

She screwed up her whole face this time and fumbled in her jacket pocket for a balled-up Kleenex. She didn't sneeze, she just dabbed her nose.

'I'm sorry. There's a new restaurant and I wondered if I could buy you dinner and talk you into giving me a lift to ... to...'

This time she did sneeze, and when she drew breath afterwards it went in with a wheeze.

I stood over her.

'Are you all right, Lara? What's the matter.'

'I'm so sorry, this hasn't happened in a long time.' She tried to breathe again, and it was an effort and she was going red in the face. 'H ... ha ... have you ha ...had a cat in here, or a d ... d ... dog?'

'What?'

'I'm all ... allergic ... to fur.'

'Thank God for that, I thought it was me,' I said without thinking.

I could tell from the way she gasped that she didn't think it was funny. Then I thought: an animal libber allergic to fur? Pull the other one. Then I thought: Springsteen!

'I'm sorry,' I said, 'it must be awful for

you. I've not been here long and I think the people before me had a cat.'

Not bad for thinking on your feet, I reckoned.

'There are cat hairs on this … this…'

Another sneeze snapped her head forward as she ran a hand over one of the cushions.

'The place came furnished,' I said desperately. 'Let me get you a drink.'

'Water … just water,' she wheezed.

I dived into the kitchen, and the first thing I did was hide Springsteen's dinner bowl and water dish in the cupboard under the sink. Then I opened the freezer door to get some ice, and half a dozen packets of hamburger meat, veal, lamb's kidneys, you name it, tumbled out on to my bare feet.

I was cramming them back into the freezer drawers and swearing fluently but softly to myself when something made me look up to the kitchen window, which on clear days gave me panoramic views over the ten-foot-square back yard.

Balanced on three legs, one paw extended like a pointer dog, was Springsteen. He was on the window-frame and must have jumped six feet straight up from the roof of the kitchen extension downstairs. He had landed on a two-inch-wide frame through a half-open window in total silence, but I knew that if he moved down onto the sink, a mere three inches below the window, he would somehow manage to smash all the plates in the drying rack, disturb the washed-up pans and send cutlery flying all over the floor. It would sound like a brass band on crack during an earthquake. Cats are like that.

He wasn't looking at me, he was looking at the packs of meat that still seemed to want to jump out of the freezer as much as I wanted to cram them back in. He showed me a millimetre of pink tongue and hissed through his fangs. From the living-room, Lara went into another round of coughing, which sounded positively terminal.

I straightened up and squared off to Springsteen with my best John Wayne voice, at the same time reaching for a pack of lamb's kidneys that were still unfrozen.

'Okay, Springsteen,' I said quietly. 'This is serious. Either you leave this kitchen immediately or I'll see you skinned and stuffed as the prize exhibit in the London Dungeon. Which'll it be?'

He hunched his shoulders as if to pounce. Reason wasn't going to work.

'Then fill your paws, you son of a bitch!' I said and flipped the kidneys, pack and wrapping, over his head like a frisbee They sailed out of the window and he turned without a sound and launched himself after them.

I bet myself that he took them before they hit the ground.

'Inhaler,' gasped Lara, which for a second I took to be some sort of bizarre instruction. Then I twigged.

'Where? Did you have a handbag?'

She shook her head, and the long fronds of her ginger mane totally hid her face.

'Didn't bring it,' she mumbled. 'It's back home.'

'Then let's go.'

She looked up at me wildly.

'But ... I...'

Then she coughed violently and clutched herself with both hands under the breasts.

'No arguments; come on,' I said. 'I'll put some shoes on.'

I dived into the bedroom and found some clean white socks, then hopped around finding my trainers, wallet and keys. I grabbed a black trenchcoat, because it was the first thing I could put my hand on that wasn't either leather or fur-lined, then I put an arm around her and helped her downstairs.

Even by the bottom of the stairs, her breathing had recovered to something like normal; well, normal for someone who'd just finished a three-minute mile. But the strain was genuine and she was putting most of her weight on me.

As I fumbled with the door catch, she pushed the hair out of her eyes and looked around.

'I'm sorry about this. It's unforgivable,'

264

she panted.

'Nonsense,' I said reassuringly.

She looked at the Christmas decorations and then the tree.

'I know,' I said, getting the door open. 'I'll straighten it later.'

By the time we reached Muswell Hill, she had recovered enough to move to the jump seat behind me, and through the open glass partition was desperately trying to talk me out of taking her home.

'I'm fine, honestly.'

I'd bundled her across Armstrong's back seat and locked open the windows in the back so she could get fresh air into her system, and it certainly seemed that the further away from Springsteen we got, the easier she could breathe.

'Come on, I'll survive. I want to take you to this restaurant. It's in the West End. I've made reservations.'

Reservations? Confident lady.

'Look, I'll be a lot happier if you get your inhaler or something, just in case. I feel responsible, you know. That's a frightening thing to suffer from. Do you take drugs for it?'

'I have some that will hold off the symptoms, but you have to take them in advance. Look, it's okay now.'

I checked her in the rear mirror. There was

anxiety in her eyes. Something definitely wasn't going to her plan.

'Let's just pick up your inhaler and then we can go straight up West. No problem; it's a straight run down through Swiss Cottage and the traffic's no sweat.'

'Well, all right,' she said slowly. 'Take a left up here, then left again.'

She gave me more instructions until we were in a quiet avenue off Ballards Lane.

'Pull in here. Will you wait here? It's my flatmate. She's not expecting me back so soon and I don't want to upset her. I'll just nip in and get my stuff. Won't be a second.'

'Okay,' I said. 'I'll turn around.'

She was out of Armstrong and sprinting towards a three-storey block of apartments before I could argue. I whipped the wheel over and Armstrong turned beautifully, as all London cabs do, within the width of the road.

Leaving the engine running, I watched the block of flats until a light came on, then another one, in the top two windows on the left. If she had a flatmate, she liked sitting in the dark.

I put my arm out of my window and opened the back door for her as she skipped across the road. She clutched a small metal canister.

'All set,' she laughed. 'And running up-stairs gives you an appetite.'

'Where to, madame?'

'Baker Street. Do you know anywhere to park?'

'With a black cab? Who needs car parks?'

'That's what I thought,' she said.

The restaurant was vegetarian, of course, called No Gravy, which I didn't think was a bad effort. The menu was imaginative, the food forgettable, and the wine list included kosher wines from Israel. We drank mineral water and talked. We talked about animals, about food, about me. A lot about me.

Lara proved an expert in turning the conversation away from herself, and by the end of the meal I knew little more about her other than that she said her surname was Preston, and that yes, she was a legal secretary and how had I known? (Three types of shorthand, good salary, negotiable working hours and familiarity with a Coroner's Court, plus a good guess.)

She insisted on paying the bill, and she did it with a roll of ten-pound notes that she produced from her jacket pocket. I'd wondered about that, with her not carrying a bag, and I'd expected a credit card or two, but it seemed she was a cash-on-the-barrel-head type.

I suggested a drink for the road or maybe a club, but she said she'd rather go home, and would I like coffee?

I said sure, thinking that if every time anyone said 'Come in for coffee' and they actually got coffee, then coffee futures were the thing to put your investments in.

It was the top-floor flat, a spacious, two-bedroomed affair decorated in pastel blues, immaculately tidy, comfortable and pretty much characterless. There was no sign of a room mate.

'Do you really want coffee?' she asked, slipping off her coat.

'No. Not really.'

I watched fascinated as she hung her jacket on a metal hanger.

'The bathroom's through there.'

She took the jacket to a built-in wardrobe and slotted the hanger in, then she crossed her arms and took her shirt off over her head, leaving the necklace of wooden beads around her throat.

I stepped up behind her and undid the metal clasp for her, sensing her shoulders tense as I did so.

'That's okay,' she said softly and relaxing a little against me. 'I can manage.'

I kissed her lightly on the shoulder and went into the bathroom like I was supposed to, but not really knowing what I was expected to do there. At least I'd been right about the brand label on her bra.

I took off my coat and then the rest of my clothes and left them in as neat a pile as I could on the old fiddle-back chair next to the bath. Then I filled the sink with hot water and washed face and hands and then took a new toothbrush from the inside pocket of my trenchcoat (well, you never know), removed the wrapping and cleaned my teeth.

On the shelf above the sink, in front of the mirror were three carefully arranged contraceptives in their shiny foil packets. Each was a different brand. I couldn't swear to it, but I was sure they were the three brands I'd last seen in the Reverend Bell's bathroom cupboard in West Elsworth. I reached for my coat again.

Lara was in bed, the only light coming through the doorway from the hall, her hair splashed over a pillow framing her white face like an aura. She turned down the duvet to her left so I didn't even get a choice in which side of the bed I had.

'Did you see what I left for you in the bathroom?' she said calmly.

I showed her what I had in the palm of my right hand.

'It's okay. I roll my own.'

CHAPTER TWELVE

'And that was it? She just told you to go and you went?'

'She said she had things to do. Hell's teeth, it was a one-night stand – and carefully stage-managed at that – not an invitation to share the rent.'

'Did you get a chance to look around?'

Prentice dunked a chocolate biscuit in his tea. We were in a scruffy, formica-lined cafe, which during the summer made a fortune selling ice-creams and soft drinks to the tourists struggling between the Houses of Parliament and Buckingham Palace. Across the road, through the bits of the window people had rubbed the condensation from, was a wet and deserted St James's Park. It was Monday morning and also Christmas Eve, so most of the offices had closed for the holiday. The few that were still working would be deserted by noon, and the staff well ensconced in the nearest pub by five past.

'Briefly, when she took a shower.'

I didn't tell him that she had insisted on showering immediately after making love. That had thrown me for a minute, but then I'd thought that as the act itself had been so clinical, why shouldn't she prefer a cold rub-down with a wire brush in preference to the more traditional sweet-nothing pillow talk? (And I hear rumours that some people still smoke afterwards.)

In any case, I was pretty sure she was going through my clothes and wallet, which were still in the bathroom, not that she'd find anything there. And it did give me the chance to pad a quick circuit around the flat.

'And what did you find? What's the matter? Who are you looking for?'

I shook my head. Maybe I'd just imagined that black BMW in the wing mirror.

'Nothing. Nothing's the matter and I found nothing in her flat.'

'What's the address of her gaff?' He made a note in a flip-top notebook.

'That was the interesting thing, of course,' I said, knowing it would wind him up. 'There was nothing to say who she was, where she worked, what she did when she wasn't at work. No cheque-books, credit cards, photographs, nothing. And there was no flatmate either; or rather, he hasn't been around for a few days.'

Prentice raised both eyebrows. 'He?'

'Yup. I had about three seconds in the spare bedroom, but it was a man's room. And I think I know why she snowed me earlier. I told you she had this attack at my place.'

'Some allergy? Was it genuine?'

'Oh yeah. When I took her back to her place to get her inhaler she made me wait outside. I thought at first she was just paranoid about me knowing where she lived, but what she was doing was improvising.'

'Improvising?'

I pretended to look around the café. 'Nice echo,' I said, and he snorted 'Get on with it.'

'She knew she couldn't stand it back at my place, so she changed plan and decided to use her own bedroom, but she had to clear away some of the obvious signs of male habitation. In the spare room, she'd stuffed a razor, a toothbrush and a can of shaving foam under the bedclothes. I deduced from their condition that they had not been used for four or five days.'

'I'm impressed. Right little Sherlock, aren't you?'

I didn't tell him that I'd opened a drawer and found piles of unmistakably masculine socks and underpants.

'So you think she had it in mind to seduce you right from the start?' Prentice said with a hint of a leer.

'I think she's a very determined lady and when she sets her mind to something, she gets it. The thing that really upset her during her allergy attack was not the allergy; she knew all about that and what was causing it. It was not being in control of herself that really bugged her.'

'Sigmund-bleedin'-Freud now as well as Sherlock Holmes! My, I did hit lucky with you, Roy, didn't I?'

'Don't push it, Sergeant. I am not, repeat not, on your payroll, and unless you've got something for me, I'm not even in your debt.'

He looked at his notebook.

'Ah yes, now, about that little favour you wanted. We've not had much luck I'm afraid. We've got this Zaria Inhadi – is that it? – as far back as the nursing agency that supplied her to the Aurora whatever-it-is rest home, but they've not kept her address from when she went on their books. They had references for her, though, and we'll follow those up ... but it is Christmas Eve, you know.'

'So I'd heard.'

He scribbled something on a page of the notebook and tore it out.

'You can get me on one of these numbers over Christmas. Ring me on Boxing Day if you see anything going down.'

I folded the sheet of paper and put it in my wallet.

'I don't know why I'm doing this,' I sighed.

'You're one of life's Samaritans, Roy. Think of it like that.'

'So who am I supposed to be the Good Samaritan to?' I asked.

'Me, of course.' He smiled, then finally let the leer come through. 'Are you sure this Lara bint didn't just simply crave your body?'

'No,' I said carefully, as if considering the idea. 'She didn't really enjoy it.'

'But did you?'

I looked at him wide-eyed.

'Now, do I look like the sort to bonk and tell?'

I broke a Rule of Life then by going into the West End to finish my Christmas shopping on Christmas Eve. Between the last-minute shoppers and the office party-goers, I'd seen quieter riots. I spotted two turkeys in Selfridges Food Store bags that had been left at bus stops, and there was a trail of streamers and abandoned party hats that made the south side of Duke Street look like the scene of a terrorist airport massacre. In the side door of Littlewoods, a couple were getting as close to copulation as could physically happen while fully clothed. As I passed by, one of a pair of elderly women watching from the bus queue said, 'I wonder if they're married?' and I said, 'Yes, but not to each other,' and they both roared with laughter.

By five o'clock, I'd had enough and loaded my shopping-bags into Armstrong. I treated myself to a cigarette to calm my nerves. Who was it said: when the going gets tough, the tough go shopping?

I meandered back eastwards, though the traffic wasn't at all bad as most people had split for the holidays; the ones still in a fit state to drive, that is.

I had spent the rest of Sunday, after leaving Finchley, touring aimlessly trying to pick up Zaria's trail. She hadn't called back at Iris's pub, and not only had the Leytonstone rest home not heard from her, but Sally the punk nurse had gone away for Christmas.

Perhaps it was just general frustration, not the least over the encounter with Lara, that made me careless. As I turned into Stuart Street, a black BMW pulled out from the kerb and stopped at an angle, blocking the road ahead. I stopped easily enough, with 20 yards to spare, and just had time for a couple of choice swear words before I found reverse.

That was as far as it went. I turned my head to look out of the rear window and got a really good view of the Transit van coming up behind, straddling the middle of the road. With traffic parked on both sides of the street, there was nowhere for me to go.

I reached around and made sure both front doors were locked – I knew the back ones were – and kept the engine running.

The van stopped up close, its headlights dazzling in the mirror until I bent it upward to kill the reflection. Ahead of me, the driver's door of the BMW opened and a tall, thin Pakistani wearing a camel coat got out and walked straight towards me.

When he was five paces away, I revved

275

Armstrong's engines but kept my foot on the clutch and my hand on the handbrake. If I was lucky, I just might take him out before I ended up on the dashboard of the BMW.

Sunil – it had to be him – raised his hands, palms out, in a surrender gesture; but he only slowed his walk, he didn't stop. He came right up to my window and put his right hand in his coat pocket.

I revved the engine again. If he produced a gun and shot me, at least I'd have a go at scratching his paintwork on the way out.

The hand came out with a white envelope. He slapped it once on the palm of his other hand, then offered it towards the window.

Ever so carefully I pulled down the window an inch. He thrust the envelope at me.

'Take it. You've caused me too much embarrassment already. I'll have the second instalment in a week's time.'

That was all he said. Then he waved at the van behind me and I heard it reverse and the light filling Armstrong withdrew. He was halfway back to the BMW when I ripped the envelope open and saw the wedge of used ten-pound notes, and even the quickest of glances said we were talking thousands not hundreds.

I lowered the window and waved at him as he climbed into his car.

'And a Merry Christmas to you too,' I yelled.

It seemed the thing to say.

Two thousand five hundred pounds.

I counted it again, sitting cross-legged in the middle of the floor. Two thousand five hundred again.

Springsteen prowled across the floor in front of me, deliberately stepping from note to note.

'Cat food,' I told him, beaming inanely and pointing at the money.

He gave me a look as if I'd just confirmed his worst suspicions, and sat down just out of range and began to nibble a rear claw. When they do their own toenails, cats can be really gross.

All that money. All the shops shut and most of central London deserted because it was Christmas Eve.

I counted it again as I stuffed it into Hugh Brogan's *History of the United States,* which had been converted into a fire-proof box safe with a small combination lock by Lenny the Lathe. Then I removed five of the notes and strolled around the corner to Stan at the local off-licence, without once looking over my shoulder.

Stan packed three bottles of champagne, one of tequila (replacement emergency present) and one of Bailey's Irish Cream, which I knew Lisabeth liked, into a cardboard box for me.

'Party, is it, then?' he asked.

'Not tonight, Stan.'

'My God, you're slipping.'

'Could be. Been a bit busy lately and the old social life has indeed slipped a mite. I'll be home in front of a log fire, roasting chestnuts and wrapping presents and watching a video.'

'Which one?' He moved over to the display of video boxes on racks between the canned beers and the chocolate.

'Got one, Stan, been saving it. *Indiana Jones and the Last Crusade.*'

'That's not out on video yet,' he frowned.

'Never said it was a good copy, Stan,' I winked.

For once, my evening went as planned. With one exception. Lara rang about 8.30 and asked if I could pick her up on Boxing Day at 6.00. I checked that she meant a.m. and, natch, she did and I negotiated up to 7.00 as there wouldn't be any traffic and she said okay, but sulkily. And I said, 'Merry Christmas,' and she said, 'Oh yes. Yes,' like I was the first to point this out to her, and then she hung up. Comfort and joy; I don't think.

I psyched myself down for what had become the traditional Christmas at Stuart Street. In Lisabeth's book, if it happens once, it becomes a tradition, and I'd made the mistake of cooperating the previous year.

Throughout the evening there was much to-ing and fro-ing between flats, though it was nowhere near as interesting as it sounds. Basically Fenella would make some spurious excuse to come up and see me so that she could wrap Lisabeth's presents, most of which she'd hidden in my flat. Half an hour later, Lisabeth would do the same. In between, I had to wrap theirs and sneak down to put them under the tree. This was even more complicated when we had Frank and Salome living upstairs and they did the same, but Doogie and Miranda were new and had been left to their own devices.

After the first bottle of champagne, I was having trouble negotiating the stairs, let alone wrapping anything, but I survived until midnight, when we were allowed by Lisabeth to stand round the tree and open one present each. There was even a card from the mysterious Mr Goodson, pinned up by the communal phone, which read 'To all at No 9 from A Goodson,' a bit like signing it 'A Wellwisher.' No-one knew where he spent Christmas and no-one had seen him leave the house.

On Christmas morning, I opened a tin of turkey catfood for Springsteen because it seemed traditional, and would have stuck a sprig of holly in it if I'd had one. I opened my presents, which Fenella had hidden from me as they'd arrived, and found a couple of interesting books, enough Body Shop male cosmetics (not tested on animals) to deal with a regiment of beards and skin problems, and, from an Irish friend, a pack of 200 Sweet Afton cigarettes that had come through the mail addressed to Duncan Torrens; Duncan Terrace and Torrens Street being the two roads nearest the Angel tube station. I knew that the third packet in the parcel, carefully re-wrapped, would contain a slab of finest Moroccan black dope.

When I heard the TV come on downstairs – Lisabeth insisted on having a carol service as background noise on the big day itself – I showered and dressed and, armed with another bottle of champagne from the fridge, trooped down to join the fun.

Lisabeth and Fenella, being veggies, substituted nut cutlets for turkey, although as a special dispensation, Fenella attempted to cook me a turkey breast fillet dotted with tarragon. It came out like a cardboard envelope with burnt lawn clippings for decoration, but it was the thought that counted. The Christmas pudding (with me in charge of flaming it with brandy – not a good move, that) was traditional, though, as were the mince pies and cream and about a zillion other calories in the form of chocolates, after-dinner mints, liqueurs, so forth, so fifth.

By mid-afternoon, we had all three collapsed into various chairs, or across the floor in Fenella's case, who had announced, 'I feel another drunk front coming on,' a line she'd learned from a visiting American friend of mine called Lewd Lulu. Eventually we pulled ourselves together enough for me to do the washing-up, and then we turned the sound on the TV right down, put on a record and broke out the Trivial Pursuit board. I won as always, though there were fewer tears than usual, then rolled a joint for us to share.

All in all, a fairly standard Christmas, no doubt typical of a million homes across the country.

'You're late,' said Lara, climbing into the back of Armstrong.

'Sorry. Had trouble starting; it's the frost,' I lied, although the weather had chilled down considerably. 'Still, no problem traffic-wise, there's absolutely zilch on the roads. Good Christmas?'

She didn't answer.

'The hunt starts gathering around ten, you know.'

'Relax. We'll zip round the M25 to the M11. There can't be roadworks on Boxing Day, and nobody uses the M11 anyway.'

She sat back in her seat as I accelerated; you don't have much choice in the matter in a taxi if the driver knows what he's doing.

'What's in the bag?'

She had an airline bag on her knee and

hadn't let it go since she got in. I guessed it was a change of clothes, as she was kitted out for action in black ski-pants, canvas deck shoes and a brown duffle coat with hood.

'Some things we might need.' She held up a series of bottles and packets so I could see in the mirror. 'Aniseed, pepper, oil of peppermint, marzipan...'

'Marzipan?'

'For the dogs. It masks scent.'

I'd heard that from my friend Trippy, whose one remaining ambition in life was to be the first drug-smuggler through the Channel Tunnel. And he was going to do it using a birthday cake with lots of marzipan on to fool the sniffer dogs at the Customs posts.

'What about your ... your allergy? Won't the dogs affect you?'

'Yes,' she said coldly. 'But we must learn to overcome physical weaknesses.' I wondered if that was part of her Kateda mantra. 'I have taken the appropriate drugs and I have my inhaler and we will all wear masks.'

She held up a white gauze mask on a metal frame, the sort that house painters and Japanese commuters use.

'Do you have one?'

'No.'

'We'll get you a scarf.'

'Is it really necessary?'

'Oh yes. Sometimes the Special Branch

have people there taking photographs of us.'

I looked at her in the mirror and she stared me out, deadpan.

I felt a twinge of sympathy for her, but only a twinge. In her case, it wasn't just paranoia; they really were after her.

We made the Reverend Bell's rectory just after 9.00. A weak and watery sun had given up the job of trying to shine, and the frost was shimmering across the fields. Our breath steamed. It was what the hunters would call a good day for it. The foxes probably disagreed.

There was a motley collection of vehicles parked outside the rectory. Several motorbikes, a clutch of Citroen 2CVs, a minibus and two Morris Minors. Exactly what you might expect. All of them had stickers on the bumper or in the back windows, ranging from 'Stop The Bloody Whaling' to 'One Planet, Don't Abuse It.' I bet none of them ran on unleaded.

Lara was out of Armstrong, bag over her shoulder and marching towards the front door before I'd killed the engine. I muttered, 'Thanks for the lift,' to myself and followed her.

Despite the weather, the front door was open and there was a general hubbub coming from the big, empty ballroom. Except it wasn't empty, there must have been 40 to 50 people in there, of all shapes, sizes and ages. They were all white, I noticed, and almost certainly all middle-class. Two couples were clearly pensioners, which probably explained one of the Morris Minors outside; they'd bought it new. All of them were dressed in jeans and bungy coats against the cold, all had scarves or masks of some sort – in a couple of cases, Batman ones – hanging round their necks. As far as I knew, I was in the middle of the Second Regiment of the Queen's Own Hunt Saboteurs.

There was a trestle-table by the French windows with two tea urns, and young Stephanie was dispensing cups of something hot and brown from them.

'Hello,' she said with a genuine smile. 'I'm glad you could come. You're fun.'

Which was the nicest thing anybody was to say to me all day.

She leaned over the table and offered me a chipped white mug.

'It's coffee, I think. Got any vodka?'

'Not this early,' I said. 'Won't your father go ape-shit if he finds you with this mob?'

'Sole purpose of exercise,' she said primly.

Lara had disappeared, so I circulated aimlessly, clutching the coffee mug in my palms for warmth. It was freezing in the ballroom, but nobody seemed to mind.

The saboteurs were greeting each other like long-lost friends, which they probably were. For many of them, it was the height of their social calendar. Some had placards, mostly homemade with a lot of red paint for effect. The best I saw said, 'If you can't eat it, don't torture it,' and the weirdest one said, 'Librans Against Slaughter.'

I caught snippets of conversation such as: '...did David ever get that hoof print out of his car door?' and '...the hounds always go for salami if you can't get authentic biltong...' And several of them smiled at me and said hello. They all had bright, expectant eyes and shiny, excited faces. They at least were ready for the chase.

Through the open front door, I saw two more bikes draw up, and these were The Business. One was a Harley, I could tell even from that distance, and the other a smaller BMW. Both riders dismounted and hung their helmets over their handlebars. Both had full leather riding gear and both wore balaclavas, which they stretched and pulled off as they walked to the door.

Lara met them in the hall, and I watched in case she threw up at the sight of so much leather. She didn't; instead she reached up and kissed the first one and then shook hands with the second as he was introduced to her. Then she led them into the milling throng.

I felt a hand on my shoulder, something that always turns my spine to jelly.

'Roy! Good of you to make it. And thank

you for bringing Lara.'

It was Bell in full cleric gear, including dog-collar and cassock, which stopped just above his Doc Martens.

'Did I have a choice?' I asked cheekily.

'Probably not. Lara is very single-minded. I see her friends have arrived.' He didn't sound too pleased about it.

'Nice disguise,' I said, indicating the cassock.

'Even our boorish local hunters think twice about riding down a man of the cloth, especially if they have to come to see me next week about their daughters' weddings or their grandchildren being christened. And anyway, it looks good on television when a vicar gets bullied.'

He was serious about this.

'Are you expecting a TV crew?'

'I shouldn't think so, not on Boxing Day. But we'll be taking our own pictures.'

'Billy's video camera?'

'Er ... yes,' he said, and flushed slightly. 'Billy's.'

He caught someone's eye across the room and headed off, saying, 'Sandra, how nice of you to turn out.' I shuffled over to where Lara was talking to the leather-clad Harley rider. His biker friend was busy introducing himself to a pair of pinch-faced young blondes, both wearing CND badge earrings.

Lara glared at me as I approached, and

not even my 100-watt smile melted her expression.

'Hello, Roy,' she said reluctantly, and as if it was at least a year since she'd seen me last. 'Meet Tony.'

Tony pulled off a gauntlet with his teeth and we shook hands.

'Hi-de-hi,' he said, in a voice that sounded as if he'd never had the silver spoon taken out of his mouth.

'Nice bike,' I said, watching Lara slide away towards Bell. 'Touch of the Electra Glides.'

He looked blank at that. 'Oh, she shifts all right. Made it here in eight minutes under the hour. No traffic, of course.'

'From where?' I asked innocently.

'Ah-ha! Nice try.' He tapped his nose with his forefinger. 'But we mustn't say, must we? Rules of the game, and all that. No surnames, no addresses. In case the Boys In Blue are around.'

'Dead right. Just checking. First time?'

He nodded and grinned inanely.

'First time this side of the tracks,' he whispered, touching his nose again. 'To be truthful, I've changed sides today. My father does a spot of hunting in Leicestershire and I have been known to jog along behind. In my younger days, natch.'

'Oh, natch.'

If he'd told me his father owned Leicestershire, I wouldn't have been surprised. From his age, accent, the haircut and the 'eight minutes under the hour from here', I had him down as a newly-commissioned lieutenant, almost certainly based in Colchester (as Aldershot was too far), and I'd even guess at the regiment: Devon and Dorsets. That was a decent enough billet for someone whose dad hunted in Leicestershire.

'So why are you turning traitor?' I asked.

'Oh, Harry and I–' he indicated his companion now deep in discussion with the CND ladies '–thought it might be a giggle.' He lowered his voice again. 'Couldn't give a tinker's toss about old Brer Fox if truth were known, but it's a good way to bugger up the fat Burghers of Cambridge, isn't it?'

'Absolutely. All good, clean fun.'

He looked at me like a fellow conspirator.

'Lara said you were the chap with the taxi. Bet you've had some laughs in that, eh?'

He flapped his gauntlet against my chest. I was having trouble taking this guy for real.

'You wouldn't believe what I've got up to in that old bus,' I said, and meant it. 'The number of women who flag you down begging for a lift is incredible.'

I said it with as much corny innuendo as I thought I could get away with, and he lapped it up.

'Have you managed to get Lara in the back seat yet?'

'One of my regular rides, you might say.'

I thought he might seize up at that. He giggled and nudged me with his elbow, then punched me lightly on the shoulder.

'Good man. Never dared myself, though always fancied her. But not good form to mess with a chap's...'

'Sister?'

'Peter's sister, of course. Don't tell me you don't know Peter?'

'Okay, I won't tell you, but I don't. Is he here?'

Tony didn't need to look around.

'Uh-huh. Lara says he's away for a few weeks. We don't see him much these days, of course, but it's not like him to miss a shindig like this. O-oh, watch out. Stand by your beds. Looks like the Vicar-General is calling us to order.'

'That was very good,' I said.

'What was?' asked Tony, bemused.

'Vicar-General. Wish I'd thought of that.'

'Really?' He was genuinely taken aback. 'Oh, thanks. I'll tell Harry.'

I left him to it and shuffled off to the side. If the defence of our realm was being left to Tony and Harry, I'd better learn Russian fast.

Bell moved into the centre of the room and clapped his hands twice for order.

'Thank you all for coming,' he boomed in his best pulpit voice. 'At this very moment, our local worthies are stretching last year's

289

red coats over yesterday's turkey and plum pudding.' There was a ripple of polite laughter. 'Some of our less worthy locals will be getting their horses ready for them, and within an hour they'll assemble at Caxton Gibbet for the traditional Stirrup Cup. That will almost certainly go on for another hour. They need Dutch Courage to do what they do.'

Murmurs of approval at this as well as more laughter.

'So we've plenty of time to get in position. The word in the village is that there are foxes in Knapworth Woods. That means the hunt will come towards us on the Elsworth road and then go into one of the fields to their right, over towards Cambridge. Everyone with banners will concentrate on blocking the road. But be careful. There will be police on duty, and remember, we're not out to hurt the dogs, and if you frighten the horses, they could hurt you.

'Lara here will be in charge of scenting the gateways and the entrances to the field to confuse the hounds. Do we have any volunteer runners this year?'

A pair of gangling hippie types – authentic ones, not the fashion crazed 'New Hippies' doing the rounds of the acid house parties in London – stepped forward.

'We've left our bait outside,' said the tallest, in a West Country burr. 'It's mostly pretty high pheasant, and it makes us not very pleasant to be near to.'

'We haven't washed for weeks in honour of the occasion,' said the other, scratching his beard.

More laughter.

'Well done, you two,' smiled Bell. 'Now then, Edna and Albert–' he indicated the couple I'd identified with the Morris Minor '–have the boot of their car absolutely stuffed with anti-hunt literature. Anyone who wants an armful of pamphlets, please see them before we set out.

'Remember, there will be lots of spectators there and we just might make a few converts. But no aggro, please. No pushing things down people's throats.

'Lastly, we have two newcomers in the shape of Harry and Tony, or maybe it's Tony and Harry. They'll have the video camera with them and they'll be filming us. But please – don't provoke anything violent just because the camera's there. Tony will be on the large motorbike, so he can make a quick getaway.'

More laughter, including a guffaw from Tony.

'So, good luck, everyone. Let's go make ourselves heard.' A wave of applause started, but Bell held it down. 'And then back here this afternoon for baked potatoes, roast chestnuts and soup. Not necessarily in that order, of course.'

Bell came through the massed ranks, being patted on the back and having his hand shaken and giving the thumbs-up sign, until he got to me.

'Roy, could we borrow you to transport the advance party?'

'Certainly. What do I have to do?'

Lara appeared at his shoulder.

'Get me and two or three others and our stuff as close to the meet as possible,' she said.

'Won't I be a bit obvious?'

'Pretend we've taken a cab out of Cambridge. They have black cabs there. We'll just be spectators and we'll mingle in. When we see which way the hunt sets off, then we'll know which fields to scent and we can zip on ahead.'

She'd got it all thought out, I had to give her that.

'Won't people be a wee bit suspicious if a taxi-load of people like that turn up?'

I pointed to the two girls with CND earrings who were helping each other into Margaret Thatcher rubber masks.

'We'll crouch down in the back,' said Lara, bristling.

'So how are you going to mingle with the spectators?'

Lara's eyebrows came together in a frown so hard it must have hurt. Behind her, Stephanie mouthed 'me' and pointed a finger at her chest.

'Tell you what,' I said, 'why don't Stephie and I mingle and see what we can find out? If I'm on my own, I'm not a threat to anybody, and Stephie knows her way around the area.'

Stephanie beamed in malicious triumph at the back of Lara's head.

'Okay, but–' she looked around '–me, Tania, Jim and Lee stay in the back.'

That seemed to settle it, not that I had any further say in the matter.

I nodded to Stephie to follow and headed for Armstrong, only to run into Tony the army type in the hallway. He was emerging from the cellar door under the staircase with Billy Tuckett's video camera under his arm.

'I say,' he grinned, 'jolly good plan, isn't it? Tactically very well thought out.'

I just smiled at him and didn't say that as far as I was concerned, the Stirrup Cup had sounded the best bit.

CHAPTER THIRTEEN

There were more spectators than I'd imagined, and more police. Whole families had turned out to see the hunt off, because it was exactly the sort of thing they'd seen on

Christmas cards and calendars for years and years. It was traditional; it was British. Show them a fox *after* a successful hunt, and they'd probably say that wasn't what they had come for. But they never saw that; they were home cracking walnuts and watching *White Christmas* or *Casablanca* by then. But who was I to judge? Let's face it, that many people gathered on the street at one time in Hackney meant there was a race riot going on.

A brace of traffic cops – you can tell by the chequerboard pattern round their hats – waved me over and told me to park where I could off the road. They were worried about double parking, not looking for hunt saboteurs.

I pulled over onto the verge of the lane, about 300 yards from the famous hangman's gibbet itself. I left enough space between Armstrong and a Ford Sierra so that I could turn him on his lock if need be. As I wasn't sure which way we would leave, I couldn't do my usual and park in the optimum getaway position (Rule of Life No 277). Behind me, a Volvo estate car – the only vehicle less aerodynamic than the London black cab – pulled in and disgorged a youngish couple and six kids, four of which were two sets of twins. It must be something in the water, I thought.

I let them troop by, the two sets of twins wearing either red or green coats depending on their age. Well, if you can't tell them apart, why not colour-code them?

'All clear,' I said through the glass partition.

Lara's task force, crouched down on the floor, looked as if they were practising for an orgy. Stephie, the only one sitting upright and comfortable, smiled a smug smile down at them.

'I'm ready, Roy. Let's go,' she said, like she was leading the local Brownie pack on manoeuvres. And I'll swear she deliberately trod on Lara's leg as she climbed out.

I got out and almost fell down some sort of drainage ditch – that's the trouble with the countryside, there's grass everywhere so you can't see where you're putting your feet – but luckily no-one was watching. As cool as if nothing had happened, I pretended to lock the driver's door and hop-skipped to catch up with Stephie.

'Morning, Mrs Jones. Hello, Fiona, I can see what you got for Christmas! Hi, Desmond, how's things?' yelled Stephie as we marched down the middle of the traffic-free lane.

'Hey, keep it down,' I snarled. 'We're not supposed to attract attention.'

'Don't be stupid, stupid. They know me. It would look really punk if I didn't say anything to them. Hello, Donna!' She shouted this to a girl her age standing forlorn in anorak and gumboots with a younger brother stuck on each hand as if she'd arrested them. 'I see you got more zits for Christmas.'

I hunched down into my coat and tried to pretend she wasn't with me. If she'd been three years older, or I'd been ten years less clever...

Near the gibbet, the hunters had gathered in a semi-circle, their coats bright and shiny, their nostrils flaring and their breath frosting on the crisp morning air. And the horses were quite impressive too.

And they were so big. Okay, some of the younger riders had ponies that could have stepped out of Thelwell cartoons, but most of the riders were mounted on huge, muscular beasts that I would have needed a ladder to get on. I have to admit to being impressed by all that power and strength, and yet they had such tiny brains. They reminded me of a lot of people I knew in the East End. The sort of people who stood outside the rougher clubs wearing dinner jackets.

I had decided that the horses must be stupid, because they allowed such a bunch of nerds to dress up in red coats and top hats and sit on their backs. But then I realised that the nerds in question had organised a Range-Rover full of iced champagne and orange juice and were giving it away in liberal quantities. By the second glass they didn't seem such a bad bunch, and by the third I was positively warming to them. Though I couldn't for the life of me see why they wanted to leave the party and go haring off over a muddy field with a bunch of noisy dogs.

And the dogs *were* noisy, barking and howling from the big horsebox transporter they were kept in. A huntsman without a horse, their equivalent of a beat policeman, I suppose, emerged from the cab of the transporter with one of the hounds leaping down out of the cab and coming to heel behind him.

'That the top dog, huh?' I asked Stephanie, glancing round for the nice maternal-looking lady with the tray of champagne I'd chatted to a few minutes before.

'He's called Rex. Leader of the pack,' she said, sipping her well-spiked orange juice.

'From the size of the footprints, Miss Baskerville, I'd have hoped for something bigger.'

'Eh?'

'Let it go.'

The whipper-in, or whatever he was called, led the dog Rex into the middle of the semi-circle of mounted huntsmen. Someone produced a plastic bowl and put it on the ground, and then a redcoated, top-hatted, pink-faced old buffer called for champagne and a bottle was produced and Rex washed down his morning Winalot with

Moet & Chandon. I took another glass from a passing tray to keep him company. I wouldn't let a dog drink alone.

A horse breathed noisily in my right ear, and I turned to look up into its frantic eyeball.

What are you doing here? it seemed to say.

'Christ, that's clever,' I said to myself.

'Hello, Father,' said Stephanie.

If I'd been expecting a red-faced Colonel, I couldn't have been more wrong. Stephie's dad didn't look much older than me, was about six foot four (though it's difficult to tell when the horse he was sitting on seemed to go up forever), bronzed and clean-shaven. Just the sort of guy you'd have on the front of paperback romantic novel. I bet myself that his tailored hunting gear cost nearly as much as the horse.

He leaned forward in his saddle and pointed his riding whip at his daughter, the leather thong bit at the end dangling about two inches in front of my nose.

'Stay away from your bolshie vicar friend, Steph. If he starts any trouble, someone'll get hurt.'

'Is that a threat or a promise?' Stephie came back, thrusting her bottom lip out at him.

'Neither,' he said quietly. My head flicked between them like a spectator at Wimbledon. 'Half these grockles can't handle a horse at the best of times. When they're half-pissed and people are yelling and screaming, they're bound to get out of control, and somebody will get hurt.'

That sounded eminently sensible to me. But Stephie just redoubled her sulk.

'And you go easy on that champagne,' he added, and she didn't deny it.

Then he pointed the whip across the road to where a blonde woman was sitting in the open tailgate of an Audi estate car. She wore a soft leather bomber jacket and Gloria Vanderbilt jeans that had been moulded on, and totally impractical high-heeled ankle boots.

'And for God's sake keep an eye on your mother. She's on her second bottle already.'

I wondered if I should volunteer; but then I thought of the whip and that big horse and those hooves and let it pass.

Mr Stephie moved off and joined a huddle of horsemen. Stephie tugged at my sleeve.

'They're up to something,' she hissed in my ear.

'You're right,' I said. 'They're closing the bar.'

We were both right. The huntsmen were gathering into formation and the whipper-in had taken the rather unsteady Rex over to the horse-box transporter where the hounds were baying louder by the minute. Local women acting as barmaids for the morning were threading through the spectators collecting empty glasses on trays.

'They're going to go early,' said Stephie excitedly, 'before Geoffrey gets here.'

The whipper-in and a couple of helpers were unbolting the tailgate of the horsebox. The hounds got louder and Rex took up a gunfighter's stance in the road, waiting to marshal his troops.

'Dammit. They must have been tipped off,' said Stephie.

'They have look-outs,' I said.

'How do you know?'

'The guys on foot, they've all got mobile phones in their pockets.' I thought everybody had noticed.

'Bastards! Somebody in the village must have told them Geoffrey's lot has set out.'

'Well, I didn't think they were using them to call up an air strike.'

Stephie tried to wither me with a look, but I'd been withered by experts in my time.

The hounds were released onto the road and they snapped and wagged around Rex, who stood stock still and tried to look imperious. He was probably as drunk as some of the riders.

'No horns,' said Stephie as if it meant something.

'What?'

'They're not blowing their hunting horns. It would tip off Geoffrey that they're on the move. They'll wait until they're off the road.'

'Well, we can certainly do something

about that. Come on.'

'Where to?'

'Back to Armstrong – the cab. We've got to stop Lara from attacking them right here and now.'

'Too many innocent spectators around, you mean?'

'Don't be daft. Too many police.'

We broke from the crush, squeezing by a horse intent on taking its rider sideways, despite what he wanted, and set off down the road at a brisk stroll.

'Don't run,' I'd told Stephie, 'it'll give the game away.'

She seemed to buy that. She was concerned about the hunters; I was worried about the cops.

'Where the hell have you been?' snapped Lara, still crouched down in the back of Armstrong.

'Mingling,' I smiled back. 'Stay where you are, the game's afoot.'

'What's he on about?' hissed one of Lara's shock troops.

'The hunt's moving off and coming this way,' I said through the glass screen as I climbed into the driver's seat. 'Now stay down and we'll turn round. There are cops directing traffic here, and I want to get clear.'

'They're early, the swine,' somebody said, which I thought was a bit rich. Don't swine have rights too?

Stephie made to get in the back, but I waved her into the front and the space normally reserved for luggage.

'Crouch down and stay down,' I said. 'You're not supposed to ride there.'

She was delighted to be doing something that was (a) illegal and (b) something Lara wasn't doing.

'Ow! What the hell is this?' she swore, having sat on my trumpet case.

'Something I brought for emergencies like this. Open it.'

As she fumbled with my trumpet, I started Armstrong and did a one-lock turn, heading down the road. One of the traffic cops actually waved me through, thinking I was being sensible and getting out of the way before the hunt appeared.

Around the first bend, and out of sight of the policemen, I slowed at the first five-bar gate into a field on our right.

'This one?' I asked.

Stephie shook her head. 'No way. That's reserved for experimental crops. Scientific farming and all that shit. They wouldn't go across there. Try the next. Hey, this is a trumpet.'

'Top of the class, kid. Find the mouthpiece. It's in the felt-covered box at the front.'

The next gate was a hundred yards away, and it was open.

'This looks like it,' said Stephie. 'That's

Knapworth Woods over there.'

She pointed to a lump of green three fields away.

'Okay, team, let's go for it,' I said into the back, and amid some choice cursing, Lara and crew stumbled out.

They had all put their masks on, and they went about their business with frenzied enthusiasm, scattering peppermint and pepper and aniseed essence all around the entrance to the field and a good way into it.

I got out and held out my hand to Stephie for the trumpet.

'You're going to play?' she asked, wide-eyed.

'I'm going to warn Geoffrey,' I said primly. 'What do you think he'll do if he hears a horn?'

'He'll get here bloody quick,' she said, cottoning on.

I licked my lips and fluffed the first three notes of the opening to 'West End Blues'. Maybe I had been a bit ambitious. So I slipped into 'Perdido', as there was nobody there to criticise the break.

The horn did me proud, ringing out bell-like over the still frosty fields. Ah, Beiderbecke, eat your heart out. They say Buddy Bolden could be heard two miles away across New Orleans on a still night. Of course, he was in a loony-bin at the time.

Stephie was tugging my arm again, and I

303

opened my left eye. She was pointing behind me. I stopped playing mid-phrase and turned.

One of Rex's offspring – and a couple of his cousins – were belting down the lane towards us. The rest wouldn't be far behind.

'It's your playing,' said Stephie, tugging even more violently on my arm.

'They like jazz?'

'They think you're calling them, dimmo.'

'Bloody hell. Let's get out of here.'

We piled into Armstrong, and in the mirror I saw more of the pack turn the corner, but the leaders had slowed and were weaving across the road trying to pick up a scent. The real huntsmen had started blowing their horns to restrain the dogs, which would act as a further signal to Bell.

Not that he needed one. His shock troops were already in sight, hurrying down the road towards us with a blue and white police panda car trying to ride shotgun on them, driving at about five miles an hour.

I looked behind again and saw the first red-coated, black-capped horsemen had rounded the bend as well as the rest of the hounds. I reckoned that both columns would meet just about where Armstrong was parked.

Definitely time to go.

I dropped the brake and turned into the field where Lara and her squad were happily running around in circles laying false scent trails like woodland fairies on the toot.

'Yeow! This is ace!' yelled Stephie, bouncing up from her crouched position in the luggage space and hitting her head on Armstrong's roof.

As long as the ground stayed frozen, I thought, Armstrong was a versatile vehicle, but a half-track personnel carrier he wasn't.

'Get in!' I shouted through the window.

Lara and her three saboteurs stared at me, then at the growing confusion in the lane, and then they dived into the back. Okay, so I didn't actually stop for them, but I did slow down a lot.

Lara came up for air and asked where the hell I was going.

'Through that field and back onto the road, which should bring us out behind the hunt,' I shouted.

'But we haven't finished scenting,' she screamed back, and then she pitched sideways as we hit another bumpy patch.

'Yee-hah!' yelled Stephie. 'Ride 'im, cowgirl!'

'Pour the stuff out of the windows,' I said. 'Look out the back.'

In the mirror, I could see the first dozen or so hounds had entered the field and were galloping round in a circle, totally confused. At the gate, the panda car had stopped to try and let the horsemen into the field while keeping the protesters at bay. Three or four made it and tried to lead the dogs away.

I slowed down and began to search for a gap in the hedge into the next field. There had to be one, I figured, so the tractors could move in and out.

I found it by following the tractor ruts in the hardened mud down the side of the hedge, going slow because the ruts were deep and Armstrong's undercarriage was scraping dangerously close to the packed dirt between them.

We almost made it, but five yards short of the gap in the hedge, Armstrong snuck his front axle in the earth and wouldn't budge.

'Everybody out, round the front and push. Now!' I ordered, and to give them credit, none of them argued.

I slammed the cab into reverse and, as they heaved, he moved back just enough for me to put a left-hand lock on the wheel.

'Right, round the back,' I shouted through the window. 'All together after three.'

They trotted to the rear, and I looked over my shoulder. Two of the huntsmen on those big, stupid, probably rather annoyed horses had spotted us and were galloping over. I didn't think they were coming to help push.

'Three!' I shouted, and they heaved and Armstrong jerked out of the rut and almost into a drainage ditch before I corrected the steering.

Lara and co dived in as we moved off. The

horsemen were 40 yards away and yelling things. I don't think they realised that almost the whole pack of hounds had set off after them.

Lara had noticed and was hanging out of a window sprinkling the rest of her herbs and spices to confuse the poor mutts even more. She almost bounced out as we crossed more tractor tracks and shot into the next field.

'Hey, this is the scientific field, the experimental stuff. They won't allow the dogs in here,' said Stephie.

'Has anybody told the dogs?' I asked.

I wasn't going to risk driving in any more tractor ruts this time, so I pointed Armstrong diagonally across the field and headed for the gate into the road.

Whatever it was they were scientifically farming in there hadn't put on much of a show; well, it was December. It could have been a con anyway, just to claim the Common Market agricultural subsidy. But whatever it was, I reckoned that Armstrong's twin tyre tracks wouldn't cause terminal damage.

Of course, I couldn't speak for the pack of hounds that followed us in there, attracted by the trail Lara was laying out of the window. Or the horses and riders, for that matter, who charged in to round up the dogs.

I slowed down as we neared the gate into the road. Round the corner to our right, it sounded as if a minor war had broken out, with car horns mixing with hunting horns and a steady chant of 'Stop the Hunt! Stop the Hunt!' In the distance, a police siren started to wail.

I told Stephie to get out and open the gate.

In the mirror, I could see more dogs and more horses tearing chaotically across the field.

'And make sure you close it after us,' I added primly. 'Remember to respect the countryside.'

Despite the howls of protest from the back seat activists, I turned left into the lane, away from the ruck around the corner.

'Is there a back way back to the village?' I asked Stephie.

'Sure. Left at the crossroads, left, left, and left again.'

'Wait a minute!' commanded Lara. 'We can't desert Geoffrey.'

I stood on the brakes.

'You go if you want to. Armstrong is far too bloody well-known round here. I'm getting him out of sight.'

'It makes sense, Lara,' said one of the others in the back.

'You're right. Come on, we can walk.'

They piled out and slammed the doors. I knew what had gone through Lara's mind: if she was caught inside Armstrong, there was no way she'd talk her way clear. On the road or in the fields, with the rest of the crowd, there would be much less chance she'd get picked up by the cops.

'I thought they'd never go,' said Stephie, trying to be coy.

'You staying?'

'Oh yes, you're far more fun than they are.'

'Do you want to get in the back?'

'No, I'm fine here.'

She spread her legs to brace herself and crouched down. She couldn't possibly be comfortable. She was even less comfortable half a mile further on, when I pushed her to the floor as the police car came out of a turning ahead of us.

The country road was just wide enough for us to pass if we slowed. He had his blue lights flashing but had turned the siren off. As we drew level, I pulled my window down and leaned out.

'Fucking road's blocked to hell back there; can't get through. Where the hell have you boys been? Christmas in the country, eh? Stuff that for a game of soldiers.'

The copper driving the car just nodded wearily at me, and accelerated as soon as he was clear without looking back at us.

'That was clever,' mumbled Stephie from somewhere under the glove compartment.

'The last thing those guys wanted was stick from a chopsy cab driver.'

She mumbled something else, which I

didn't catch. Then my leg was tapped and I looked down.

'Want some?'

Stephie had found the emergency vodka.

I stashed Armstrong behind the Parish Room, as he would be out of sight from the road there.

'No sign of the Animal Army,' I said, indicating the deserted rectory.

Stephie stepped in front of me, her hands clasped behind her back, shoulders hunched. I could see the up-from-under look coming a mile off.

'How should we fill in the time?'

I thought of her father and how big he'd looked on that horse and made the only really sensible decision of the day.

'We'll go and have lunch. I'm starving.'

We were almost at the door of The Five Bells before she stopped swearing under her breath. Once inside, her face lit up, especially when the landlord recognised her and said hello. It was only just after noon, but the pub was filling rapidly, mostly with men escaping from cold turkey and visiting relatives.

'A pint of bitter, please,' I said, 'and–?'

'A coke, please, Mr Jenner,' said Stephie sweetly.

'Certainly, my dear,' said the landlord. 'Would that be a coke or a Coca-Cola?'

He winked at her as he pulled my beer. I

wasn't following this at all.

'Oh, a Coca-Cola to begin with, I think,' she said.

He took a long glass and squirted about an inch of coke from a mixer dispense unit into it, then added some ice cubes from a bucket behind the bar. And then, almost as if he just happened to be passing it, he hit the vodka bottle for a double shot and zapped the glass on the bar.

As I paid, I asked her: 'As a regular here, if not the actual captain of the darts team—'

'Vice captain,' the landlord chipped in.

'– what do you recommend for lunch?'

'Steak sandwiches,' she said without hesitation. 'Rare.'

I sneaked a glance out of the pub window across to the rectory. All clear.

'Make that two.'

What was fascinating about the rest of that afternoon was not just the variety of alcohol that was consumed, nor the fact that I seemed to pay for very little of it. It was the mix of people who visited the pub.

Apart from the locals, there were spectators from the hunt and the huntsmen themselves, along with their dog-handlers, stableboys or whatever they called them, and the hunt saboteurs too, or at least the less fanatic ones. And because the huntsmen had changed out of their red coats and the saboteurs had left their placards outside, they mixed without friction. Sure, there were the occasional dirty looks flashed across the bar, but the landlord kept his eye on things, and while they weren't actually buying each other drinks, they didn't seem likely to try and kill each other. Maybe it was just a game to both sides.

Quite a few of the saboteurs wanted to buy me drinks for my valiant action during the morning's campaign. I pooh-poohed most of the compliments and told them to keep their voices down in case any of the hunting fraternity suddenly remembered who'd been driving the black London cab, but I accepted most of their drinks, and Stephie took her share of Coca-Colas (saying 'It's the real thing' after each one.)

The two army types, Tony and Harry, appeared at about two o'clock and stood us another round.

'You wouldn't like to stage your charge across that field again, would you?' Tony asked me. 'We didn't get there in time to video it, unfortunately. But everyone was talking about it.'

I sighed with relief. I'd forgotten about these two prats and Billy's video camera.

'No action replays, I'm afraid. Don't think the locals would approve.'

'I'll say,' said Harry, eyeing Stephie with ill-concealed lust. 'The word is that the company that owns most of the land round here is slapping the hunt organisers on the wrist in no uncertain terms about that field you ruined.'

'It wasn't just me–' I started.

'Of course not,' soothed Tony. 'Tactical expediency on your part; bloody great cock-up on part of the Hunt. They'd been warned off going in that field – some special crop or other. But it was really just a put-up. The farmers don't really like the Hunt; makes too much mess and all that. So they'll use it as an excuse to stop them in future.'

'The farmers couldn't give a shit about foxes,' said Harry knowledgeably. 'They prefer to shoot the little beasts.'

'Talking of little beasts,' said Tony, lowering his voice, 'have you seen that vixen Lara?'

'Not since this morning,' I said truthfully. 'I 'spect she'll be back at the ranch.'

'You could be right,' Tony nodded. 'Must have a word with her before we disappear.'

He checked his watch.

'My God, we'd better be off, young Harry me lad. We've some serious partying to do down in London tonight.'

They made their farewells. Harry even went to the extent of leaning over and kissing Stephie's hand, despite Stephie's 'Oh, gross!' reaction.

No sooner had they gone than Stephie announced she too had to put in an appearance at home.

'Will your father be mad at you?' I asked, because I was lubricated enough to be concerned.

'I hope so,' she said chirpily. 'We've wasted the morning if he isn't.' There's no arguing with that sort of logic. 'You sticking around?'

'For a while,' I said. I knew I would have to sober up considerably before getting behind Armstrong's wheel again. The old 'It is better to travel hopefully than to arrive' motto only ever worked for Kamikaze pilots.

'So you'll be at the disco tonight?' She stood up and started to button her coat and finish her vodka and coke in the same blurred movement.

'Disco?'

'Wayne. The Flying Fenman. Special Boxing Day disco here tonight. Thought you'd stick around to see how the professionals do it.'

Everyone's a critic these days. And they're getting younger.

It was already dark by the time I wandered back over to the rectory. Nearly all the cars, and the army types' motorbikes, had gone. Only a couple of Citroens and the Morris Minor stuffed full of anti-hunt pamphlets remained. The half-dozen or so people who remained were cleaning up the big ballroom, which looked like a soup kitchen after a bomb had gone off. The Reverend Bell, still in his cassock – although liberally splashed with mud – was organising the filling of black plastic sacks with used paper plates, the remains of baked potatoes and other assorted rubbish. Two motherly figures were collecting cups on trays and ferrying them to the kitchen.

Bell looked up and saw me, but he refused to hold eye contact. Some of the others smiled and nodded and said 'Well done' at me, but it was hardly the hero's welcome I'd expected.

'Where have you been?' said an icy voice behind me.

Lara was standing, legs apart, hands on hips.

'Keeping a low profile,' I said with a smile.

'Well, get your coat off and help with the washing-up.'

Her face cracked into a half-smile as if she'd just thought of something funny, then she held out her hands for my coat.

'Wash or dry?' I asked, trying to look cheerful.

'Mavis will tell you.' She nodded to one of the middle-aged women carrying a tray of cups towards the kitchen.

'Reporting for duty right away, sah!' I snapped, flicking her a mock salute, which turned out more casual than intended as I missed my forehead first time.

She ignored me and disappeared into the

hall with my coat.

Mavis turned out to be a proper diamond. She took one look at me and decided not to trust me with the crockery, so I was put to work drying teaspoons and carrying plastic sacks of rubbish out to the rectory's back door. In between chores, she made me cups of strong, sweet coffee, asking delicately if I wanted it black, and I'd said no because it was the milk that soaked up the alcohol.

Actually, it was Mavis's constant chatter that sobered me up more than anything else. And could she rabbit. She turned out to be the astrologist of the gang, convinced that small, furry mammals were all born under the sign of Aries, carnivores were Taureans (I didn't argue) and reptiles were Aquarians. As the others gradually departed, they would put their heads round the kitchen door and say 'Cheerio, Mavis' or 'Happy New Year,' and she'd give them titbits of advice such as 'Prepare well for long journeys' or 'Remember to think of the colour blue next year.' I wondered what tablets she was on, and where I could get some.

When it was time for her to go, Lara helped her on with her raincoat and Bell hovered near the front door, offering to show her to her little Citroen with the aid of a torch. I got the distinct impression he was still avoiding me.

'Goodbye, Roy,' said Mavis. 'Remember

always that pride comes before a fall.'

'I will, dear, I will,' I said, putting an arm around her shoulders and squeezing lightly.

Bell held the door for her and followed her out into the night.

'Sweet lady,' I said to Lara.

She looked blank and then said 'Oh yeah' in a vague way, then she curled a finger at me and indicated the door under the stairs to the cellar where the video gear was.

'Come and see what we got today,' she said, opening the door and reaching inside for the light switch.

I think I really must have thought it was a different sort of invitation, especially as Lara's voice had gone quite husky and she was breathing deeply.

Whatever, I took an expectant step towards her, and when I was opposite the cellar doorway, she swayed to her left and crouched and then her right foot came up into my stomach with a force something akin to sticking your fingers in a power point.

There wasn't much comfort in thinking that I saw it coming, even though I couldn't do anything about it. I never even saw the heel of the hand smash into my forehead or the back elbow into my right-side kidney as I doubled up. But I felt them.

Then I think it was her right foot, but I wouldn't swear to it, which came down on my right foot, just below the ankle, and then there was real red pain everywhere. It must have been relatively easy for her by then just to lash out once more and send me tumbling down the hard cellar steps to the incredibly hard cellar floor.

CHAPTER FOURTEEN

I landed on my left shoulder. I remember that, because it was the one bit of me that didn't hurt up until then.

I must have more or less bounced into a kneeling position, and I know I stayed there for a while as it seemed the only option open to me. My right foot was pure agony, and for the life of me I couldn't remember stepping on a six-inch nail. I didn't seem able to breathe well at all, my left arm was dead to the world, my side hurt as if someone had inserted a burst appendix into me, and I couldn't focus on anything as there was a sheet of perspex in front of my eyes. I shook my head to try and clear my vision. That hurt as well, and it still seemed as if I was looking through a jar of honey.

Don't pass out, I told myself. Stay awake. There's an awful lot of crap in books and the movies about people getting knocked out and then coming to with little more than a

318

headache. If it was that easy, how come the first thing they ever ask at the hospital is, did you lose consciousness or not? And if you say yes, they panic and jam on the electrodes.

Try and be sick, I told myself; it'll take your mind off things.

Someone was talking to me.

It was Lara, from the top of the stairs. I couldn't focus on her, but at least I could hear her, so something was working.

'Now stay there,' she said, through rapid pants of breath. 'Or I'll come down and really hurt you.'

She didn't get any argument from me on that one.

At least she left the lights on.

The video equipment, the piles of cassettes, the fake studio setup all swam into focus eventually. I still couldn't make it to my feet though, so I crawled across the floor until I reached the desk. By clawing at that, I managed to get somewhere near upright on my left leg, and it didn't take me much more than an hour.

That was about the sum total of my achievement. I scanned the place for possible weapons. Short of throwing a television set at her, and I didn't give odds on me being able to lift it, there was nothing. I dismissed any notion of using some of the electric cables, or video leads, as a strangler's noose or garrotte.

That would involve getting too close to her. And if I was that close to her, she was that close to me, and she played rough.

I decided that my best policy was to try and hide, or at least make myself as small a target as possible. I tipped the desk onto its end and drew it around me in the corner of the cellar, crawling over the legs to weight it down. The desktop was half-inch thick plywood, and that made me think of the Kateda demonstration I'd witnessed, and suddenly it didn't seem like such a good plan.

But it was the only one I had. At least I could keep my right foot behind the desk. That worried me. Even the slightest pressure on it was nerve-shredding, and my grubby Reebok trainer was bulging at the laces. I knew if I took the shoe off it would never go back on. There was no blood, though, which was good, I told myself. My shirt was spotted with it, but mostly from scratches and cuts picked up when bouncing down the cellar steps. I felt carefully all over my head and scalp and found several egg-sized lumps but no cuts. My right side ached, but there was nothing I could do about it.

Apart from all that, I was in pretty good shape.

If they'd left me alone for another hour, I might have made myself believe it. But they didn't.

The two of them appeared at the top of

the stairs dead on seven o'clock. I don't know why I was worried about what time it was; I wasn't going anywhere.

I hung on to the leg of the desk. If they were going to pull it away, they'd have to take me with it, but I didn't think that was beyond them.

'There he is,' I heard Lara say as she led Bell down the steps.

Between the edge of the desktop and the wall I had my back against, I could see them clearly. Bell paused at the bottom of the stairs and looked anxiously in my direction. In his mud-spattered cassock, he gave me the impression that he had just finished digging a grave.

Come on: think positive.

Lara stood next to him, pulling on a pair of black gloves, the sort gardeners wear. Perhaps that meant I'd hurt her hands when she did me over. If that was the only positive thought I could manage, I was in trouble.

'Go on,' Lara was saying to Bell, 'ask him, if you don't believe me.'

Bell held out his hands, palms up, towards me. I flinched.

'Roy, you've been very stupid,' he said slowly.

'That's been said before.'

Watch it. Don't provoke them.

'Lara says you've taken one of our video tapes. A very special tape.'

321

'Oh, does she?' I said, far too cockily.

There was a scream that wasn't me, and then one that was.

Lara gave a war cry and lashed out at the desktop, her gloved fist coming through the wood as if it was paper, stopping two inches from my nose. I yelled because I was genuinely frightened now.

'Lara, that's enough!' shouted Bell.

'Ask him again,' she said calmly.

He didn't have to.

'Yes, okay, I took a tape. I just picked one at random.'

'Why?'

'I thought it might be something Billy Tuckett had done, and I was going to show it to his mother,' I flannelled quickly. It's not easy to concentrate when you're trying to make yourself small enough to slide through the cracks in the concrete.

'You didn't know what was on that tape when you took it?'

'No, swear to God,' I said, hoping to prick his conscience.

'But you do now?' said Lara menacingly. She was menacing and I couldn't see her.

'Yes, I saw it when I got home.' There was no point in lying.

'Did anyone else see it?'

'No,' I lied.

'Where is it now?'

'In the dustbin. I threw it away. I didn't

want to be caught with that in my possession.'

'I believe him,' said Bell.

'You believe anybody,' she said nastily, and he flinched from her tongue as much as I had from her fist.

'Whether he's telling the truth or not, he knows too much. I'm bringing things forward to tonight.'

'But you can't,' spluttered Bell.

'I can and I am doing. Remember this, Geoffrey, it was Peter and I who founded this cell. You and your little friend Billy asked to join us. It was always understood that I gave the orders when Peter was not here.'

He bowed his head in defeat. I wanted to urge him on to stand up to her, but I also wanted to keep my head on my shoulders.

'Don't worry, you won't be involved directly. I can manage things from here on in.'

'But how will you get to London?' asked Bell, despite my screaming silently for him to shut up and let her go.

'I'll drive.'

'But you can't!' he came back petulantly.

For God's sake, I'll lend her the bus fare! Just let her go!

'I told you I don't have a licence. I never said I couldn't drive.'

'And what if you're stopped for any reason? By the police?'

She won't be; she won't be.

'Not having a licence will be the least of my worries.'

Good, that's the spirit. *Bon voyage.*

'All you have to do is keep him here until after midnight.' I could feel her pointing at me through the desk.

'Then what?'

'Then you have to look out for yourself, Geoffrey. It's what we agreed.'

Why didn't she just go?

'What about Harry and Tony?'

She made a snorting sound.

'What are they going to do? By the time they realise the fourth tape is a blank – well, they're hardly going to report it to their commanding officer, are they?'

So that was it. That was why Tony had been so keen to see Lara before he left. She'd somehow talked him into borrowing the training films on explosives for her and he'd wanted them back. That's when she'd noticed one was missing and my card – as the only person from outside the cell to have access – had been marked from then on.

'Goodbye, Geoffrey. It's not going to be how we planned it, but I'm going through with it and you can't stop me.'

I watched her climb the stairs and close the door at the top behind her. She didn't look round and neither did Bell. He stood with his arms limp at his sides, head bowed.

He could have been praying.

When I heard the front door slam, and I was more or less sure she'd gone, I exhaled loudly.

'You can come out from behind there if you wish,' said Bell. 'I won't hurt you unless you attempt to leave.'

'I don't think I can,' I said truthfully.

Most of the muscles I had left without bruises on them seemed to have knotted with the tension. My buttocks ached and my right leg had decided against adopting the vertical ever again.

Bell took hold of the desk by its edges and eased it back; I howled as one of the legs caught my right foot slightly, but by curling my left leg under the right one, I was able at least to shuffle into a sitting position facing him. He backed away and sat on the bottom stair, elbows on knees, chin resting on his clasped hands.

'I'm sorry about Lara,' he said.

'Not half as sorry as I am,' I said wearily. 'You know what she's up to, don't you?'

'Yes,' he said, averting his eyes.

'She's got a bomb, hasn't she?'

'Yes.'

'Semtex, plastic explosives. The stuff they had on that video.'

'Yes.' Quieter now.

'Where did she get it?'

No answer.

'Was it her brother, Peter?'

'I can't say.'

'Where is this Peter, Geoffrey?'

'I can't say.'

'Is Lara going to meet him?'

He snickered at that. 'Oh no. She's doing this all by herself.'

'Doing what, Geoffrey?'

'I can't say.'

'Stop playing the broken record, Geoffrey. She's gone after Professor Bamforth, hasn't she?'

His head snapped up and his eyes glowed. 'How did you know that?'

'Billy left notes. Not much. The name, Brian Bamforth–' I tried to remember exactly what I'd found at Billy's, but the old brain wasn't exactly speeding into action '– and the word "transgenic" and a date: New Year's Eve. She's just brought things forward, that's all, isn't it?'

'I can't say any more,' he said.

'You haven't said anything yet, Geoffrey. And you might as well, because tonight – one way or another – it's all over. It can't have been easy, playing at urban commandos. You're not cut out for it. Billy certainly wasn't.'

He sat in silence for a minute. Then he said: 'Are you really here because of Billy?'

'That's why I came originally, yes.'

'Was he a close friend?'

'Not particularly. Hadn't seen him for years, then suddenly he's dead right in front of me. I didn't like that.'

'Why not?' He seemed genuinely curious.

'Damned if I know for sure. It just seemed such a waste. The whole thing does. You'll never get anywhere hurting people to stop them hurting animals.'

He nodded his head.

'I know that. I think I always have known it. But much of the time, there simply seems to be no other way. Have you ever felt really angry about something? Not jealous, or shocked, or annoyed, but really *angry?*'

'I try not to, Geoffrey. Life's too short.'

I don't think he heard me.

'Even when you're in the right, anger is a terrible thing: a destroyer of relationships, of happiness.'

He was either getting maudlin or rehearsing his next sermon. At least he didn't look dangerous.

'Is Lara that angry with the world, Geoffrey? Angry enough to kill someone?'

'She already has,' he said softly. 'Indirectly. But God knows she was responsible.'

I licked my lips. I had to be careful. The guy was so guilt-ridden I could turn it to my advantage. Alternatively, he could react the other way and blow a fuse.

'It was her at the Dwyer Street school, wasn't it? Lara and Billy.' I said it softly. 'She was the one Billy was running from when he fell. That's what happened, wasn't it?'

'Yes,' he said with relief, 'it was Lara. She'd suspected Billy for some time – suspected him of possibly betraying the cell. When we got to the school and we found the animals had gone, she thought it was Billy setting us up.'

'So she took him aside for a few choice words; the sort of conversation she had with me earlier this evening, eh? But Billy knew about the Kateda. Knew what she could do. And what? He tried to jump her, get in first?'

'I think so. He was very frightened. I saw him going across the roof. Lara was chasing him.' He looked at me, and there was a flash of fear across his face. 'She didn't get to him. He fell – he just disappeared – while she was still yards away. You've got to believe that.'

'That's okay, Geoffrey, I do.'

I tried to change position, because I was cramping up and he was suddenly alert again. I showed him the palms of my hands to indicate I wasn't going anywhere.

'Did you teach her the Kateda?' I asked for the sake of getting him talking again.

'No, she taught me.'

I wasn't sure whether that made me feel better or worse.

'Was Peter with you that night at Dwyer Street?'

'Yes, he was driving.'

'Where is Peter?'

'In prison.'

'Prison?'

'He was arrested just a few days ago, at a demonstration. He was sentenced to a month in prison because he refused to say anything.'

This was rich. If only Prentice knew. His fearsome Action Against Animal Abuse cell was already at half-strength. One dead, one inside.

But Lara was the one at large.

'You've got to stop her, Geoffrey.'

'I can't.'

'I lied to her, Geoffrey. I have been talking to the police. They know I'm here and they know Professor Bamforth is a target and they know you've been playing with explosives.'

'Then they'll stop her,' he said, more to himself than me. Then, looking up again: 'Can you forgive her, Roy?'

I made a play of looking at my foot and checking my cuts and bruises.

'Of course I can,' I said, because I felt it the right thing to say. 'I'll live.'

'I'm sorry she's taken your taxi,' said Bell.

What? The lousy bitch. I'll see her in hell. Now it was war.

'You've got to let me out of here, Geoffrey. I think I can stop her.'

'I can't,' he said simply.

'Why not?'

'I promised her I would keep you here.'

'That's it? You'll let her go after this Bamforth guy and stick a bomb through his letter-box when I could—'

Something in his face gave me an awful thought.

'The bomb's in Armstrong, isn't it?'

He said nothing, which was like speaking volumes.

I twisted round to try and get a grip on the wall and pull myself up. I don't know how I did it myself. My side hurt as I twisted, my left arm hurt as I tried to tension myself against the brickwork, and I was trying to keep my right leg away from anything.

'You'll hurt yourself,' said Bell.

I'd heard that before as well.

'Please don't hurt yourself any more, Roy. There's nothing you can do. I'm going now, and I'll lock the door, so there's no point in struggling.'

He started up the stairs. He was right, and I almost cried in frustration. All he had to do was leave and lock the door. It would take me a day and a night to climb those stairs alone.

Okay, then. No more Mister Nice Guy.

'It won't be just you, Geoffrey. They'll get you, but it won't be just you. They're after Lucy as well. Lucy Scarrott, Geoffrey, remember her?'

That had stopped him in his tracks,

halfway up.

'The police think there's a connection between her and Billy, and they've been looking for her. I could tell them where she is.'

I was almost upright now and sweating fit for a Turkish bath. Each time I tried to put my right foot down, it was pure agony.

'What?' He'd said something I'd missed.

'You've seen Lucy?'

'Oh yes, I've seen her. She wasn't involved with Billy at all, except as a friend, though he probably loved her madly. I'll bet he went for Lara as well, just like you did.'

I'd lost him again. He wasn't listening any more. I had to find another chink in him, but without it rebounding in violence, against me.

'I met Lucy's daughter as well, Geoffrey. Lovely little kid.'

A guess, but a good one.

'What's her name?' he asked quietly.

'Of course, she'd be taken into care if anything happened to Lucy...'

'What's her name?' he shouted.

Bullseye.

'Cleo. She's a beautiful little girl. Really.'

He stayed where he was; frozen on the stairs. I tried an experimental hop, overbalanced and touched the floor with my right foot. I almost fainted and went into a one-legged crouch a bit like a Cossack dancer after a heavy night.

He was talking again.

'I promised. I can't let you out.'

There was a definite emphasis on the last 'I,' but before I could plead again, he had gone. Five steps up and then the door slammed and I heard a bolt shoot home.

More in despair than anything, I threw myself at the stairs, and to my surprise I got my arms onto the bottom one. If I could haul myself up them, all I would have to deal with was a bolted door, a 60-mile jog to London and a black belt female psychopath with a car bomb.

Should do it by midnight; no problem.

I was two steps from the top when the bolt was drawn back. Exposed, unarmed and helpless, I cowered down behind the step so at least he couldn't get a straight shot at my head.

The door opened and a female voice said: 'Bloody hell, you look like the pits, man.'

I risked a glance over the step. Bright yellow high heels, black fishnet tights, gold lurex figure-hugging strapless dress and a brown leather bomber jacket hung dead casual over one shoulder.

'Hello, Stephie,' I smiled. 'Boy, am I glad to see you.'

'I still think we should have called the police,' she said for the tenth time.

'Where's your spirit of adventure? Light

me another cigarette, will you?'

I should have listened more closely to the Reverend Bell. He'd said *he* couldn't let me out, because he'd promised Lara, and some weird and wonderful bond, which I couldn't fathom, had held him to that. So he'd gone over to the disco at The Five Bells and told Stephie to come and do it. When I'd asked where he was, she'd said she'd last seen him heading for the church and the lights coming on there.

I hoped for his sake that God had left the answering machine on over the holiday.

'Who gave you the black eye?' she'd asked.

'Nobody gave it to me, I had to fight for it,' I'd said, and made her help me out of the rectory.

With great presence of mind, she'd left me sitting on a flower tub while she went back inside, to emerge with my anorak (and wallet) and a walking stick she'd purloined from the hat-stand in the hall. It appeared that all rectories of that age came with a hat-stand full of walking sticks. It must be in the contract somewhere.

I had to admit it helped, but it was still comforting to have a lean on her as well. When she'd said 'What now?' I had taken 20 pounds out of my wallet and told her to go over to the pub and buy a bottle of whisky, some cigarettes – to hell with good intentions – and find someone willing to drive me to London. And to offer however much cash, paid on arrival, they wanted.

She'd come back after no more than ten minutes, unscrewing the cap on the whisky bottle as she click-clacked her high heels up the path. I'd taken a pull on the bottle as she'd unwrapped the cigarettes.

'I got matches too,' she'd said.

'Initiative,' I'd replied, between drinks.

I'd taken a cigarette from her and broken off the filter tip and thrown it away. As I'd exhaled smoke, I'd asked her about a driver.

'No chance,' she'd said. Then she'd held up something bright in the moonlight. 'But I talked Wayne into lending me the keys to his van. Do you think you can drive it?'

'Has it got wheels?' I'd asked.

She passed me another cigarette, having carefully snapped off the filter, and lit it for me so the match glare didn't dazzle me.

'I don't think Wayne ever drove this fast,' she said, tugging her seat-belt for added security.

I didn't complain. I'd told her to keep talking to keep me awake. Despite the old van being Wayne's travelling advert, with 'THE FLYING FENMAN' painted down both sides, it had neither radio nor tape-deck.

Stephie's task was to feed me smokes and occasional nips at the whisky bottle, which she did with a great show of distaste as she didn't like it.

'Keep talking,' I said.

'What about?'

'Anything. Just keep me awake.'

'Do you think fishnet tights are tarty? My father says they're in the same league as ankle bracelets, but Sindy Johnson, who's in my class, has been wearing one for...'

Hunched uncomfortably over the wheel of Wayne's van, with the walking stick instead of my right foot pressing the accelerator to the floorboards, we sped down the motorway.

If I got stopped and arrested now, they'd never believe me.

There was zero traffic about, which helped. Probably helped keep us alive.

I stayed on the M11, which was easier for getting to Hackney, and by some miracle we made it to Stuart Street, intact, by 10.30. Lara had left me my house keys, so we wouldn't have to disturb anybody.

'Is this where you live?' Stephie asked, not sure at all about getting out of the van.

'Yes, but don't worry, I just want to collect something.'

'What?'

A weapon. But I didn't say it.

She helped me up the stairs and into my flat, and the first thing I did was slip the latch on the cat flap in the door. Then I told Stephie to go straight into the kitchen and close all the windows.

I hobbled into the living-room and hit the lights. Springsteen was stretched full length on the Habitat sofa-bed. The remains of a turkey carcass, still with a couple of pounds of meat on it, were spread over my one good rug.

'Hi yer, kid. Good Christmas?'

He opened one eye and watched me limp over to the bookcase where I stashed my booze. I selected the bottle of Bailey's Irish Cream, which I'd bought for Lisabeth emergencies, and took the top off as I hobbled back into the kitchen.

'Fancy a night-cap?' I said.

'Well, if you've got any...' started Stephie.

'Not you,' I said a bit sharpish, jerking a thumb towards Springsteen, who was stretching his front paws to test if ground level was where he'd left it. 'Him.'

'He's eaten the left-overs from your turkey,' said Stephie indignantly.

'Wasn't my turkey,' I said.

I put down a bowl and poured a good slug of the Bailey's into it. Springsteen flitted through my legs, avoiding my damaged foot but indicating that he'd noted it was a weak spot. His face disappeared into the bowl.

'Chug-a-lug, my son,' I encouraged.

Stephie was horrified.

'Isn't it dangerous to get a cat drunk?' she whispered.

336

'I certainly hope so.'

I didn't want to do Springsteen any harm, of course, but I did want him compliant enough to get him into his travelling basket. And until they make a cat basket out of the steel they use to keep the Great White sharks away from Jacques Cousteau, the only way to do it was get him tipsy.

While he was on his second dishful, I changed into my leather jacket, dug out a pair of leather gloves (however relaxed, he still had claws) and ransacked the bathroom cupboard. In a bottle marked 'Multivitamin' I kept a supply of benzedrine tablets, which are legal in Germany but not exactly on prescription in Britain. I took two and put two more into the pocket of my jacket.

They wouldn't kill the pain in my foot, but they'd make me forget about it for a while.

I unearthed Springsteen's basket from the back of my bedroom wardrobe (putting that in there is one way of keeping him out) and checked the locking mechanism. Now or never.

I limped up behind him and scooped him in head first.

'Let's go!' I commanded Stephie, and she ran ahead of me, opening doors and even carrying the basket down the stairs as I couldn't manage it and my walking stick.

By the time we got to the van, he'd stopped

hissing and trying to turn full circle. We put the basket in the back. If he did anything unspeakable, it would be Wayne's problem.

'We should have called the police,' Stephie tried again, as I started the van's engine.

'We will,' I said. 'Soon.'

'Why the big macho man?' she said nastily. It wasn't a game any more. 'You're going after her because she beat you up and humiliated you, aren't you.'

'Not at all,' I said, jamming the walking stick on to the accelerator again. 'She stole my cab.'

I used up a year's traffic luck on that ride over to Finchley, with few cars on the road and no sign of a policeman.

I drove by Lara's block of flats once without saying anything to Stephie. There was a light on in the top flat on the left.

Then I threw the van into a U-turn and pulled up outside a telephone box.

'Got any money?' I asked Stephie, who was sulking but still not quite ready to shout that she wanted to go home.

'No.'

I gave her a handful of silver from my jacket and the piece of paper Prentice had given me with his private numbers on.

'Ring these first and ask to speak to Detective-Sergeant Prentice. Got that? If you can't get him, dial 999 and say there is a bomb in a car – yes, say it's in a car – at the home of Professor Brian Bamforth. Okay?'

'Where is that?'

'What?'

'They'll ask where this Professor Prentice lives.'

'Professor *Bamforth* and *Sergeant* Prentice. Do try and keep up. And I don't flamin' well know, but they will. Just keep saying it until they believe you.'

'Where will you be?'

'Over there.' I pointed to the block of flats.

'Be careful.'

'We will.'

The bennies were taking effect and the pain seemed almost bearable as I limped across the road, walking stick in one hand, Springsteen's basket in the other. He'd adopted the basic cat defence of increasing his weight at will and seemed intent on wrecking the last remaining muscles in my left arm.

I made it, though, and my luck held. The main door to the flats wasn't security locked. If nothing else, I could always grass on them to their insurance company.

I took the lift up to Lara's floor and, just in case, I held the walking stick aloft as the doors opened. There was nobody in the corridor. Two doors, the one on the right Lara's.

Without the benzedrine and the whisky, I would probably have stopped there and asked myself how I would get her to open the door. But in my state, I don't think it occurred to me.

I put the basket down, leant the stick against the wall, and removed a semi-docile Springsteen, who by now weighed about a ton and seemed to be at least six feet long.

He stretched out a paw lazily. It seemed to go on forever, and I had the distinct impression he was reaching for the doorbell.

I wasn't having any of that. That was my job. I pressed once, and the dull ding-dong echoed from inside.

The door handle turned and a lock snapped and I was watching it in slow motion.

She was saying 'Who...?' when I put what was left of my shoulder muscles to the door, and as she flashed into view, I threw Springsteen at her face with as much force as I could muster.

CHAPTER FIFTEEN

It worked better than I thought it would; in fact, it was altogether quite spectacular. Springsteen hit and stuck like a limpet.

The reason was twofold. He found a neutral purchase in the material of her sweatshirt, locking his claws in above her breasts and swinging as the shirt stretched but didn't rip. Lara helped by flapping at him, desperately wanting to swat him but determined not to actually touch him if she could help it.

She didn't scream, but it looked as if she was, with the sound turned down, lips curled back and mouth open wide as she back-pedalled across the room. Springsteen hung in there, his back legs digging into her stomach to get a better grip. He wanted to go up and over her. By backing away, she was trying to make him fall backwards and down – two directions not found in a cat's operational manual. It looked as if he was trying to get at her neck, like an illustration I'd once seen of the legendary Japanese cat vampire. (They have two tails, though; that's how you can spot them.)

They were almost across the room when she met the coffee table with the back of her knees and went over backwards herself. The table collapsed under her weight and the back of her head hit the carpet with a dull thud. Springsteen rode her fall and then bounced loose up in the air, landing about an inch from Lara's face. That showed at least that his reactions weren't totally shot. Most cats at that point would have dived for cover. Springsteen stayed where he landed, looked down at Lara's face with precision rather than malice and flicked out his right front paw. It had always been his best punch. Three parallel sets of claw marks appeared on her right cheek, about half an inch apart. Then she screamed.

I think Springsteen was more surprised by that than by anything else that had happened so far. He leapt sideways and began to look for escape routes.

I stepped into the room and slammed the door just as Springsteen was about to dive through my legs. I grabbed him and hugged him to my chest more to immobilise his claws than out of affection. His tail, fluffed up to four times its normal size, swished at my thighs, and just to show he wasn't pleased, he playfully bit my gloved thumb.

Lara sat upright and touched her cheek. She was still in silent scream mode, mouth wide open and nostrils flared, and she was looking at her hands in disbelief.

It wasn't the few small droplets of blood, little more than specks, that worried her, it was hair. Springsteen's winter coat, quite luxuriant at its best, was prone to moulting, and the relatively mild winter we were having in London hadn't helped.

She rubbed her hands down the front of her sweatshirt, and that just made things worse. Then I realised she wasn't trying to scream, she was trying to breathe. And then she started shaking. She was having a panic attack trying to avoid an allergy attack.

I took a step towards her and said, 'Hello again.'

She shuffled backwards, still in a sitting position, kicking at the wreckage of the coffee table as if it were somehow restraining her.

I took two more steps, and she went back further until her spine hit the wall near the bedroom door. She flung out her arms, and her fingers scrabbled at the paintwork. I heard a nail break.

'Where's Armstrong, Lara?' I said slowly.

She wasn't looking at me; she hadn't looked at me at all. Her gaze was fixed on Springsteen.

Then her breath came in long, ragged wheezes almost as if she was trying to blow bubbles in her throat. It sounded awful, and each heave of her chest made her upper torso quiver. She sneezed then, and the effort racked her more.

'Where did you leave the cab, Lara?' I asked again, moving to sit on the edge of an armchair within five feet of her. A few hours before, I would have settled on five miles being the safest distance between us.

She sneezed again, then wheezed. The bubbling sound was giving way to a dry rasping noise that seemed to fascinate Springsteen. He stopped kicking against me and turned his head to look at her. She turned her head away quickly as if trying to sink into the wall, but her eyes flashed back immediately.

I edged forward as if offering Springsteen to her.

'Don't want to make friends?'

'Get ... it ... away...' she gasped, then sneezed twice. Her legs, splayed out in front of her, were quivering now.

'Where did you leave the cab, Lara? Just tell me and I'll take him away.'

'Aaa .... aaa ... Abberton ... St ... str...'

Abberton Street? Christ, I'd just driven past that.

'Abberton Street? The one round the corner?'

She nodded, and the air rattled in her throat. It was like watching somebody drown, without the water.

'Does Professor Bamforth live there? Professor Brian Bamforth?'

Another nod. Springsteen said 'Yeeeow,' and that brought two more nods in rapid succession. The sound of her breathing filled the room.

'Is it a timing device, Lara?'

Nothing.

I stood up and took a step towards her, holding Springsteen in front of me.

'Yesssss,' she hissed.

'Set for midnight?'

She nodded. If she'd been planning for

New Year's Eve, it would have been midnight, and she probably didn't know enough to mess around with a timer.

I started to back off, and then I noticed a plastic shoulder-bag in the chair I'd been leaning against.

Holding Springsteen with one arm, I opened the bag's clasp and tipped its contents into the chair. Among the usual female detritus were her inhaler and a plastic tub of pills with one of those child-proof locks only children can open without swearing. The pharmacist's label on the pills said '12 hour protection per dosage'. She'd told me that morning – was it only that morning? – that she'd taken her drugs. Luckily for me, she hadn't thought a top-up dose necessary.

'Keys, Lara. What did you do with the keys for the cab?'

'D ... d ... dr ... drain...'

'You dropped them down a drain?'

Nod.

'Okay. I'm going now,' I said, putting both inhaler and the pills in my jacket pocket.

She didn't say anything. I don't think she could.

I left her sitting against the wall, face turned into it, arms outstretched, fingernails clawing gently at the paintwork. A martyr crucified by the one weakness she couldn't overcome with sheer willpower.

There was no way of locking the flat door

from the outside, so I grabbed Springsteen's basket and hurried to the lift. My foot didn't seem to hurt at all any more. Springsteen even went back into his basket without a struggle.

I was on a roll. Things were going my way.

As the lift doors opened, I realised I'd forgotten the walking stick. The hell with it. I took my two reserve benzedrines instead and hobbled out of the building and across the road towards Abberton Street still crunching them.

I thought about what else it said on Lara's bottle of pills: the small fact that the prescription had been made out for a Miss L Bamforth. And I wondered what had happened to make someone so angry, as Geoffrey Bell would have understood. Angry enough to blow up her own father.

But that was her business and I didn't think of her again, because then I was in Abberton Street and there was Armstrong parked 50 yards away outside an unpretentious, snug, middle-class detached house. And that was my business.

The street was deserted apart from parked cars. Most of the houses still had lights on downstairs, including the one Armstrong was outside. People staying up late watching the television or playing idiot board games that then get put away for another year.

I left Springsteen's basket inside the front gate of the first house, where he would be protected by a concrete gatepost should anything go wrong.

'Don't worry,' I whispered to him, 'nothing will go wrong.'

He turned around inside the basket and showed me his tail. It was a good thing I wasn't looking for volunteers.

There was a street light across the road from Armstrong, which allowed enough light for me to see inside him. I walked – limped – all the way round him, peering in the windows, but there was nothing untoward at all. It had to be in the boot. That's where I'd have put it. Near the fuel tank.

I went down on my knees behind the rear nearside wheel and felt around in the mud and rust and muck until I located the magnetic pad I'd welded there. Still attached, despite our cross-country ramble with the hunters, was Armstrong's emergency key.

I looked at my watch. Eleven minutes to midnight. No sirens, no robot half-tracks, no helicopters hovering overhead with searchlights. Where the hell was the Bomb Squad when you needed them?

I slipped the key into the boot and carefully twisted the handle, lowering the boot flap as if I was taking a soufflé out of an oven.

There's not that much room in a black cab's boot, because the spare wheel stands there in the middle. So that's where she'd put it.

Actually, the bomb itself was in an old red biscuit tin with the words 'Chocolate Assorted' printed across the lid in yellow letters each decorated with little sprigs of holly. It had been jammed half behind the spare tyre and held in place by black insulating tape. Inside the spare wheel frame itself was the detonator: a cheap travelling alarm clock with the back removed, taped to a square of hardboard. Two thin, red wires led to a small alternator and a 2.5 volt battery taped next to it. From that, two thicker wires, each with a jack plug like you'd find on a stereo speaker, ran to the biscuit tin and disappeared into two holes punched crudely in the side.

The clock had its gold alarm arm fixed straight up on 12. Its timer arms said it was ten to, but could you ever rely on those things?

I reached out both hands and gently eased the jack plugs from the tin. The ends were covered in grey, putty-like stuff. It was only a smear on each, but for all I knew it was maybe enough to set things going. I let the leads dangle over the edge of the boot and set about the battery, cursing my gloves, but not wanting to take them off. The idea of touching the thing was to me what touching Springsteen had been to Lara.

I eased back the thin metal flap that held it in place at the bottom until I was sure it wouldn't give a connection, then I peeled back the insulating tape until it fell out and rattled into the rim of the spare wheel with a loud clang. Or at least it seemed loud. I realised I had forgotten to breathe recently.

I ripped the damned thing free then and carried the clock part in one hand and the battery and leads in the other into the short driveway of Professor Bamforth's house. I put them down a good yard apart on the gravel and then went back for the biscuit tin.

I laid that down another yard away from the other bits and thought about ringing the doorbell. In the distance, I heard the siren of a fire-engine. Let them break the news.

Armstrong started first go, his engine still warm. I reversed down the street to where I'd left Springsteen and put the basket on the floor in the back.

'They wouldn't have made it in time, you know,' I told him excitedly. 'That probably makes me a hero.'

He was asleep.

I climbed back into the driver's seat and put my arms around the steering-wheel, giving it a big hug of relief.

'Let's go home, kid,' I said in my John Wayne voice, and I smiled in the dark at the two fire-engines and three police cars we passed on the way.

'That's him,' said Lisabeth, pointing an accusing finger. The Gestapo officers pushed by her to get at me and drag me from my hiding place.

Well, it wasn't quite like that, but it was close.

My hiding-place was under the duvet, stretched across my bed where I'd fallen, pole-axed, when I'd got in. I had remembered to open the cat basket, because it was there in the middle of the floor, its door hanging open as if Springsteen had busted his way out. Taking my clothes off, however, had been beyond me.

Lisabeth was at the bedroom door, and behind her was a uniformed police sergeant.

'That's him,' Lisabeth was saying.

I struggled up to sit on the edge of the bed, and as soon as I put my right foot on the floor, it reminded me that it still hurt.

'Mr Angel, is it?' asked the policeman.

I put my hands up to my head and realised I was still wearing gloves. Sheepishly I pulled them off.

'I told you it was,' Lisabeth said indignantly, looking up at him.

'Er ... quite. Looks as if you were having a good time last night, sir,' he said.

He was looking at the bottles of Bailey's and tequila that were rolling around the bedroom floor. I think I must have had some idea about a celebration when I got Springsteen back home, but somehow I hadn't quite made it.

'Yes, great party,' I said cheerfully, 'You should've been there, Lisabeth, you'd have loved the...'

From the stairs came the sound of a struggle followed by what I knew instantly was the Christmas tree in the hall crashing over again.

Then a shrill female voice.

'That's him! Let me get at the bastard!'

Stephie.

'We didn't forget anything when we were out last night, did we, sir?' asked the sergeant politely.

The hospital X-rays found three small broken bones in my foot, and they splashed a partial plaster on it and told me to stay off my feet for a week or two. The cuts and bumps on my head didn't deserve stitching and they couldn't find any internal damage. What really hurt was they didn't believe I'd done it falling down stairs.

Still, it got me out of organising the house New Year's Eve party, apart from a few administrative phone calls, and Lisabeth and Fenella – and even Miranda – took to their new roles as nurses with relish. There was one sticky moment when I had to explain what I'd meant when Lisabeth overheard me telling Fenella I could get her a nurse's uniform, but I blagged my way through.

A whole procession of friends turned up to see me, and I held court from an armchair with my right foot on a pile of cushions, playing it for all it was worth.

Prentice turned up and spent a morning filling me in.

Stephie had done her bit, yelling and screaming and threatening to hold her breath until she went blue if the police didn't come. Then, when she'd heard the sirens, she'd thought of what her father might say if she got involved in whatever was going down, so she'd gone into panic.

I'd left the keys in the Flying Fenman and so, being a gutsy girl, she'd started it up and found first gear. The only problem was, she couldn't find any of the others. Steering wasn't her strong point either. She'd turned left to get away from the sirens and found herself in a cul-de-sac.

And there she stayed until morning.

'She climbed into the back of the van and made herself comfortable and put her head down for a few hours,' said Prentice. 'Then she struck up a very interesting relationship with a passing milkman and he gave her a lift on his milk-float to the nearest police station.'

'I wonder what she was doing so far from home?' I asked innocently.

'Funnily enough, that's what her father said when we rang him. Well, that was the gist of it. There was an awful lot of other stuff he said as well.'

I'll bet.

'So what actually happened the other night?' I tried casually, but he wasn't taken in for a minute.

'It looks – looks – as if certain members of Action Against Animal Abuse were trying to assemble a bomb from six pounds of Semtex H outside the home of Professor Brian Bamforth, when for some reason they were disturbed. There was an anonymous tip-off and officers from the Metropolitan Police, along with fellow officers from the Bomb Squad and the London Fire Brigade, were able to arrive in time to prevent any damage to life or property.'

Huh! Thanks a bunch!

'Acting on other information received, a certain Miss Lucy Bamforth–' Lucy? I wondered if she'd changed it deliberately to get in with the Reverend Bell. Two Lucys in his life would have been too much – 'otherwise known as Lara Preston, was apprehended and, after medical treatment for a respiratory condition, was questioned by police.'

'And what did she say?'

He held up a thumb and forefinger made into a circle.

'Zilch. Didn't even want a solicitor. The

Reverend Geoffrey Bell, however, was questioned and arrested yesterday by Cambridge police. He admitted to the illegal possession of military property, to whit, high explosives. The forensic boys have already found traces from where they hid it. In a coal bunker, if you must know.'

I raised an eyebrow but pretended it was all going over my head.

'He won't, of course, say how he got them, but it's clear they came via one Peter Bamforth, alias Peter Preston, a former army officer and brother of the better-known Lucy-stroke-Lara.'

'How did you find him?' I asked wide-eyed, trying to suppress a grin.

'We had him all the time,' he said through clenched teeth. 'He was in Wormwood Scrubs. He was arrested following a disturbance outside a fur shop in Wigmore Street just before Christmas.' Prentice allowed himself a smile. 'He was wearing a rabbit costume when he was nicked.'

'He wasn't carrying a sledgehammer as well, was he?' I asked before I could stop myself.

'Yes,' Prentice answered, his eyes narrowing. 'How did you know that?'

'Shot in the dark,' I said dismissively. 'So what happens now?'

'Justice takes its natural course,' he said airily.

'Which means?'

'We screw the lid down tight to make sure it doesn't make the papers. Well, think about it. Bamforth the mad professor about to take his seat on loads of scientific committees, having signed the Official Secrets Act in triplicate. His loony children – their mother died, by the way, and he's remarried – go animal-activist and try and kill him. One of them an ex-army officer pinching munitions, the other a martial arts expert who was Young Secretary of the Year a while back. All that and furry animals in nasty experiments – Christ, can't you just imagine what the newspapers would do to it?'

'And don't forget the muscular Christianity element: Karate Kick Vicar in Bomb Plot Horror.'

Prentice put a hand to his brow as if testing for fever.

'Don't. Not even in jest. I had his bishop on the phone yesterday. Really pissed off about having his Christmas interrupted he was, too. Still, the Military Plod want to talk to the Reverend Bell; I won't have to.'

'So how much do you reckon I'll get from the papers for my story, then?'

Prentice leaned over and patted my stretched-out leg.

'What story, Roy? You weren't there, were you?'

'Oh no, of course not. I was forgetting.'

He winked.

'Good. Oh, by the way, we found Billy Tuckett's bicycle in the back of Peter Pres ... Peter Barmforth's van. It was in a lock-up garage in Islington. You can take it back to Mrs Tuckett if you want. I'll have it dropped round when we've finished with it.'

'What about his video camera and stuff?'

'That's up to Cambridge, but it'll be released eventually. There was some interesting stuff on those tapes, by all accounts.'

'I'll see how I feel,' I said. I had no burning desire to see Billy's mum again, but there might come a time when I needed free meat.

He stood up to go.

'Incidentally, what with all this excitement, I never checked how our inquiries were going on what's-her-name, your friend ... Zaria?'

'Forget it.'

'Really? I mean, I suppose I owe you one...'

'Put *that* in writing and let me carry it around in my wallet,' I suggested. 'But otherwise, forget it. That particular problem solved itself.'

'Fair enough. We'll ... er ... run into each other sometime. Maybe.'

'Maybe.' He raised a hand in farewell. 'Hang on a minute.'

'Yeah?'

'You said you'd found Billy's bike.' He nodded. 'Which puts Peter Bamforth at the Dwyer Street school, doesn't it?'

'Yup. Pretty much.'

'I'm sure in my mind it was an accident, you know. Billy being on that roof.'

'So I understand from what the Reverend Bell has been saying.'

'And what about Lara?'

'We've no physical evidence to put her there, but she's well tied to the bomb at her daddy's place.'

'Really? How?'

Prentice stroked his chin.

'It was funny, really. You see, there wasn't a single makeable fingerprint on the bomb. Not on the explosive, the timer or anything. But where it was laid out, just as if someone was going to put it together, somebody had dropped some pills and an inhaler thing. And they were just covered in young Lara's prints. Even had her name on them – her real name, and address.'

'Lucky, that,' I said.

'Yeah, it was. I wondered when you'd ask.'

As I was still classified as walking wounded by New Year's Eve, I got out of my rash promise to get a band together for the house party. It was just as well, as there wouldn't have been room, given the number of people who turned up.

The compromise was that the speakers of my CD player were strapped to the banister of the landing outside my flat and the volume turned up so that the whole house (and most of the street) could benefit. Doogie and Miranda opened their place up for the eats – and Doogie excelled himself there – while Lisabeth's and Fenella's place was cleared and darkened for anyone fancying a dance. Mr Goodson was away for the holiday – I'm pretty sure someone had checked – so we used the old communal kitchen next to his flat as a bar.

Needless to say, as always happens with parties, most everybody remained in the hallway or on the stairs until the need for more booze or a lavatory forced them to move.

My friend Duncan the Drunken, probably the best car mechanic in the world, turned up with a case of very good French wine that a satisfied customer had given him for Christmas. He handed it to me and headed straight for the kitchen muttering 'Where's the beer?' Doreen, his wife, pecked me on the cheek, took off her fake fur coat and draped it over the box of wine I was holding. Then she took an engraved pint tankard from her capacious handbag and followed Duncan shouting: 'Duncan, you've forgotten your Christmas present!'

I staggered upstairs to put the wine in my

flat, stepping over the elongated figure of Bunny, who was saying to a slim, diminutive blonde, 'Cats have at least eight erogenous zones, whereas humans...'

I presumed Springsteen had given him his cue. He'd be downstairs in the thick of it somewhere, as he loved parties.

I dumped the wine in my kitchenette and wandered into my living-room to check that the CD player was programmed to continue to boogie.

'Oh, hello, Roy,' said Fenella, scaring me half-to-death as she leapt up from the sofa. 'This is Josie,' she said, starting to blush. 'An old school chum.'

Josie was a smaller Fenella, and she wore round, John Lennon glasses.

'Hello,' she said, without a hint of a smile.

'We were just coming downstairs to join the party,' said Fenella.

As they trooped out, I followed Fenella and whispered in her ear: 'Lisabeth's upstairs in among the food.'

'She would be,' she whispered back. Then she took Josie's arm. 'Roy got us our Christmas tree. Isn't it pretty?'

Josie looked over the balcony at the assorted drunks milling around the battered conifer.

'It's not straight,' she said to me.

'Stick around,' I said. 'Nobody will be.'

The front door opened downstairs and a

familiar figure in an ankle-length overcoat entered. It was Nassim Nassim, our esteemed landlord.

'Bloody hell,' I said to myself. 'Who asked him?'

'I did,' said Fenella. 'I thought it would be a nice gesture. I don't know who the power-dressing girlfriend is though. It's certainly not Mrs Nassim.'

No, it wasn't. It was Zaria.

'I can explain,' she said, when I finally got her alone in my bedroom.

I'd told Fenella to get them upstairs as quickly as possible, to where the food was. Nassim wasn't much of a drinker but he would certainly freak out over Doogie's buffet.

Fenella did me proud, leading Nassim by the arm with Zaria following, and as she went by, I nipped out of my flat and grabbed her hand, dragging her inside.

'Sit down and start then,' I told her.

She perched on the edge of the bed. Fenella was right about the power-dressing. Her suit coat had shoulder pads an eagle could have landed on; the matching skirt stopped half an inch above the knee; and she wore red stockings with black seams and black three-inch heels.

'Have you got a cigarette?' she asked.

I gave her a cigarette, found her an ashtray,

thought to hell with it and lit one myself, then got her a drink as well.

'Well?'

'Well, you know that packet you gave me to post when we were in Leytonstone?'

'It has crossed my mind in the last week or two,' I sighed.

She suddenly reached out a hand and touched my leg.

'You're limping. Did Sunil's people do that to you?'

'It's nothing,' I said, shrugging it off but not enlightening her. 'Go on.'

'I assumed the packet was drugs,' she said firmly. So had I.

'And I do not approve of drugs or the people who traffic in them,' she went on. 'So I decided not to post the packet to you.'

'But you couldn't resist opening it?'

She shrugged her shoulder pads.

'I was surprised to find the disks, I have to admit,' she said.

'The what?'

'The computer disks. I ran them through the word-processor at the nursing home.'

'It wasn't drugs?'

'Oh no.' She was wide-eyed at the thought. 'It was Sunil's own private double-entry ledger.'

'Come again?'

'You know he manages – managed – some of Nassim's property for him. Well, he'd been systematically fiddling Nassim out of I guessed 20 percent of his rentals for two years. He kept one set of books on his personal computer and gave Nassim a completely different set of figures.'

I sat down on the bed next to her.

'And you started to blackmail him, and he thought it was me. I thought he was after me, and all he wanted to do was give me money.'

'That was my first idea,' she smiled, putting a hand on my knee. 'But then I discovered that Nassim is a distant relation – I'm his great half-niece. I think. Anyway, I made contact with him and chatted him up and he was impressed by my business knowledge and my evaluation of his property assets, which was bigger than he'd ever thought. So I got in touch with Sunil and told him not to try and buy me off with money. I did try and get to you to tell you.'

'It's a good job he never got to me then, isn't it?' I asked carefully.

'I suppose so, as things turned out,' she said, and went on without pause, 'I told him the stakes were raised and if he didn't want exposing and the family disgrace and all that shit, then he'd better resign from Nassim's business and go back home and manage his own.'

'And he went?'

'Oh yes. He knew what was on those disks, and he knows my branch of the family doesn't mess about.'

'I'll bet. But still, it's a bit much, isn't it? Packing up and moving back to somewhere north of Peshawar or wherever.'

'Where's that?'

'Pakistan. Isn't it?'

'Who said anything about Pakistan? I said he'd gone home. To Leicester.'

'Oh. Sorry. So now what?'

'So I'm the new property manager for Nassim, that's what. And he'll make me a director within a year.'

I gave her the suspicious eye.

'You're our new landlord.'

'You could say that,' she beamed.

'And would I be really way off base if I said I wouldn't be at all surprised if our rent was to rise suddenly?'

'Well, you have to admit that at market values, this particular area of the city has been long—'

I put a forefinger to her lips.

'Unless nice Mr Nassim finds out about one cousin on the fiddle and one great half-niece who's a blackmailer, perhaps?'

She sucked at her bottom lip.

'Perhaps we could arrange something,' she said, as if thinking hard. Then she cracked into a lecherous smile and her hand moved up my leg.

'What about nursing?' I asked.

'I've given that the elbow. Business is far

363

more rewarding. I've got a company car, did I tell you?'

'No, I meant that I could use a nurse for a few weeks. Someone to wait on me hand and foot, you might say.'

She looked at her watch.

'I have to run Nassim home, but I could nip back later perhaps.'

'I'll try and keep the party going.'

It was Lisabeth who remembered to turn the radio on at midnight so we could hear the bongs of Big Ben ushering in the new year. Then, by popular demand, I had to play 'Auld Lang Syne' on the trumpet from the top of the stairs outside Doogie's flat. Everybody linked arms and sang and the whole human snake turned into an impromptu conga line that once again threatened the Christmas tree.

I was sharing some of Doogie's fine 12-year-old malt whisky and munching on a turkey leg when Miranda rushed in just before one o'clock.

'Do come and see, Doogie,' she yelled, her face flushed, tugging at his drinking arm.

'Whisst, woman,' he snapped, and carefully took the whisky glass with his other hand. 'What have you got your knickers twisted about now?'

'Come see, come see. That nice Mr Tomlin from No 23 came round. We thought he was going to complain about the noise. Well, he did, actually, but he also left something for you, Roy.'

'Me? I've never met the man.'

'Well, come and see, then.'

She bounded out, dragging Doogie with her.

I followed them down the stairs and from the first landing I could see the group of people gathered near the front door. There were still people drinking and dancing and lounging about on the stairs, and Bunny was explaining to the straight-faced Josie that the most common place to find an erogenous zone was...

Miranda forced the crowd apart, and I could see Fenella on her knees in the hallway, a large cardboard box in front of her.

Springsteen sat a foot away from her. He was motionless, looking at the box in horror.

'Angel! Come see,' yelled Fenella, as I eased my way downstairs. 'Mr Tomlin brought them. You know, the man who breeds pedigree Siamese down the road. He said they were our responsibility now.'

She dug her hands into the box and came up with a pair of mottled black and white kittens.

'Springsteen!' I yelled above the music as he disappeared like a black bullet down the hall towards the kitchen. 'I want a word with you!'

The publishers hope that this book has given you enjoyable reading. Large Print Books are especially designed to be as easy to see and hold as possible. If you wish a complete list of our books please ask at your local library or write directly to:

Magna Large Print Books
Magna House, Long Preston,
Skipton, North Yorkshire.
BD23 4ND

This Large Print Book, for people
who cannot read normal print,
is published under the auspices of

THE ULVERSCROFT FOUNDATION